CODE BLUE

THE CONNECTION TRILOGY - BOOK 2

ANITA WALLER

www.bloodhoundbooks.com

Print ISBN 978-1-914614-55-2

ALSO BY ANITA WALLER

PSYCHOLOGICAL THRILLERS

Beautiful

Angel

34 Days

Strategy

Captor

Game Players

Malignant

Liars (co-written with Patricia Dixon)

Gamble

Epitaph

Nine Lives

SUPERNATURAL

Winterscroft

KAT AND MOUSE SERIES

Murder Undeniable (Book 1)

Murder Unexpected (Book 2)

Murder Unearthed (Book 3)

Murder Untimely (Book 4)

Murder Unjoyful (Book 5)

THE CONNECTION TRILOGY

Blood Red

To Peter and Janet Stubbs,
long-time friends and wholly supportive of my work.
Thank you.

Blue has no dimensions, it is beyond dimensions.
— **Yves Klein**

But the sky was never quite the same shade of blue again.
— **Anne Rice**

PROLOGUE

SUNDAY 10TH MAY 2015

S itting at traffic lights wasn't John Coates's idea of a valuable occupation; he wanted to be home with Caroline, his wife of two years, talking and dreaming about their hopes, their wishes, following the planned caesarean birth of twins in a couple of weeks. Little girls, they had been told, identical...

He tapped his fingers on the steering wheel, waiting. If the game of golf hadn't been a long-standing meet, he would have been at home all day, but the others had insisted he take a break from being a putative daddy, because when the twins arrived he wouldn't be able to swan off and play sports.

The driver in front seemed to be anxious to be away; his engine revved several times, and he watched as the man first adjusted his interior mirror, then straightened his wing mirror, before combing his hair. The lights changed to green, and the Kia barrelled across the junction and away up the main road at an ever-increasing speed.

John touched the accelerator and his BMW moved smoothly forward, following in the wake of the car now some distance in front of him. He trailed the Kia's disappearing tail lights until he reached his left turn, leaving him with a two-minute drive to home. John Coates felt happy; not deliriously, ecstatically euphoric, simply wrapped in happiness. For one thing he'd won at golf, and for another the child he'd longed for had turned out to be two. He felt as though he smiled a lot.

It sometimes seemed as if he'd loved Caroline for ever, but in reality they had met four years earlier when he had interviewed her for the job of his PA. He knew he would employ her as soon as he saw her. Fortunately, she had been more than qualified for the post as well as being stunningly attractive, and two years later their wedding had been the talk of Sheffield. They had spoken of having two children, so had bought a house that could accommodate a family of that size easily; it had been a major source of hilarity when the two children were found to be arriving at the same time.

His thoughts drifted to the room they had set aside for the nursery, the one overlooking the back garden; decorated in lemon, pink and white, two white cots placed against opposite walls. Winnie the Pooh would enhance the twins' lives, or so Caro had convinced him.

He pulled his car on to the drive; Caroline usually came out of the front door, laughing and waiting for him to take her in his arms, but he guessed it was getting to be too much now. With no sign of her, John hoped she was resting on the sofa; the baby bump was huge.

The front door was slightly open and he smiled. He knew she would have opened it ready for him coming home. He closed it quietly behind him. If she was asleep he didn't want to wake her, she had to be finding it so tiring at this late stage of the pregnancy. So many nights he had watched her rubbing the bump, trying to ease the discomfort a little, and very often she could be heard talking to her daughters as they waited to make their entrance into the world, to be with both Mummy and Daddy.

He hung his coat in the cloakroom, and headed for the lounge but she wasn't on the sofa, so he climbed the stairs. She had admitted with a laugh to having what she called 'nanny naps' in the early afternoon, having half an hour in bed to ease the aches and pains caused by the weight she was carrying inside her. He was guessing it had morphed from being a nanny nap into a nanny sleep. He smiled again. She would be mortified at missing his arrival back home.

He quietly opened the bedroom door, but the bed was untouched. No sleeping Caroline there. He moved along to the only other room with a bed in it, the guest room, and quietly opened that door. No Caroline.

'Shit,' he mumbled. His thoughts escalated, and he prayed she hadn't gone into labour. He ran downstairs, tripping the last two as he missed his step. He followed the hallway to the far end, to the kitchen. Still no Caroline, and he walked into the dining area, to the French doors. He opened one side and stepped out onto the paved patio.

'Caro...' The word left his mouth as a croak. Louder. 'Caro!' and he ran across to her, then reeled back in disbelief as he rounded the end of the table. His world went silent. His brain, for a second, froze. His first reaction was that someone had tipped over a tin of red paint, but then he saw his wife's head, her body almost totally obscured by the upturned garden table.

Caroline was lying on her back, a towel still fastened around her swollen breasts, still damp from the shower she must have been taking when something made her go outside. Bruising was showing on her body, shoe imprints, and between her legs two bloodied lumps of flesh, still, unmoving in any way. John dropped to his knees, taking out his phone at the same time.

'Ambulance,' he gasped. 'Police as well. My wife... she's been attacked.' He gave his address; he struggled to remember it.

He lifted Caroline's head and cradled her. 'I think she's dead,' he whimpered. 'Please, hurry. My babies, both dead.'

'Can the ambulance crew get to you, sir? Is your door unlocked?'

'No, but it's quicker to go down the side of the house. Please, hurry. We're in the back garden. I can't leave her.'

'Is your wife breathing, sir?'

'I don't think so. Our twins...'

'How old are they, sir?'

'They were due in two weeks. They're born but they're not breathing. Oh, God,' and he dropped the phone and pulled Caroline towards him.

The ambulance was there within three minutes, and he hadn't moved. His whole life was on the patio with him, and he was going nowhere.

The paramedic felt at Caroline's neck, then repeated the action.

'She's alive,' she said, and it seemed to John that the god he had been ambivalent about up to that point, really did exist. More paramedics arrived; a shake of a head confirmed that his beautiful girls hadn't drawn breath, and they were moved away from Caroline's open legs so that she could be placed on a stretcher.

She was stabilised and moved very quickly. John heard the sirens as his wife disappeared to a hospital on the other side of the city, and he became aware of multiple photographs being taken. The babies, fully formed but bloody, seemed to be holding hands now they had been moved slightly. Photos had been taken before Caroline had been stretchered away, showing the full horror of the situation, but now the photographer had shifted to more routine pictures. Pictures were taken of the entire patio area, the French doors, the kitchen – how had he not noticed the blood on the kitchen floor?

John stared at it; she must have already been losing her babies inside the house. Had the man chased her out into the back garden or had she gone there hoping for a neighbour to help?

John felt a huge rage building inside him. Everything had been destroyed in a matter of a couple of hours. She had been fine at three when he had rung to check on her.

'Mr Coates?'

John turned and saw the DI who had arrived earlier. He couldn't remember his name. He stared blankly at him. 'I'm sorry... your name...'

'DI Alex Mason, sir. And the lady organising everything is DS Tessa Marsden. I need five minutes with you, and then you can get off to the hospital. One of my lads will take you, I don't recommend you drive.'

John nodded, almost an automatic action.

'Your wife, John. Caroline? Had you spoken to her today at all? I understand you've come in from work to find this.'

'I spoke to her around three, and she was fine then. She said she felt tired, so she was going to have a shower and then a nap until I arrived home. I sometimes ring her to tell her I'm on my way, but because she'd actually admitted to feeling tired, I didn't today. I wanted her to sleep, not be woken up by me. And I wasn't coming in from work, I was at a bloody golf match.' The bitterness showed in his voice.

He dropped down onto a kitchen chair and rested his elbows on the table, his head on his hands. 'Who the fuck would do that to a heavily pregnant woman?'

'I have no answers, not yet, John,' the DI said, 'but believe me, this case is a priority. You'll be seeing a lot of us. Have you had chance to check if anything's been stolen?'

'You think it was a burglary?' John looked shocked.

'Do you have anything of specific value in the house? Anything top of the range? Computers, games consoles, smart TVs? That's what they normally go for.'

John nodded. 'We have everything like that. Electronics is my business. He's killed my babies for a smart TV?'

'He?'

John hesitated. 'Sorry, assumption. I simply can't see a woman doing this to a heavily pregnant woman.'

Alex Mason paused for a moment to let John collect his thoughts. 'Do you keep money in the house?'

'No, cash is something that's always an issue with us. We've never got any. We're always having to nip up the road to Sainsbury's to use their machine.' And then he stopped talking. 'Oh my God...'

He moved across to a kitchen drawer and pulled it out as far as it would go. He rummaged around inside it and then slammed his hand on the work surface.

'He didn't kill them for a smart TV,' he said. 'He killed them for fifteen thousand pounds.'

'You had fifteen thousand pounds in a drawer? Fifteen *thousand*?'

'We did. My wife sold her Lexus yesterday, because we knew it wouldn't be big enough when the twins came. She's... she was... picking up a new car next Wednesday, one that's got a boot big enough for a double buggy, and a large back seat. The buyer bought the Lexus for cash. He drove away with it last night. I have his details...' His voice faded away. 'His details were with the money.'

'How did he contact you?'

'He didn't contact me, he contacted Caroline. And before

you ask, we don't have his number. It came through as No Caller ID, and Caroline answered it because when the hospital calls it shows as that on her screen. It proved to be this man, who said he had fifteen thousand cash, ready and waiting, and would she take that. She'd advertised it for sixteen thousand, expecting to have to come down on the price. She said yes, but asked him to call after five, knowing I would be here. He did, and drove the car away with him after handing over the money. We've got CCTV everywhere, it should show him on that, and what's happened today.'

'Did he see where you put the money?'

'No, I'd still got it in my hand when he went.'

'Then presumably your wife told him it was in the drawer to try to get rid of him, if indeed it was the same man. I'll not keep you any longer, Mr Coates. I'm going to ask DS Marsden to go with you to the hospital. And if you remember anything else, tell her. There will be someone here overnight, this is a major crime scene. Now go to your wife.'

1

'You look smart.' Luke looked at Fred and grinned. 'It's either a woman or a job interview.'

'Don't get cocky, young Luke,' Fred growled. 'I've only been in this job a couple of weeks, so I'm hardly likely to be job hunting. Mind you – it's been a fraught couple of weeks, so maybe...'

'So it's a woman then?'

'I can wear new shoes, can't I?'

Luke eyed the older man up and down. 'And new jeans, and a Gucci sweatshirt. You had a good shop at Meadowhall then?'

'I did. I was celebrating two jobs well done. Thought I'd treat myself, and I kind of liked the sweatshirt. If I'd gone for something to eat first before doing my shopping, I wouldn't have bought it. I met Amy Barker and her two-faced sister in the Oasis, having a coffee. They didn't know what to say to me. It seems, reading between the lines, that they set Tony Barker up big style between them. I let them know I'd worked it out, and they didn't deny it. Their smiles and giggles disappeared damn fast I can tell you. And then, when I opened up my newspaper, it was to see Harley King's photo plastered on the front page, the one thing Ernest Lounds was trying to avoid. I'm telling you, if I hadn't already finished my little spending spree, I'd have been a thousand pounds better off now.'

'Well, I think you look very smart,' Cheryl joined in. 'I need to nip across the road to stock up on milk and stuff, so can you man the phone for me for ten minutes, Luke, please?'

'I'll go,' Fred said, a shade too quickly. 'Tell me what you want.'

Cheryl looked at him for a moment, then pushed a small piece of paper and a twenty-pound note in his direction. 'Thank you.'

'Don't sound so suspicious, I need to get a few bits for home. I don't want to get a reputation for being nice, I'm simply being practical.'

Luke laughed. 'And my mum works there.'

Fred growled again, picked up the money and note and walked out of the door, holding it for Tessa to enter.

'What's wrong with our Fred?' she asked.

'Nothing much, don't mention Mum's name to him, he's a touch sensitive about it. Beth still in the North East?'

'She is, and Simon. They went yesterday so they would be fresh for the work they still need to do before the meeting when they break the bad news to the Board. I've a couple of appointments for both of you, I've emailed the details.' Cheryl glanced down her list. 'And that's it for the moment. Slow day, methinks, with two of our team away for a couple of days.'

'Don't say that,' Tessa called over her shoulder as she headed for the lift. 'You'll jinx it.'

Fred smiled at Naomi Taylor as he packed the shopping into bags. 'You're sure tomorrow's okay with you?'

'It's fine, and I never have to worry about somebody to look after the girls, because Mum never goes out. I'll look forward to it, Fred.'

'I'll text you later when I've sorted out the table booking. Thank you, Naomi, you've brightened up my day.'

She laughed. 'Good. That's what I like to hear. And can you tell Luke if he wants to stop by for a meal tonight, I'm doing a curry. There'll be plenty for him and Maria if they want it.'

'He seems smitten.'

'That's a lovely old-fashioned word. I think he is, and it's something he needs instead of working all the time.'

A customer began to empty her basket onto the belt, and Fred took his leave, clutching onto the list Cheryl had given him because it now had Naomi's mobile number on the back of it.

Tessa read through Cheryl's email, feeling a little bemused. Although it wasn't a blast from the past, the interaction between her and John and Caroline Coates had been sporadic; always warm, because she had become close to them after the case involving the two men who had caused the deaths of their babies, but she hadn't heard from the Coateses in a while other than a Christmas card exchange. She had, though, sent them a card notifying them of her decision to leave the police and become a partner at Connection...

John's message, according to Cheryl, had been not to ring him back, he would ring her later as he wasn't ready yet to involve Caroline. Tessa opened her browser and typed in John Coates, feeling she might need to refresh her memory. She didn't. Every word was ingrained, every image from that most horrific crime etched into her brain and never likely to leave it.

With a deep sigh she closed her laptop and picked up her coffee, sipping it and thinking. Whatever John wanted, it couldn't be anything to do with the twenty fifteen crime. The two men had been caught two days after the event and couldn't be out of prison yet. Yet the unease sat heavily on her. What could John possibly want that he needed to keep from his wife? Tessa stared at her phone willing it to ring, but the silence hung heavily in the room.

'Alexa, play classical piano.'

The little round Echo Dot obliged, and Tessa reduced it to volume two. She let the music wash over her, and tried to get her mind away from the crime scene photographs of that day in May, twenty fifteen, that would never leave her. So much blood, a desperately near-death woman with her dead babies between her legs, expelled by a huge kick to her eight-month pregnant stomach, and the heat from the sun. Always the heat from the sun making the whole scene surprisingly unreal.

And every year it was brought to mind briefly as she wrote their Christmas card, one of the very few she actually sent. It always seemed important that she remained in contact with the couple she had come to know so well, to support through the worst time of their lives.

Their Christmas card to her had spoken of things going well, their new baby was now a one-year-old, a little girl adopted at birth, and a new company for John. Immediately after the deaths of the twins, John had sold his extremely successful IT and security company so that he could be at home with Caroline, and now it seemed a new company that John had named Code Blue had been born and was producing top of the range games.

She picked up her phone. 'Luke, you ever heard of Code Blue?'

He laughed. 'What's Maria been saying?'

'Nothing, I haven't seen her. What is it?'

'It's a game. One of the most successful on the market at the moment. It cost me an arm and a leg to buy it, but it's worth it.

We play it most nights on the PS4. I've been doing it for some time, but we've set everything up in my bungalow now, and I've shown her how to manoeuvre and track in it. It's not an easy game, but it's so clever. Wouldn't have thought it was your idea of fun, but...'

'It's not. I don't play games, but I actually know the inventor, if that's the right word for him.'

'It's good enough. What do you mean, you know the inventor? You've never told me you moved in such exalted circles. Hang on, I'll come through.'

Luke produced the chocolate digestives, and Tessa handed him a coffee.

'Okay,' he said, 'is he a criminal?'

Tessa laughed. 'Hardly. He's a very clever man who owned a massive company in Sheffield specialising in selling electronics, installation of security systems, but only high-grade stuff. Then he and his wife lost the twins she was carrying in horrific circumstances, and he gave up the business, sold it and stayed home with his wife to help both of them heal. I was a DS at the time, and grew very close to both of them. Now it seems he wants to speak to me, but I don't know why yet. His Christmas card explained he'd started a new company, and it's called Code Blue. It rang a very small bell in my mind that it was the name of a game, but other than that I know nothing about it. I'm assuming it's a game produced by his company...'

'It is. That's what it says on the back, and it's a company in Sheffield. Is that where he lives?'

'Yes, right on the Derbyshire border, which is why we got the case five years ago. I take it you'll want to shake his hand if he turns up here then?'

'Too right I will. And I'm going to bring in the case, I want it signing.'

Tessa reached across for another biscuit. 'I must stop eating these,' she said with a sigh. 'Why don't you get the plain ones, without chocolate? That would help.'

'I don't like them as much,' Luke explained, 'and they are *my* biscuits. You could always get your own.'

Tessa's eyes widened. 'Buy biscuits? Never. They're fattening. I never buy them.'

'You don't have biscuits at home? What sort of house doesn't have biscuits? And can I point out you eat biscuits at work?'

'That's different. I eat them here when I'm thinking.'

'Or when I put them in the middle of the table. I'll stop bringing them.'

Tessa leaned towards the centre of her desk and grabbed the remaining half packet before dropping it into her drawer. 'I'll look after these, in case you carry out that threat.'

Luke stood. 'He's ringing you, your friend?'

'He is. Why?'

'If you need an accomplice...'

'I'll send for you. Promise.'

The phone call, when it came, was brief. Had Tessa an hour to spare at two that afternoon? She confirmed she had and asked if it was in connection with an investigation he required. When he said yes, she said her colleague would be there as well. He said that was fine, but if she could limit it to the two of them that would be good.

Luke didn't even take the car, he sprinted up the main road, ran into his house and brought the cover for the game back with him. On his way back down to the office he met his mother heading home after finishing her shift at the Co-op. The excitement was evident in his voice as he told her about his planned afternoon, and she smiled as she listened to him. 'Don't fan-boy him, ask for his autograph politely and then put it away. I'll see you and Maria tonight, I'm going to do the curry now.' She turned to walk away before saying, 'Oh, and I'm going out with Fred tomorrow night.'

Luke was some distance away from her before he realised what she had said, and he turned around to respond but she had disappeared, and he frowned. Had she really said she was going out with Fred? In all his life he had only known her go on a date once, and she soon got rid of him. Should he warn Fred his mother was a bit fickle, or should he leave them to get on with it...

2

_____

John Coates's hair had started to turn grey at the sides, and Tessa felt that it suited him, turned him from the handsome younger man of five years earlier into a man of a more distinguished appearance, still remarkably good-looking with his deep-brown eyes and ready smile, but maturing very nicely.

She met him at the lift door, and held out her hand. 'John,' she said. 'It's good to see you. Follow me.'

John Coates looked around her office and smiled. 'This is good, very smart. You're happy here?'

'I am. I couldn't stay in the police, it was time to move on.'

He nodded. 'I can understand that. It's why I sold Coates Electronics, I couldn't have gone back there. Not after...'

Tessa handed him a coffee, and placed a second cup on her desk. 'Luke, my colleague, is joining us. And we'll be recording our conversation if that's okay with you. It saves us being distracted by having to take notes.'

'That's fine. It really is good to see you again, Tessa. It brings back awful memories, but through it all you were by our sides, supporting us, especially through the trial. We knew the two of them were bang to rights, caught face-on with our CCTV system, but juries can be so unpredictable...'

Tessa laughed. 'Tell me about it. But in your case, they reached the guilty verdict very quickly. And now you have a baby, the beautiful Casey. Time to put it behind you?'

'I would,' John said with a sigh, 'if only Caroline could.'

There was a gentle tap on the door, and Luke popped his head around it. 'Sorry, I was on the phone. Mr Coates,' and he held out his hand.

John shook it. 'Call me John. Is that Code Blue?'

'It is. Will you sign it for me, please?' Luke handed over the game case and a Sharpie pen. 'I play this most days, best one on the market at the moment.'

'So the charts tell us. We send new games out to beta testers before we release them to the sales floors, and our team couldn't wait to get the finished version.' He signed both the case and the disc with a flourish and handed it back to Luke. 'I take it you're a fan of the game?'

'A big fan. I feel honoured to meet you.'

Luke sat down, and Tessa placed the recorder on the table, switching it on as she did so.

'Okay, John we're now recording. You'll get a transcript of the conversation. So begin when you're ready.'

John turned to Luke. 'I don't know how much you know, Luke, but five years ago my wife was pregnant with our twin daughters. In May of twenty fifteen she was attacked in our home, and almost died. The twins were basically kicked out of her body, and never drew breath. The back story to it is that the day before this happened Caroline sold her Lexus to a man for fifteen thousand pounds. He paid cash. He drove the car away with him, and I put the cash in a drawer until I could take it to the bank. It all seemed to be above board, we filled out the log book details for DVLA and it was all bundled together with the money.'

He paused for a moment. 'We never saw him or the car again, and neither did the police. The following day two lads, late teens, arrived at our house while I was out, and pushed their way in. Our house is well-covered by CCTV and it caught it all, including the previous day's visitor who had bought the car. They said at the trial they had been sent to get the money back but they didn't know who he was.'

Tessa interrupted. 'The police always thought they did know, but were too scared of him to reveal the name.'

'From what the police gleaned from the CCTV images, Caroline refused to tell them where the money was and tried to escape from them by running outside. They caught her, knocked her over and began kicking her. We can see she speaks to them, and then they give her one last kick to her stomach and go back inside. Caroline did confirm she told them where the money was, and they grabbed it and ran. Caroline was unconscious when I found her, our twins died before they lived, and our world was simply destroyed. It's taken a long time to achieve anything approaching normality, but now we have a beautiful adopted daughter. However, things are definitely not right.'

He picked up his coffee and emptied the cup, before handing it to Tessa. 'I could use another one.'

'You haven't changed,' she said with a smile. She refilled his cup, took Luke's biscuits out of her drawer, and arranged them on a plate. 'Chocolate biscuits,' she said, 'Luke doesn't like plain ones.'

'A man after my own heart,' John said with a grin. There was a brief pause while he gathered his thoughts. 'Caroline isn't sleeping. She appreciates the fact that the two who did all the damage are safely behind bars, on remand before she was even brought out of her induced coma, but she knows the real culprit, the one who bought her car, is still free, and possibly doing the same to others as he did to her. He chose a couple of lads who were high on drugs to get his money back, but presumably he'll have learnt from that and uses more reliable people now. This man is invading her dreams, she looks worn out, and it's not because of Casey. Casey came to us as soon as she was born, so she's fifteen months old now and has never been a baby who took a lot of hard work. She sleeps through the night fortunately, but her mummy doesn't. And that's because the second she closes her eyes, he's there. Sending her for counselling hasn't helped, and then we got your card saying you'd moved here, and I knew you could help us.'

'What do you want us to do?'

'Find him. Get him put away. He's as guilty, if not more so, than the other two bastards. The police aren't looking, they got the people who attacked Caroline, and they let it go at that. He never lifted his head all the time he was at our home, so we had him on CCTV but nothing showed clearly.'

'You think he was aware of where your cameras are?' Luke asked.

John looked a little surprised by the question, and pursed his lips before answering. 'Possibly, but I thought he'd kept his head down deliberately in case there were any. But thinking about that, when he rang our door bell he stood with his back to the camera. As if he knew...'

'I know it's some time ago,' Luke pressed, 'but who fitted your system?'

'My own company, Coates Electronics. It's part of what we did. I can't speak for now, of course, because it's no longer my company, but we had one section dedicated to security systems, and had the highest level of security in place for protecting details of our clients' installations. Including my own. Our cameras have been upgraded since then, but I did it myself. Nobody gets beyond the gates now, and even then we have to know them very well before we let them through. Our daughter is the most precious thing in our lives, and nobody will get to her.'

'Caroline doesn't know you're here?' Tessa asked.

'Not yet. I didn't want to build her hopes up until you said yes, you would take the case. I'll pay anything, Tessa, if you'll say you'll do it.'

'You'll be billed according to our usual rates, John. I'll need you to sign a contract, and place a deposit, then we'll get on with the work. Don't expect quick results, this is a five-year-old dead end that we have to open up, but we'll try our hardest to find him.'

'Get me the contract.' He smiled. 'I'm getting used to signing my name using this desk.'

'So,' Luke spoke, taking advantage of Tessa finding a blank contract, 'tell me about Code Blue.'

'When Caroline eventually came home from hospital, we employed a nurse to take care of her medical needs, and I began to feel a little superfluous. On the day I signed Coates over to its new owners I became a multi-millionaire. Very multi. I've always messed around with games, and decided to try my hand at one. I developed three very quickly, and they really took off. Then the old chap who lived next door to us died, and his house went on the market. I bought it, knocked all the insides out of it, and turned it into premises for a company I called Code Blue, which was the name of the new game I was working on. I employ six people at the moment, a receptionist and five technical wizards, and it's very much a growth industry, I can tell you. It means I have direct access from our house to work, because I had a connecting corridor built, and Caroline can reach me at any time.'

'Awesome,' Luke said. 'You're developing one at the moment?'

'I am. It's got a working name of Ice White, completely different to anything we've released so far, and I keep dropping hints in the industry magazines. There's been a lot of interest shown. You and Tessa are very welcome to come and see what we do, I'll make sure you get beyond the gates.'

Coates pulled the contract towards him, gave it a cursory glance, and signed it. He handed it back.

'Thank you. I'll go down with you as you leave, and introduce you to Cheryl, our receptionist. She deals with deposit payments, she'll sort you out. Luke and I will work together on this one, so my first action will be to make sure he is fully conversant with the attack on Caroline. You're going to tell her you've spoken to us?'

'I am now I've been to see you. It's possible knowing you're helping will give her a little peace so she can sleep at night. Thank you, Tessa, Luke.'

He finished his coffee and stood. 'Come on, let's go and hand some of this Code Blue money over to Connection. Contact me anytime, whether it's with information or you simply want to know something.'

'He wasn't a bit like I expected,' Luke said, leaning back on his chair, and staring at the name autographed on his game case. 'Seemed really down to earth, and clearly loves his family.'

Tessa closed her eyes for a moment. 'You should have seen him when it all happened. He was devastated. Completely broken. Nobody expected Caroline to survive, but those surgeons fought for her. They had to remove her womb, along with other bits of her, and then had to tell her when she did eventually surface, that she could never have another baby.'

'Hence the adoption.'

'That's right. It seems strange I didn't know about that, because if she's turned one now, little Casey, and she was adopted from birth, why didn't they mention her on last year's Christmas card? They did on this year's, and she's now fifteen months.'

'I suspect that's maybe Caroline's insecurities. Her and John needed to get used to the baby first, and it sounds as though they're completely cut off from the rest of the world in their fortress. That's the damage the crime did, not the beating Caroline took. She's probably scared all the time, and he's clearly worried and scared for her. We have to find him, Tessa, don't we?'

She glanced at her watch. 'It's getting late now, and I want to go into detail with you over the attack. The pictures are horrific, so I'll give you a night of peace. Nine tomorrow morning?'

Luke stood. 'I'll be here.'

3

Luke pulled up outside Connection, and waved across the road towards the vets as he saw Maria London get out of her car. The previous night had been spent at the cinema after Naomi's curry, and he had dropped Maria home before returning to his own place higher up the village.

They had tentatively planned on meeting for half an hour at lunchtime for a quick sandwich in the village café, but both knew such arrangements could be cancelled at a moment's notice because of their jobs. He hoped today's meeting could go ahead, and he turned and went into the office.

Tessa was already at her desk and was glancing through the files she had resurrected the night before. She had looked through them so many times in the past, that she now knew every word, every picture, but Luke knew little of the crime that had shocked a nation five years earlier.

She looked up as he walked in. 'Good morning. Coffee?'

'I'll get it. You want one?'

'No thanks. I'm having alternate days when I only drink water.'

He laughed. 'Yeah, right. This your first day on the new regime?'

'It is. I had hot water with lemon in it with my breakfast toast, and now I have this.' She tapped the bottle in front of her.

Luke poured himself a coffee and sat opposite Tessa, who handed him some pictures. 'Don't look at these for a moment, they're horrific. They're the crime scene photographs from when Caroline Coates was attacked. This,' she waved a USB stick in the air, 'is the stuff we recovered from CCTV. It basically shows everything that happened in the short time frame between the two men attacking her and John arriving home from his golf match. Prior to that segment there's CCTV of the man we are now looking for, from him walking up the drive to leaving in the Lexus. At no point do we see his face fully. He didn't wear a hoodie, but he did have a hood that he kept up until he walked through the front door. Then he took it down. We have a sketch of him provided by John sitting with our police artist, and when Caroline was sufficiently recovered she confirmed it was very much as she remembered him. The other two men, still only lads really because they were both nineteen, were quickly identified and in custody two days later. They hadn't been in trouble of any sort before, but quite rightly the judge didn't let that affect his sentencing decision. The main man, the one who paid out the fifteen thousand pounds, then calmly took it back the day after, has never been traced.'

'They wouldn't talk?'

She shook her head. 'Not a word. They were scared. No, stronger than that, they were terrified. He gave them five thousand to share between them, and he disappeared with the Lexus and ten thousand pounds.'

'Did he ever repeat it?'

'We believe so. Everything went into HOLMES so all forces can access the information, and we had several contact us saying they believed our case, which appeared to be his first one, was similar to something that had occurred in their part of the country. He got smarter, and there wasn't a recurrence of the violence used against Caroline, but he seemed to buy a car in the evening, then he got somebody else to steal the money back during the night. He targeted high-end cars like the Lexus, always paid cash obviously, and in a couple of cases the ones who took the money back were caught, but like our Sheffield pair, were too scared to talk. The case became a cold case, that is one that will immediately be opened up if ever there's a strong lead from some other police force.'

There was a brief tap on the door, and Fred popped his head around. 'Morning, you two.'

'Fred!' Tessa smiled. 'Come in a minute. Did you work on the Coates investigation five years ago?'

He closed the door quietly. 'I did. One of the worst things I've ever come across and I've seen some bad stuff. They're in prison though, aren't they?'

'They are, the thugs, but the chap who hired them has never been tracked down. We've been asked to find him and it's a request from John Coates. His wife is struggling, mentally, and he thinks it's because this man was never caught.'

'You want me in on this, I'm there,' Fred said grimly. 'They could have coped with being burgled to get the money back, but I can understand them not coping with everything else that happened. I can say this now I'm not in the force, but we didn't have the most competent DI in the world either.'

'Alex Mason? Mr Charm?' Tessa gave a short laugh. 'He took the glory for solving this case, then left. And really he didn't solve it. It was information from the public that told us who the attackers were. Once he'd got them, he considered it closed. I tried to extend it, but as a DS I didn't have the clout that he had as a DI, and it was allowed to drift away to the cold case section. Every so often it came out when a similar robbery cropped up, but it's simply never been solved.'

Fred turned to leave. 'As I say, if you want me, even if it's simply to use my memory, I'll make myself available. I'm popping up to see Ernest Lounds this morning, I want to make sure he really wants to leave this investigation as a closed case. Now the newspapers know his son-in-law committed suicide and the information is out there, he might want us to continue with it.'

'Thanks, Fred,' Tessa said. 'And I'll certainly pull you in if we need anything. Enjoy your evening with Naomi.'

Fred's eyes turned to Luke. 'You have a big mouth, young Luke.'

'Too right I do.' Luke laughed. 'I remember what everybody was like when I started to see Maria – if you think you can take my mother on a date and not have consequences in the workplace, think again. And I hope you're taking her somewhere nice...'

Fred's eyes flashed. 'I am... bed.'

Fred crossed his fingers as an aide-mémoire to remember to tell Naomi what he had said to her son, knowing she would continue with the joke. First stop before going to see Ernest would be a two-minute trip across the road to the Co-op.

He closed Tessa's office door as he heard Luke saying, 'Did he say what I thought he said?'

Fred couldn't hide the laughter as he reached Cheryl's desk, and he explained what he had said.

She grinned. 'He'll be unbearable now. Best go and confess to Naomi before Luke rings her.'

Fred needed no further excuse to nip across the road; fortunately, Naomi saw the funny side, and promised to continue to wind up her son if he should venture to mention Fred's comment.

'I'm really looking forward to tonight, Fred. Don't tell me where we're going, I'll enjoy the surprise. See you at seven.'

Luke finished looking through the crime scene photographs, and listened as Tessa went into more detail than the pictures revealed. He felt sickened, and understood how and why Caroline Coates was finding life, and sleep, impossible. There had been three criminals involved, and one of them had never paid the price for what he set up.

'You think we might need to speak to your ex-DI?'

'Possibly. He took himself off on more than one occasion to interview people, and all we had was his word for what he had found out. He was an idle bastard, believe me. Delegated all the time, and seemed far too friendly with the criminal fraternity. When he handed in his notice, there was a general feeling of relief. I was promoted to DI when he went, and Hannah was made up to DS. It all worked out fine for us, but by the time he went this case had been archived.'

'What's he do now?'

'Not sure. I'll leave that with you, your internet skills are far greater than mine.'

Luke glanced at his watch. 'Okay, I'm going for a half-hour lunch break at the tea rooms up the road, then as soon as I get back I'll make a start. You need a sandwich bringing back?'

Tessa opened her bag and brought out a plastic bag containing Ryvita biscuits. 'I would love a sandwich, but I'm trying to be good. Don't rush back, John isn't expecting quick results on this. You meeting Maria?'

He laughed. 'Who knows. That's the plan, but it only takes a poorly rabbit or an underweight cat to throw any arrangements out the window. The animals definitely take precedence over me.'

'Enjoy your sandwich, whether Maria arrives or not. And think of me with my crispbreads...'

Maria was waiting for him as he walked through the door. She had chosen a table for two, and was studying the menu. She stood as he walked towards her, and she leaned forward to kiss him.

'We did it! Lunch break at the same time! I'm having a ham salad sandwich.' She handed the menu to him.

He placed it on the table. 'I'll have the same, although after the photographs I've been looking at, there's half a chance it might not stay down. It's been a bad morning.'

'Want to talk about it?'

He shook his head. 'Maybe later when we're on our own. I don't want to risk being overheard. I'll go and order our lunch. You want tea or a cold drink?'

'Tea, please.'

Luke gave their orders, and returned to his seat. 'You had a good morning?'

'Not really.' She sighed. 'We've had to put two poorly cats down today, and I hate having to do that. Both of them had tumours, and it was the kindest thing to do, but I imagine their owners are sitting now crying their eyes out. It can be such a lovely job most of the time, and then we get days like today.'

'What time are you finishing?'

'It should be about four. Why?'

'Thought we might have a takeaway, and cuddle up with a movie. This is the first time we can walk in without having to do some sort of furniture construction, or go and buy something we need and can't live without, and I thought it would be nice to behave like normal people for a change.'

The café owner appeared at their side. 'Luke, Maria, good to see you. Two ham sandwiches, and a pot of tea for two. Luke, are you available this afternoon?'

Luke took out his phone. 'I can be. What time?'

'We close at three thirty. I can come straight down then.'

'Perfect. You're booked in, Amanda. Don't worry if you're delayed, I'm there till five.'

She nodded and squeezed his shoulder. 'Thanks, Luke. Enjoy your lunch, you two.'

'She sounded serious,' Maria whispered.

'She certainly had an edge to her voice,' he agreed. 'Let's hope it's something simple she needs advice with, I like Amanda.'

They ate their sandwiches, speaking very little after that. The small tea room became busier, and eventually they left, walking back down towards their workplaces.

They stopped outside Connection and he stood at the pavement edge as she prepared to dart across the road, busy with tourist traffic even in January.

'See you at mine?' he said. 'Now that Amanda is coming here, I can't predict what time I'll be done.'

'We'll not have a takeaway. I'll do us a spag bol with candles.' She grinned at him.

'Brilliant.' He leaned across to kiss her, as she prepared to run.

'Oh, and by the way,' she said, as she stepped off the pavement, 'I'll be staying over tonight.'

. . .

He was relieved when Amanda Gilchrist rang to postpone her meeting with him until Thursday morning, saying they had a late booking for a coachload of visitors.

'It's not urgent?' he asked.

'No, something on my mind that needs resolving. I'll be there Thursday at half past eight if that's okay.'

'I'll book you in,' he promised. 'Like you, I have to be versatile with appointments, so if you need to change it, it's fine.'

4

Beth and Simon checked out of their hotel and loaded their bags into Beth's car before heading for the final meeting with their clients, Goldex. They carried their laptops into the meeting, in case any further information was needed, but Beth knew today was the day when it was all going to be delivered into the hands of the Cleveland Fraud Squad.

They had grown to like the people they were working with, and Beth felt a degree of anger that so much money was involved. They had narrowed the field down to two people, one in accounts, and one who worked for the company on the legal side. These two, in tandem, had set up a tight system for transferring money to an offshore account that currently held slightly over six million pounds, money that had been filtered there over the previous couple of years. It had only been a request to Connection to recruit a top-class accountant for the company that she had first had concerns about the finances, and the subsequent meeting with the CEO had resulted in the full-blown investigation.

The day before had drained Beth and Simon; when they had

shown their findings to the Board, and now it was time to bow out and let the legalities begin.

Seated around the table were five Board members, and three police officers. Simon was using Beth's laptop for the presentation being shown on the large screen, and after an hour he sat down.

Gregory Ellerman immediately rose to his feet. 'Thank you, Beth. As CEO of this company, I am speaking on behalf of the board when I say a massive thank you for the work you have put in to uncover this. I'm sure our police friends will also acknowledge the work you have done, in partnership with Simon.' All the officers nodded their heads in agreement, while wondering which incompetent fools had allowed six million to be squirreled away without noticing it.

Gregory continued. 'When we called in Connection it was simply to recruit a first-class accountant for us, as our current one is retiring next month. I suspect he will be going sooner than that.' He turned to Beth. 'Beth, I think this is the point where you, Simon and myself disappear with your files, and hand everything over to the officers.'

'What happens next?'

The question came from an earnest-looking dark-haired man who so far hadn't said a word. His facial expression matched his voice.

'Nothing of this leaves this room. I am assuming the first step will be to block that offshore account before they can transfer those funds anywhere else. You'll all be kept fully informed but not by email. I will contact all of you by phone before the end of the day. Coffee and tea are available in the anteroom. Feel free to discuss the issues amongst yourselves of course, but please don't take anything home yet. The time for that will come.'

He stood, as did Beth, Simon and the three police officers. Nobody else spoke, nobody else moved.

Luke couldn't concentrate. His typing up of the transcript of the conversation with John Coates was somewhat erratic, and he had a smile on his face that came from deep within him as he heard the echo of *I'll be staying over tonight* rampaging around his brain.

The tap on his door was soft, and Tessa's head appeared. 'You busy?'

'Typing up the transcript.'

She gave a slight nod, and the rest of her followed as she entered his office. 'It's buzzing around my brain.'

'Mine too.' *Alongside other things...*

She swung a chair round to face him, and sat. 'Where do we start?'

'I've no idea. It's why I decided to get this typed up, I thought it might trigger thoughts, but so far there's nothing. I'm assuming you have the *entire* police file?'

'I do, unless anything's happened to add to it in the last two months, and I can't see that having happened. What we have is what we've got, but at least we have a starting point. I'm hoping John has told Caroline he's involved us, because I think you need to meet her. You need the whole picture, it's not enough to know he's the brains behind Code Blue.'

'Have you played it?'

Tessa laughed. 'No. The last game I played was Snake on a Nokia phone.'

Luke's eyes lit up. 'You've played Snake?'

'You haven't?'

'No, it's sort of folklore, I've never even seen it. There is something I should mention. I think he's built Code Blue

33

around what happened to them. We have to trap a killer. The man victim of a crime in which his partner was seriously hurt and his children killed is the one doing the searching, and the killer is very ghostlike. As the game progresses he becomes more real, but the slightest misstep loses a fraction of him. That's simplifying it obviously, but basically it's a mind game, following clues, getting weapons...'

'Sounds delightful. I really came in to try to sort where we start with this. Everything was so well checked at the time. The CCTV was examined several times but there was nothing.'

'I'm going to look at it. Maybe it needs fresh eyes, fresh thoughts from somebody who knew absolutely nothing about the case. Whoever this mastermind is, he must have had some hold on the two lads who were sent down for the assault or they would have given him up. Maybe that's where we need to start looking. Did he threaten their families? They must be pretty pissed off that they are doing long stretches for a share of five thousand, and he got away with everything plus ten grand and a Lexus. And if what you say can be proved, it seems he's carried on getting away with it.'

'So what's the plan?'

'Think there's any chance of a prison visit?'

'None whatsoever. If I still had DI in front of my name, the answer would have been yes, but I don't.'

'Okay, let's put ourselves in their places. What would be the one thing that would keep your mouth zipped?'

'Exactly what you said – a threat to my family.' Tessa nodded as if in agreement with herself.

'And nobody is likely to say we can't talk to them?'

'No, we are bona fide investigators when all's said and done.'

'Is all the info on their lives in here?' Luke tapped the thick file.

'Yes, but we've moved on five years. Things will have

changed. I think we'll need to do some internet trawling, update the files with any extra stuff we find, and then decide where we're going from there. In the meantime, we need to pay a visit to the Coates' home, get some thoughts from Caroline now we're five years on from the attack, and see if there's anything we can trigger in her mind given the distance in time.'

'And if nothing comes from this?'

'Then I move to plan B, but I don't want to do that. That would involve contacting somebody from my police days that I don't want to contact. An informer. There's nothing to stop us talking to the DI who was in charge when this all happened because he's now a civilian, but if I'm being brutally frank, he was a waste of time. I believe he retired before he was told to go. He wasn't bent or anything like that, merely too bloody lazy to do the job.'

Luke was making notes while Tessa did most of the talking, and eventually he pulled the file towards him. He opened it and looked at the pictures of the two nineteen-year-olds locked away.

There was little to choose between the photographs; both had the same glassy-eyed stare, thin chiselled features, hooded brown eyes and lank hair.

'They related?'

'Second cousins,' Tessa said.

'You can tell.'

Tessa nodded. 'They even spoke alike, same phrasing, used the same swear words. At the time it felt uncanny. But neither of them gave up anything. They simply said he was a random man they met in a pub. When you listen to the interview tapes, you'll be shocked at how alike they sound, even to the slight lisp they both have. The relationship is via their mothers. They were direct cousins. They said they didn't know who their father was, but they were only three months apart in age so I suppose it's perfectly possible they had the same father. When we interviewed their mothers, both said the boys were the result of one-night stands and they didn't know the name of the father. We got nothing else out of them, but it seemed strange they both came up with the same story. We ran the DNA from the lads through the database but didn't come up with anything on the system. They called him Skinny, but that was their name for him because he was. Skinny, I mean.'

'Then Skinny it is. And I think we should talk to this ex-DI of yours. When did he leave?'

'Virtually as soon as we got these two imbeciles locked up. He considered it case closed, so the higher-ups deemed it go into cold storage. We occasionally got it out and looked at it, whenever a similar case was reported to us, but nothing ever came of it. We'll solve it, though, won't we?'

'Too damn right we will,' Luke said forcibly. 'I've a lot of reading to do on it, but I'll do as much as I can tonight...' He hesitated.

'You had plans?' Tessa laughed.

'I'm not sure... I hope so, but...'

'Then I'll leave you alone to get a head start on it. Don't push yourself too hard, they've waited five years for answers, so we take this at our own pace. I suggest you start with the CCTV, take your time, watch it carefully. Your eyes are fresh to it, and you might spot some mannerism, some mistake he made, that tired police eyes missed or glossed over. While you're doing that, I'll try to find out where Alex Mason is living now, in case we want to meet with him.'

Beth and Simon pulled up outside Connection, and both of them sat for a moment.

'I'm knackered,' Simon said.

'Me too. Tomorrow morning we'll have a late start, say eleven, and we'll have a de-briefing. We've a report to produce and an invoice for our costs. I have to say, Simon, you've been a star. This would have taken me at least two days longer if you hadn't worked alongside me. I didn't anticipate anything like this when I offered you the job, I wanted you more on the recruiting side, but this has been massive.'

Simon gave a short laugh. 'I'll be honest, I didn't expect this either, but it's certainly been an eye opener. We'd certainly spot fraud on this scale a lot sooner if it happened again. You'll be required to attend court?'

'One or both of us will, I assume, as we discovered it in the first place. Greg wanted us to find him an accountant, he didn't know we were going to be saying where's this random six million gone.'

Simon opened the passenger door. 'Come on, let's get all this stuff inside and locked away till tomorrow. Then I'm going to change into my running gear and run home. I need to loosen joints that have hardly moved for the past few days.'

'I can take you home.'

'I'd rather run. I run most days, so I need to do this. Thanks anyway.'

Cheryl lifted her head and smiled at the two of them. 'Our wanderers return. Good to see you back. Beth, you've a few messages on your desk. Simon, you have one. Fred is at Ernest Lounds' place, Luke and Tessa are in their offices. I've notified everyone that our weekly team meeting is being moved to Thursday at ten, as you asked, Beth. Would you like a drink making?'

'Cheryl, you're a smart lady. I'm sure we could both manage a coffee. We decided not to stop on the journey back down from the North East, but that might have been a mistake.'

'Then go into your office, I'll bring them in. Welcome home. It's been quiet without you.'

Beth laughed. 'Cheeky monkey. I imagine the two upstairs have made up for it.'

'They did have rather a nice-looking man come in to discuss a case. I expect they'll bring you up to date very quickly. I think they're working it together.' She stood. 'I'll make those coffees.'

5

Luke put his arms around Maria's waist as she stood at the cooker stirring the bolognese sauce. He kissed the back of her neck. 'That's a welcome sight. I'm glad to be home, it's been a long day.'

Without turning, she said, 'I meant it.'

He hesitated before speaking. 'Good. I hoped you did.'

She carefully lowered the heat, placed the wooden spoon on the side and eventually turned to face him.

'I love you,' she said.

'And I love you.'

Maria smiled. 'And that's why I'm staying tonight.'

Fred opened the passenger door and Naomi squeezed his hand in thanks. He walked round to the driver side and settled into his own seat. 'I'm taking you to a new Chinese restaurant in Chesterfield. That okay?'

'Chinese is my favourite. Did you ask Luke?'

'No, but I once heard him say about all the different parts that make up a Chinese meal for you when you order a takeaway because you liked everything, so I figured if I could find a buffet style, I'd win your eternal gratitude. This has only been open a couple of months, and our table is booked for eight, so we can get a drink first.'

'Maybe I should have worn a cheong-sam,' she said with a laugh.

'You're absolutely stunning as you are,' Fred said as he started the car. 'Please forgive me, Naomi, if I'm a bit rusty with how I treat you, I'm basically having to learn everything from new. You're the first lady I've taken out since I lost Jane.'

Naomi touched his hand as it rested on the gear lever. 'And I'm happy to learn with you. Let's go and enjoy ourselves, Fred, at our age we've earned it.'

Luke leaned on his elbow and stared down at the sleeping girl by his side. His Maria. He had a feeling inside him that his life had changed for ever and in an incredibly good way. They hadn't spoken of a future, only the present, but the whole situation, although overwhelming, felt so right.

He gently stroked her cheek, and she stirred. 'Time is it?'

He looked at the digital figures on his clock. '3.23.'

And she was asleep again. He smiled. He didn't want to sleep. He wanted to look at her beautiful face, remember it glowing as it had done a few hours earlier as they had made love for the first time, and he wanted to be with her for ever.

Fred delivered Naomi back to her door at eleven, and they sat in the car and talked for a few minutes.

'You're very welcome to come in for a coffee, Fred.'

'Not tonight, thanks, Naomi. I have an early start tomorrow, and I've some reading to catch up on for a case Luke is working with Tessa. This is my life,' he said simply.

'I know. And I'm happy with it. Don't forget I've had a couple of years of Luke wandering in and out at odd times of the day and night, sometimes being away overnight, sometimes surveillance jobs with Doris, so I am fully aware of what your job entails. And if you have to cancel Thursday evening for any reason, don't worry about it. We can change it to another time.'

'You know,' he said, his voice pensive, 'when I lost Jane I thought my world had ended. I never imagined I would take another woman out for a meal, couldn't even begin to think I would want to. And then I saw you at Cheryl's house. I'm sorry if this sounds a bit forward, but I knew we would be good for each other. Luke being your son was a minor complication, but he'll get over it.'

'Fred, you're such a lovely person. And we will enjoy each other's company, I know we will, so we'll have to forget Luke and his protectiveness towards me. What I do in my life is my decision, not my son's. And I'm really looking forward to the cinema on Thursday, but I'll understand if we have to postpone. Let's take whatever we have one day at a time, and enjoy the journey. Yes?' She held up a hand for a high-five, but he gently lowered it, pulled her towards him and kissed her.

'Yes,' he said quietly, 'oh very much yes.'

Wednesday the fifth of February twenty twenty began quietly. Fred was first to arrive and immediately became immersed in his computer, printing out things to add to his file on the Coates case. Back in twenty fifteen he had been infuriated by the lacklustre investigation, but had assumed when he left the force that he wouldn't ever hear of it again, unless it accidentally came on to someone's radar from another case.

Now it had come on to the Connection radar, and although he wasn't involved, he needed to be up to date with all they knew, just in case... He had experienced flash backs to the sight of the two dead babies for months after the event, and remembered feeling anger at being diverted to a different case, with even more anger when the Coates one was relegated to being a cold case.

His radio was playing Classic FM in the background, and a Strauss waltz faded gently away to make way for the nine o'clock news.

He listened to the headlines, feeling uncomfortably aware that news programmes seemed to be leading with the virus that had originated in China, and was now spreading. Covid-19 seemed to be flavour of the month with the major stations, and he hoped to God somebody would get it under control shortly. Already so many deaths in China...

He picked up the papers the printer had stacked up, and quickly read through them. He had concentrated on newspaper reports from the time of the attack, and he placed them into date order, before clipping them into a separate file.

Fred refreshed his coffee and pulled his laptop towards him. The long discussion with Ernest Lounds the previous day needed putting into a report, and the final bill prepared now that Ernest had said a very definite no to a continuance of the case. It niggled Fred that Ernest was firmly saying no, but he was the client. To make everything worse, Fred felt that Ernest knew more than he was saying, and was hiding something important, but it was clear from seeing his wife that the man had more than enough on his plate at home.

He reluctantly closed it not only on his laptop, but in his mind. He let his thoughts roam to the strains of Schubert, and opened a new file for a client he had visited after leaving the Lounds' home the previous afternoon.

．　．　．

Ken Freeman had filled the doorway when he answered Fred's ring of his bell. Easily six feet six inches tall, he towered over Fred, his heavy build seeming to add to the appearance of height.

With a strong Yorkshire accent, he invited Fred into his home, gave him a cup of tea and sat down opposite him at the kitchen table.

'Reight,' he said.

Fred waited.

'This cottage. As tha can probably tell, I'm not from these parts. I've lived all mi life in Sheffield wi' mi grandparents. Nah I live 'ere in Bradwell, which is a lot posher than where I grew up. An' I'll be honest, I want to know what I know nowt about.'

Fred took out his recorder and switched it on. 'Ken, I'm going to record this because it's easier for me when I come to write everything up. Is that okay?'

'Fine. Do whatever tha needs to do, but get me some answers.'

'Okay. Tuesday, fourth of February twenty twenty, client Kenneth Freeman, Whitelilac Cottage, Bradwell. Begin at the beginning, Ken, and tell me why you need me here.'

'Reight. I'll try and talk a bit posher. I've always worked in't steelworks at Stocksbridge, and never bothered 'ow I talked, we all spoke same t'language in all that noise. But nah I've talked to one or two folks round 'ere, and I'm going to 'ave to smarten up. Have to smarten up,' he corrected himself.

'Mi granddad got me t'job when I left school, and I only left a couple of weeks ago. I'm forty nah. I'm tekkin' a few weeks off while I decide what ter do next, 'cos nah it seems I've got a bob or two.'

Fred waited. Ken was clearly building a picture of himself, wanted Fred to know the full story.

Ken took a deep breath. 'I went to live with Nan and Granddad when I were nowt but a babby – I were two. I never 'ad a dad, and I was told my mum died. Car crash they said. When I got older I asked 'em to take me to her grave, but they said she'd been cremated and her ashes scattered in some bluebell woods. I 'ad no reason to doubt 'em. They loved me, gave me a good life, and we weren't poor. We weren't rich, don't get me wrong, but they owned that little house we lived in, and when they both died in the same year it passed to me. In the meantime I'd got married, divorced – all within three years – and kept goin' to work.'

Fred smiled. 'Pretty straightforward then.'

'Yep. After t'divorce I lived on mi own, but then Granddad died first, so I moved back in to look after mi nan. She'd been diagnosed with cancer before Granddad died, so I did as much as I could for her, but I was glad when she finally passed. She became reight thin, was dependent on morphine to keep the pain away. That's no way to go. An' I've been on mi own ever since.'

'And now you're here, in Bradwell?'

'That's why I need your Connection agency. Four weeks ago I 'ad a letter. From a solicitor, asking me to contact him urgently, 'e 'ad summat to tell me.' Ken stood. 'Let's 'ave another cuppa. We getting' to t'problem now, an' it's at least a two-cup problem.'

Fred pushed his empty cup across to him. He was beginning to enjoy this huge man's company, and hoped he wouldn't posh up his accent too much, just to feel as though he could live in Bradwell. Fred wandered across to the kitchen window and looked out at the back garden. Daffodils were already showing leaves that were quite tall, and the garden itself was well laid out and clearly loved.

The kettle boiled, drinks were made, and both men re-took their seats at the table. Ken placed a pack of chocolate and jam tea cakes between them. 'Help yourself,' he said. 'My favourites, and just about posh enough for Bradwell, I reckon. An' if they're not, well that's tough.'

Fred took one, bit into it, and said, 'Well posh enough, I reckon.'

6

Ken looked down at his half-eaten tea cake and gathered his thoughts. 'I wasn't worried about seeing this solicitor chap, more puzzled. I've kept it, so I'll show it to you in a bit. It said nowt other than contact them. Anyways, when I did, the receptionist made an appointment for two days later for me to see this feller who was so desperate to see me.' Ken put the rest of his tea cake into his mouth and was silent for a bit while he chewed it, gathering his thoughts. Fred waited for him to continue.

'I booked a day off work, put on mi suit and went down to Paradise Square. Yer know Paradise Square?'

Fred nodded. 'Very well.'

'That's where their offices are. Nice place, nice desks. Nice people as it turned out. I went in, found out this Harley Lowell-Raine was a woman and not a man, and came out with this 'ouse. She 'eld a will my mother made in nineteen eighty-five leaving the house and bank account to me. There was almost a million in the bank, and heaven only knows what this house is worth. I couldn't take it all in at the time, and she kept insisting all she knew was what was in t'will. Mum had a carer towards the end, a live-in carer, who was tasked with notifying the solicitor once my mother passed. I have spoken to this carer, and she's quite happy to talk to you, but she knew nowt really. She was only here for about four months, and I don't think my mother spoke too much about her life. My mother's name, by the way, was Joanne, Joanne Freeman. She never married, so I've no idea where the money came from.'

'You thought your mother died when you moved to live with your grandparents, you said?'

'That's what I was told. I need ter know the truth, Mr Iveson.'

'Fred, I'm Fred.'

'Can you 'elp, Fred?'

'I can, I'm sure. You're prepared for anything?'

'Owts better than nowt.'

Fred finished his tea, and switched off the recorder. 'I'll get this written up, work out a plan, and I'll give you a ring tomorrow. If you're happy at that stage to employ us, I'll ask you to sign a contract and pay a deposit. Is that okay?'

'I'm 'appy to sign now, and will a cheque do?'

Fred opened his briefcase and took out the form. 'I hope we can give you what you need, Ken. I'll certainly give it my best shot.'

'I've got some paperwork that woman gave me, so tek it and look through it, and let me 'ave it back when tha's done.' He handed a large envelope to Fred, and Fred eased it into his briefcase.

'Thank you. I'll copy everything and return it in the next couple of days.'

Fred finished listening and transcribing the recording, then took the cheque and contract through to Cheryl.

'Morning.' She smiled. 'You came in early this morning.'

'Wanted to get started on this. Quite a fascinating and interesting case. Am I right in thinking you worked in Paradise Square before you stopped soliciting?'

With a straight face, she said, 'I normally do all my soliciting on the Town Hall steps, but I'm getting a bit old to pull in the punters now.'

'I used the wrong phrase...'

'Slightly, but yes, I did work in Paradise Square. Why?'

'Did you know a solicitor called Harley Lowell-Raine?'

'I did. She was a partner in the offices next door to where I worked. Nice lady, did a lot for the Children's Hospital charity. Why?'

'Her name's cropped up in this new case and I may need to speak with her. Only wanted your thoughts on her.'

'If you do, pass on my regards. I liked her.'

He nodded, and went back to his own office.

'DI Heaton! Good to see you.' Cheryl smiled at the man she had a lot of time for, both as the husband of her Kat Heaton, her church deacon, and as the police contact for the Connection team.

'Good to see you too, Cheryl. Is Tessa in? Or Luke?'

'They're both in their offices. I'll tell Tessa you're here.' She pressed Tessa's internal line. 'DI Heaton is here to see you.' There was a pause. 'I'll send him up.'

'Thanks, Cheryl,' Carl said as he headed for the lift.

Tessa met him in the corridor, and led him back to her room.

'Is Luke here?' he asked. 'You might want him in on this one.'

'It's really only a courtesy call, I felt you should know before you read it in the newspapers.' Carl took a sip of his coffee. It was worth the visit for the quality of the coffee. 'It's Martin Synyer. He died in the early hours of yesterday morning.'

'What?' Shock was etched onto Tessa's face. 'Dead?'

'It's been confirmed from two sources – his girlfriend in Spain and the Consulate. It seems he contracted coronavirus from his girlfriend. She made it, he didn't. She's still poorly but over the worst and expected to survive, he was put on a ventilator but ultimately succumbed. As you know from the news, Spain is being overrun with the virus, and he chose the wrong place to hide.'

'Does Phyllis know?'

'Yes, the girlfriend rang her. It was Phyllis who told her to contact the British Consulate. They got in touch with us as it flagged up he was wanted.'

'So it's over, our unfinished case. Thank you for telling us, Carl. It almost feels like justice for Denise and Lorna in an odd sort of way. And I am glad we didn't see this in the newspapers first. I'll complete our records. Will his body be returned?'

'Doubt it. Phyllis doesn't want him back. I went out to see her after we heard from the Consulate, but the girlfriend had already rung her, so she knew. I don't know how bad it affected her when she first found out, but she was quite cool about it when I told her. Sort of a "good riddance to bad rubbish" attitude. She's taken over the Synyer business, blocked all his income from it, so I got the impression life was good for our Phyllis.'

Carl stood. 'I'll head off. I've a meeting at eleven where no doubt this will be discussed, but we can also close our files on it now. We've asked for DNA proof it is Martin Synyer as he was a wanted criminal, but I don't doubt it is him. Have a good day, you two, I'll see myself out.'

. . .

'Don't you hate it when somebody cheats justice,' Luke said quietly. 'I don't feel any sort of sorrow that he's dead, it's more that I'm angry. He was a killer, he's served no time at all for it, it's bloody infuriating.'

'I agree. He'd still be alive if he'd stayed in this country. This Covid thing is becoming a bit more worrying every day. It must certainly be worrying in Spain. Italy has a high rate of deaths as well.'

'Thank God we're an island.'

Tessa looked at him. 'For such a smart guy you can be a bit dim at times. Ever heard of aeroplanes?'

The outer door was locked and all members of staff were seated around Beth's desk by eleven, ready to give reports on closed cases and new activities.

Beth began by giving details of their three days spent in Middlesbrough, the passing on of the case to the Cleveland Fraud Squad, and the successful conclusion of their side of the matter. Simon came in for some praise, and he blushed.

'Ignore his blush,' Beth said. 'He was a star. He took up the slack when I was weakening. It's been a definite learning curve for both of us, but we got through it. I can't give you any final figures yet because I don't want to close it until we know whether we'll be needed again, but bonuses may be on the cards. We're back to our bread and butter work now, recruiting. I'm sending Simon off for a couple of days with Joel, to sit in on what he does, and to learn from him, so I'm taking a couple of days off to get this wedding sorted. We haven't even booked a venue yet, and we can't have a wedding when the only thing secured is the church.'

'Awesome,' Tessa said. 'Well done, you two.'

She then went on to explain in detail the Coates case, saying that she and Luke had decided to work it between them as it had the potential to be big. The criminal element was the driving factor in that decision, and she had made Luke fully aware of all the facts. Fred had also volunteered his services should they be needed, as he had been involved originally.

'Okay,' Beth said when Tessa sat back. 'That sounds... big. If you need IT help, give me a shout, but if you have the original police files you'll probably not need me. You're happy to go ahead with the three of you?'

Tessa nodded. 'We are, but if we get any sort of inkling of who he is, we may need help at that point.'

'Fred? You're happy with what Tessa has reported?'

'I am. I'd give anything to find the man who caused the deaths of those babies. If Tessa needs me, I can run it alongside a new case I took on yesterday.' He then spent several minutes reporting on Ken Freeman and his search for details about his mother, before sitting back.

'Fascinating,' Beth said. 'I wouldn't know where to start, so...'

'And I can't add up,' Fred said. 'We all have our strengths and our weaknesses, Beth. I'm a ferret, I'll sort this, but you, you'll probably recruit the next Prime Minister.'

'If only,' Beth muttered. 'Cheryl? Are they behaving?'

'More or less. I'm starting to organise everybody, and I pretty much know where everybody is at any given moment. This is the point where I say a massive thank you for giving me a chance with this job, because I love coming to work every morning.'

There was a round of applause at her words, and her blush matched Simon's from earlier.

'Are we done?' Beth asked.

'Think so. Can we get off to work now?' Fred asked.

'Not quite,' Luke said. 'Tessa asked me to fill you all in on the Synyer case from a couple of weeks ago. Carl popped in earlier today to give us the news that Martin Synyer has died in Spain, from this Covid virus thing. He apparently contracted it from his girlfriend. She made it through, but he didn't. The Consulate, and his girlfriend, have both confirmed it, and the police are waiting for DNA confirmation. It'll be hitting the papers anytime now because the case was so recent. On a personal note, I feel angry that he's dead and has escaped the justice that should have been meted out to him, but I guess it was a bad way to die, attached to a ventilator that wasn't helping him to breathe.'

There was a silence in the room.

Beth shook her head. 'Good grief. Maybe we should be thinking a bit more seriously about this... Are we not hearing enough about it? I know Spain is fighting a losing battle with it, and we tend to be stoic and British about it, but it's going to arrive here eventually.'

'What can we do?' Fred spoke quietly. 'I suggest we avoid crowds, and wait for guidance from the government. In the meantime, we do our jobs to the best of our ability, and support each other.'

Beth looked around at everybody, their faces concerned after the news about the death of Synyer. 'I can't grieve for that man, he was a killer, an adulterer, and everything that is horrible in a person, so let's close the case and forget him. I'm sure his wife will have. It must be doughnut time.' She reached behind her to the window sill and lifted a large white box. 'I'll pour fresh coffees. Thank you everybody, an enlightening meeting indeed.'

7

Luke and Tessa didn't have long to wait at the gates of the Coates home, and Tessa drove through, parking outside the front door.

'Smart house,' Luke said approvingly. 'One day...'

'I don't doubt,' Tessa laughed, 'but you may have some time to wait.' She locked the car as the front door of the house opened. John stood there, a smile on his face.

'Welcome,' he said. 'Caroline is making coffee.'

He led them through to the lounge where a fire burned brightly in the grate, casting flickering shadows around the walls of the tastefully decorated room. Leather chesterfield sofas surrounded a coffee table of dark wood, and Tessa and Luke sat side by side, looking around appreciatively.

'This has changed,' Tessa said.

'We changed everything. The kitchen was ripped apart and a new one installed before Caro even came home from the hospital. I didn't want her coming back to the bad memories of running through the kitchen to try to save herself, so that was all brand new for her. We redesigned this room between us.'

'It's beautiful. But it's more than that, it's comfortable.'

'Good,' John said with a smile. 'When we started to bring this together, that was the priority.'

The door opened, and Caroline Coates joined them, pushing a small tea trolley.

She had changed little over the five years. Still remarkably beautiful with her long blonde hair framing a petite, almost elfin-like face, and a slim figure to die for, Tessa briefly wondered if Caro too had to have alternate days of water.

Luke stood. 'Can I help?'

'Oh, I like you already,' Caro said with a smile. 'No, I'm fine thanks. We found this little tea trolley in the Antiques Quarter a few weeks ago, and I've only used it once since then, so let me have the pleasure of wheeling it.'

John closed the door behind her and moved back to his chair.

'Is Casey not joining us?' Tessa asked.

'No, sorry,' Caro responded. 'She's having her morning nap. I still have days of pain, and I do encourage Casey to stick to her sleep routine when I'm not too good. She's a very well-behaved child, fortunately.'

Tessa looked accusingly at John. 'You should have said. We could have delayed this until Caro felt better.'

Caroline held up her hand. 'Honestly, it's fine. John has explained what he has done in asking you to find the man who destroyed me, and believe me, the sooner that happens the better. I want to see him face to face, tell him what he caused and that I consider him to be the murderer of my babies, not the two thugs currently locked up for it. Please, Tessa, do your best.'

'You know I will.' Tessa took the cup and saucer handed to her. 'I needed Luke to meet you, we'll be working this together. We've both read the police files on the case, and I know this is complete up to me leaving the police at the end of the year. I'm pretty sure nothing will have been added in the couple of months since then. But we need to think outside the box now. The one thing that has shown up is that he's a smart man. He targets high-end cars and buys them with real money. He always seems to have a good reason for paying cash – usually a gambling win. And let's face it, cash is cash, and he does leave a name and address for the form to be sent to DVLA that he is the new owner of the car you're about to hand over to him. He works a little differently now in that he only sends one person to retrieve the cash. The police always thought that you were the unlucky first target for him. He practised with you, then honed his skills as time went on.'

Luke sipped at his drink before speaking. 'We also think he researches thoroughly. He's been caught on CCTV several times, but seems to know where cameras are. His face has never been captured, so therefore he hasn't either. Security is strong at companies who deal with alarm and CCTV installations, so...'

'You think he befriends somebody who works in that department?'

'Either that, or he blackmails them, or he works there himself. Do you have the files dating back to when you owned Coates Electronics?'

John smiled. 'Everything. But I do have to say that everybody who worked for me on the management side was interviewed by me, and very extensively. We held a lot of data about our clients, and I couldn't take chances. Everybody was CRB checked, and employed on a six-month trial basis before being given a full contract.'

Tessa put down her cup. 'We need it. We need all the information on everybody who was working for you at the time of the assault. I accept the man didn't work for you because you would have known him, but he knew the layout of your home enough to tell the two who entered that afternoon exactly where everything was. He knew somebody in your security office. If he hadn't chosen two addicts to recover his fifteen thousand, I don't doubt they would have been careful to be out of CCTV shot. How long was the car advertised, Caro?'

'About two weeks. I got a paltry amount offered for it as a trade-in, so I decided to sell it privately.'

'So he had two weeks to perfect his plan. Out of interest, was he the only one to view the car?'

'He was the only one to turn up. I had two other people contact me, but neither of them turned up. That's annoying, because you tell anybody else who rings that you've got somebody coming to look at it, and then you've lost a potential sale.'

'Smart move on his part, wasn't it,' Luke joined in.

'What do you mean?'

'I'll bet anything that those two calls were made by his accomplices, for that exact reason. He had to perfect his plan before making a move, and he bought time by getting them to ring up and make enquiries about it.'

'Shit,' John growled. 'He played us so well, didn't he.'

'Not really. You wouldn't be expected to think like a criminal. It took him two weeks to get prepared, and the only way he slipped up was in the two idiots he chose to do the burglary.'

'Why was none of this said at the time?'

Tessa looked down at her hands. 'I'm almost embarrassed to say it,' she confessed, 'but it was felt that when we'd caught the two who assaulted Caroline, it was game over. Our DI decided to cold case it, and then he left the force. Whoever this man is, I'm convinced he's still working the scam because it's happened since, but he moves around the area. I personally never picked up another of his, but we were informed about them because of the similarity in MO. This time, I promise you we'll find him.'

Caroline leaned forward. 'I never understood why they took

the entire blame for it, those two lads. Why didn't they give him up?'

Luke and Tessa exchanged a glance. 'We've talked about this,' Luke said. 'It's possible he had something on them that would have sent them down forever, or he used some sort of threat with them. Maybe he promised to hurt their families unless they kept quiet – who knows. It's never going to happen that they give him up now, because they're well into their sentences. They need to ride it out for a couple more years and they'll be released.'

Caroline stiffened. 'But they got fourteen years each!'

'And they'll do half.' Tessa spoke gently.

Tessa and Luke followed John along the corridor linking the two houses, and through the door with the Code Blue sign affixed to it. They found themselves in a small reception area, and the middle-aged woman manning the desk swung round with a smile.

'Shelley, this is Tessa Marsden and Luke Taylor. They have an open-door invitation to visit whenever they want or need to, they're doing some specialised work for me.'

'No problem,' she said. 'I'll prepare key fobs.' She turned to Tessa and Luke. 'They'll be ready for when you leave.'

John nodded. 'Thank you. Okay, follow me, you two, come and meet my gang.'

The main room was a large open plan office, separated by head-height screens. There were five people working quietly at computers, and Luke and Tessa were introduced to them as they travelled around.

John eventually led them towards his own office, mainly glass, and with a bank of computers to keep him busy.

'Wow,' was the first word from Luke's mouth.

John grinned. 'I know. It's like working in my own personal toy box. Give me five minutes and I'll transfer all the files you want to see onto a disc drive. The home set-ups in these files are probably out of date now – I did sell Coates over five years ago. But if it was somebody working for me giving out information, this is the information that would have been given out.'

Tessa looked around her. 'This seems a very peaceful place to work. Calming, quiet.'

John gave a slight laugh. 'It is at the moment. It can be hectic and noisy when somebody comes up with a breakthrough on a particular problem, but I was careful to recruit the right people. Three of them worked for me at Coates Electricals – Dom, Ivan and Flora. The other two, Kathy and Brad, I recruited personally from my beta-testing team.'

'Can you give Luke their full details, please?'

'But...'

'John, we check everything and everybody. You said three of them came from Coates, so they'll definitely be checked.'

'Sorry – I'm not used to feeling out of control. I'll add the employee file to the disc drive.'

They watched as Flora stood and carried her cup to the coffee station. She saw them looking, held up her cup and mimed to ask if they needed a drink. All three declined, and fifteen minutes later John was leading them back to the main house, where they said goodbye to Caroline before heading out to their car.

Tessa shivered as she climbed into the driving seat. 'Feels like snow, it's that cold. Take care, John, I'll be in touch as soon as we need to start asking questions. The next two days will be spent going through that disc drive.'

'We've waited nearly six years, Tessa. There's no rush, just find him. I see Caroline dipping lower and lower every day.'

. . .

Tessa pulled out onto the main road, and Luke sank back in his seat. 'I can't believe I've been in the headquarters of Code Blue. Wait till I tell Maria, she'll be so jealous.'

'When we've solved John's puzzle of who the attacker is, maybe you can get permission to take Maria for a visit.'

'Oh my God! You're right. If there's anything meant to inspire me to crack on with this, that's it.'

'It's not going to happen in a rush. There'll be loads to trawl through on that disc drive. It's going to be a quiet couple of days for us. Plenty of biscuits, plenty of tea and coffee...'

'And water for you.'

'Water's not cutting it with me for giving me extra brain power,' Tessa admitted with a laugh. 'Think I might be back to the hot stuff by tomorrow morning, and I feel a Chinese takeaway coming on for tonight. Damn. And I've been so good...'

Silence descended, each lost in their own thoughts of the afternoon with John and Caroline, each letting their imaginations roam as to what had happened in the two weeks prior to the attack on Caroline. As they pulled up outside Connection, Tessa stated the obvious.

'This one's not going to be easy, biscuits or no biscuits.'

8

Thursday was a grey day. A miserable feel to it, with a promise of rain later, cold, and inhospitable. Fred shivered as he got out of his car and walked across to open up Connection. He wanted to finish early, knowing he was taking Naomi to the cinema, and apart from all that the Freeman case was proving to be fascinating.

He switched on his kettle to make his first cup of tea, and placed the large envelope on his desk. He had glanced through the contents the previous evening, but knew they needed closer inspection as well as a few minutes being fed through the photocopier.

The main door opened and Luke walked in, holding a hand up in greeting towards Fred.

'We're a couple of early birds, aren't we.'

'I thought it would be quiet,' Fred said with a grin.

'It will be. I'm meeting Amanda from the teashop at half past eight, so I thought I'd get my coffee machine working before she arrived. Maria had to be in early as well, so we stopped off to get her a clean uniform before coming in...' Luke's voice trailed away as he realised what he was saying.

'That's interesting. You dropped Maria off at home at eight in the morning?'

'Don't tell Mum.'

'What's it worth to keep it quiet?'

'Whatever you want...'

'I'll think about it. I might get a lot of fun out of telling your mum.'

Luke groaned as he stepped into the lift. His big mouth had revealed the exact thing they'd decided to stay quiet about.

Amanda was a few minutes early, and she gratefully accepted the coffee Luke handed to her.

'It makes a nice change for you to be giving me a cup of coffee.' She smiled at him. 'You feeling okay now?'

'I'm good. Occasional twinges in my shoulder, but apart from that I've recovered.'

'The whole village was concerned about you, you know. I think Naomi got cheesed off with everybody popping into the shop to get an update on your condition.'

'It'll take more than a two-bit thug to kill me off.' He held a chair out for her and walked round to his side of the desk. 'Right, tell me why you're here. What your problem is.'

'I'm not really sure. We've got planning permission to extend the teashop, turning it into an evening eatery, a bistro, as well as a daytime tea and coffee shop. It's taken for ever to get the permission and we've jumped through more hoops than the hoop manufacturers can make, but finally it's in place – as is the finance. That's the part I want you to look at for me.'

Luke waited. She was clearly gathering her thoughts before speaking them aloud.

'I was contacted by a really nice man, Josiah Lightwood, who had heard of my plans to expand. He wanted to buy into my business, and on paper it made sense. It meant I wouldn't have to borrow money to finance the new build, and it would halve the worry. He was really nice, gave me lots of time to consider his proposal, left me with a full plan when he had one professionally done, and I handed it to my partner to read through it. Neither of us could find anything wrong, and it seemed to answer any concerns we might have had about the whole idea of growing the business. He's retired, sold the business he was in, and now is looking for an investment. He doesn't want to work in the tea rooms, merely be a silent partner.'

'And you're happy with that?'

'Of course. I have my own way of working, so don't really want somebody muscling in who I might not be able to work with. I want to set on my own staff when the time comes.'

'So what's worrying you?'

She paused and sipped at her coffee. 'I don't know. I'm expected to sign a contract next Monday that will tie me to him, and I don't know him. I see the smart man, the business man, the softly spoken man, but I don't see concrete proof that I can trust him. Do you understand?'

'Have you brought his business plan?'

'I've brought everything. Our planning permission, the architect's plans, anything you could possibly need. I want you to tell me I'm being an idiot, and to grab what he's offering with both hands. What's bothering me is that I can't reach that conclusion on my own.'

'Okay, here's what I'm going to do. Beth is our mathematical genius. She knows people, she understands contracts, and she may even know this Josiah Lightwood. Leave everything with me, and we'll have something for you by Sunday. Don't sign anything until Beth has gone through all of this with a fine toothcomb – she's an expert with fine toothcombs.' He laughed. 'All I have to do is get her into the office, because she'd booked a couple of days leave.'

'Tell her afternoon tea for two on the house by way of apology.' Amanda smiled at Luke. 'You've taken a load off my shoulders, Luke. I've not been sleeping at night worrying about it, and it was like a sign from the angels when I saw you in the café on Tuesday.'

He removed a contract form from his desk drawer. 'And now I have to think about my business.'

Beth looked out of her lounge window cradling her first coffee of the day, and felt reluctant to head out of the door. She'd found the ideal venue for the wedding the previous day, and knew she was paying lip service to carrying on with the search, but she wanted to have two or three options to show Joel.

'How many calories in a bacon sandwich,' she murmured softly. 'Too many? Or not enough? Could I manage a bacon sandwich right now? Too right I could.'

She carried the coffee through to the kitchen, opened the fridge door and took out the bacon box. Ten minutes later she was sitting down with a sandwich and a fresh coffee, prepared to take her first bite. Her phone rang.

'Luke Taylor, I'm on holiday.'

'I need you. You said...'

'I know what I said, but I didn't mean it. Besides, I've got a huge bacon sandwich halfway to my mouth, so I can't think of anything else right now.'

'If I said afternoon tea for two with all the trimmings, would you be tempted to listen to me?'

She took her first bite of her bacon buttie. 'Might be,' she mumbled.

Luke talked as Beth ate her way through her sandwich.

They both finished at the same time, and she wiped the crumbs from her mouth. 'I'm on my way in. If she's feeling uncomfortable, then something isn't right. Can you photocopy everything she has brought in? I don't like keeping originals with us, we can let her have hers back. What's your take on it?'

'Concerned. She didn't approach him, he approached her. I don't think she's asked enough questions of him, she doesn't really know him and that's what's worrying her the most. It may all be genuine, he may be what he purports to be, a retired company director with money to invest, but she doesn't know anything beyond that. Anyway, I've built you up to be the world's biggest expert in detecting fraudsters and conmen, so I think you should follow through on your promise to help any of us if we needed an extra pair of hands. I do.'

'Has Amanda signed one of our contracts?'

'She has, which is another reason for you forgetting these few days you've booked off. Your business needs you, Beth.'

'Don't pull that one. I give in. I'll be there in half an hour, so get photocopying.'

Fred was switching off the copier when Luke peered over his shoulder. 'You done?'

Fred nodded. 'Just. I think I move on to computer work now. I need more information, so I'm going to lock myself into the office, top up the teapot, and get to work. Has Amanda gone?'

'She has, and Beth is on her way in. I've persuaded her she doesn't need a holiday, bribed her with afternoon tea for two at Amanda's place. It's financial problems, and I figured Beth was the best one to sort it, especially as we've only got until Sunday to work out if it's genuine or not. Contracts are being signed Monday.'

Fred frowned. 'She's left it very late to be having these sort of thoughts. Throw me a name, just in case...'

'Josiah Lightwood.'

Luke could see cogs churning inside Fred's head. 'Nope,' he finally said. 'Doesn't ring any bells, so if he's a conman he's not done it before using that name. Let's leave it to Beth, she seems to have a knack for recognising when things aren't right.'

'My thoughts exactly. Amanda brought some paperwork in, so I'm going to photocopy it, deliver the originals back to her, and pass the copies to Beth. I can then get back to the Coates enquiry.'

'Smart move.' Fred picked up his copies. 'And I thought it was going to be a quiet day. There's only Simon not in.'

'You're taking Mum out tonight, aren't you?'

Fred's smile was huge. 'I most certainly am. We're going for a drink first, then we'll decide what film to see. It's years since I've been to the cinema.'

'And you'll keep quiet?'

Fred guffawed with laughter. 'That's for me to know and you to worry about.'

It didn't take Luke long to copy Amanda's paperwork, and he heard Tessa's voice as he switched off the hum of the copier.

She was talking to Cheryl, checking diary appointments. 'We need today and tomorrow totally free, and we'll work in Luke's office because it's bigger and he's got biscuits.'

'Fair enough,' Cheryl said. 'I'll cancel this hairdresser booking, see if I can get you in for next week at the same time. That's the only thing that you have booked in. Is there anything I can help with?'

'We'll let you know. We're going through CCTV footage, statements from the Coates's, and anything else we need to check. My plan is to start from the beginning of the investigation and work through to the day it was cold-cased. This will be so big for us if we manage to find this... this bastard. I didn't want the investigation to be stopped, I felt we hadn't given it everything, but we had this DI who was so bloody idle...'

'I can hear the frustration in your voice. Ah, here's young Luke. Offering my help, Luke, if you two need an extra pair of hands.'

'Thanks, Cheryl. You're a star. Did I hear you say we're in my office, Tessa? I'll nip over to the Co-op and get us some doughnuts.'

'For all of us?' Cheryl's eyes lit up.

'Definitely for all of us. So far this morning I've pulled Beth back into work when she's supposed to be on holiday, and I've got some serious bribery to do with Fred. Tessa I have to keep sweet because she's cancelled the diet, and you just like doughnuts.'

'Serious bribery?' Both women spoke in unison.

Luke blushed. 'Never mind. Let's say it may be a three-doughnut bribe.'

'Good grief.' Tessa was laughing. 'Our mission today, Cheryl, is to find out what Luke has done wrong, and how Fred managed to find out about it. Three doughnuts indeed!'

9

By ten all the staff of Connection, with the exception of Simon who was drinking a Starbucks latte with Joel Masters in the centre of Manchester, were ensconced in their offices, doughnuts in their hands.

Luke had downloaded the contents of the data file on to his computer and was watching the CCTV gathered at the time of the assault on Caroline Coates. He was surprised to discover extra footage taken from neighbours of the couple, but it showed the man who had bought Caroline's Lexus walking to the property, some time after John arrived home from work. Luke slowed it until he was watching it frame by frame, and made notes as he did so.

The man was wearing a North Face jacket in black, and had his face hidden by the hood that was pulled onto his head, despite the warm weather. The hood remained in place until he entered the house, and his back was towards the outside camera the whole of the time he waited at the front door.

Once inside the house he carefully avoided any of the interior cameras, and Luke found himself talking to himself. 'He bloody knew the location of the cameras. This has got to be connected to Coates Electricals. Somebody has given him information about this security set-up... we need to check employees. I need to see what DI Mason discovered about the employees...'

He looked up startled as the door opened, and Tessa entered. 'It's daft us working separately, I've brought my stuff in here. You okay with that?'

'Of course. I assumed that was happening anyway. You'll have to ignore me muttering away to myself – this stinks. This bloke knew where the cameras were without any doubt.'

'Which leads us straight back to Coates Electricals. I think John doesn't want to believe any of his carefully vetted employees would give out information about security systems. I said as much to DI Mason, but he told me to stop wasting my time, we'd got the lads who'd done the damage. By the time he left the job it was already a cold case.'

'Would it be stupid of me to suggest this DI Mason could be involved?'

Tessa gave a short harsh bark of laughter. 'He wouldn't have that much energy. Honestly, Luke, he was the laziest man I've ever met. He controlled from his desk, not from being out on the streets talking to witnesses or rallying the troops to go door-knocking and talking to neighbours. He squashed almost every suggestion I made until in the end I had to let it go. John bringing it to my doorstep again is almost like a dream come true.'

'I'm going to get the clearest shots we have of him, and get them printed off. There'll not be many, but if we can compare them against other crimes that are deemed to be similar, maybe we can pick up something else. How do we get access to the others that are felt to be the same man? Beth?'

'No, let's try to stop her being sent to the chain gang,' Tessa said with a grin. She held up a second memory stick.

'What's that?'

'Five other sets of CCTV images from five other cases, all believed to be the same man buying the cars, all expensive cars, and all bought on Friday evening, with the cash stolen back during Friday night. He perfected his system after the practice run at the Coates' home.'

'Really?'

'I still have friends on the force,' Tessa explained. 'This is a copy, not the original. He's stayed pretty much in this area, but different forces. Lincoln, Manchester, Wakefield, Hull and Derby. Within an hour's journey of Sheffield, which leads me to think he's still living in the same city. This CCTV hasn't been looked at in its entirety, only job by job. My friend put everything on one stick for us and said good luck.'

Luke slid the stick into the USB port and downloaded the contents. He then passed it to Tessa who did the same.

'So, you want me to start with this new information,' Luke asked, 'or shall I go on to the employees? John gave us everything on them, so I can soon formulate a spreadsheet for us which hopefully will make something jump off the page and smack us on our heads.'

'Take a break from the CCTV, go for the employees. Staring at CCTV for hours on end will give you a massive headache. Go back to these new images when you've had a rest from the first lot.'

'So, we're looking at employees that were there at the time of the attack?'

'Not really. I would go back a year earlier than that, because John had his system put in around six months before the event. We can discount anybody who left his employ before the date of the installation, which was the beginning of November, twenty fourteen. From that date onwards we need to consider every name.'

'Think I'd better up the strength of the coffee, I need to stay awake.'

Fred straightened out the birth certificate pertaining to Joanne Freeman, and made notes of her parents' names, Sybil and Donald Freeman. He then looked at Ken's birth certificate; it stated his mother's name was Joanne, father unknown.

Fred typed in Joanne Freeman on Google, and came up with several hits, none of which seemed to have any bearing on the late Joanne, Ken's mother. He tried going onto Facebook and putting in her name, once again without success.

He did, however, find Ken's Facebook account, but used so rarely that Fred knew it would be of no help. He smiled at the thought of the gruff and blunt Yorkshireman using Facebook.

Ken had a small number of friends – nine in total, and it had been over a year since he had commented. Patiently, and without rushing anything, Fred clicked through each of the friends and quickly realised that they were all much more prolific than their friend Ken.

He made a list of the names, then clicked on each one. They seemed to be workmates, but none of their comments were directed towards Ken, probably because they realised he would never see their words or reply to them.

Fred meticulously worked his way through and decided there was nothing to cause him to think clues would be in there, so he left Facebook and returned to the small pile of paperwork he had brought with him from Ken's cottage.

He stared at the name of the carer, Debra Burford, and wondered how close she had been to the woman she had nursed for the last few months of her life. Time to find out.

He dialled her number, and was a little put out when it went through to voicemail. He left a message explaining who he was and that he was working for Ken, and would like a chat with her. He left his number, and disconnected with a sigh.

His thoughts turned to the large amount of money Joanne had left for her son, and wondered how she had accrued such a vast amount. Where had she been employed? Had she had her own business? He once again picked up his phone, this time ringing Ken.

"Ey up, Fred.'

Fred smiled. "Ey up, Ken. I've made a start on looking at your mother's life, but not having much luck. She didn't use Facebook so no clues there, and despite googling her name, nothing showed there either. So now I'm following the money.'

'I might be able to 'elp. I'm starting to clear stuff out, and there's a little roll-top bureau in t'lounge. I found a few bank statements, just last year's so maybe there's others somewhere else filed away. I can drop them into your office?'

'That would be more than helpful, Ken. I'll make you a cup of tea this time.'

'Reight. I'll be there in half an hour.'

He chuckled as he replaced his phone on the desk, and went back to the pile of papers he'd photocopied. He could give the originals back to their owner, along with a cup of tea.

Ken seemed to fill the office, and Cheryl smiled at him, having been warned of his size.

'Mr Freeman, Fred is expecting you. His office is the one at the end of this short corridor.'

'Thanks, love.'

Fred made the tea, and Ken sat down, patiently waiting, and clutching yet another envelope.

'I wasn't really looking for anything, hoped she might have a book of stamps in there, when I saw these.' He waved the envelope. 'I've not touched owt else, because I think you should go through it. You're more likely to recognise summat that might 'elp find out why she dumped me.'

'I don't think she did "dump you", as you so elegantly phrase it. Let's look at the facts that we do know. She's lived at that cottage since nineteen eighty-two, which was when you went to live with your grandparents. She didn't move to the other end of the earth, she lived a mere ten miles away, which is nothing, is it? No, she didn't dump you, she kept you close enough if she were ever needed during your childhood. And she left everything she had to you. There's a lot more to this than is obvious at this point, but I'll track down your story. And it may well start with these bank statements.'

Ken stared thoughtfully at him. 'She didn't dump me?'

'Let's look at the facts. You said on Tuesday that you weren't poor, that your grandparents owned their little house. Who worked?'

'My granddad. He got me my first job at the same place.'

'So there was only one income?'

'Yes, until I started work, then obviously I added to the pot.'

'You went on holidays?'

'Every year, usually Cornwall, we all liked surfing.'

'So every year you visited the most expensive county in the UK, on a steelworker's wage. Bet you went more than once, didn't you?'

'We did. Usually June and September...' Ken's voice trailed away as he realised what Fred was saying.

'My mum sent them money? Is that what you're saying? And they never told me?'

'When you inherited your grandparents' home, did you have any paperwork from there?'

'I did, but I had a big bonfire and burnt it all one night, when I was feeling too down to cope. I missed 'em, hated being on my own. And I felt guilty for being relieved that Nan was gone, because she suffered so much. It was a bad time.'

'You presumably still own the house?'

'I do, but it's on t'market. I've accepted an offer on it. There's nowt in it, I got rid of all the furniture to St Luke's, and had a skip for t'rest. Everything came with my new place at Bradwell, so I brought nothing with me except mi clothes.'

'Okay, I think the first thing I need to do is go through the bureau, so if you're in tomorrow morning, I'll go straight to you instead of coming in here, and we'll go through it piece by piece. Somewhere there is a clue as to why she felt she had to leave you with her parents, when she was always easily within reach for any emergencies. There could be any number of reasons, and that bureau could be the key to it all. Did you find a book of stamps?'

Ken grinned. 'I did. The postbox is a couple of steps beyond mi front door, so it saved me a walk to t'shop to buy some. Us Yorkshire folks don't throw money around, tha' knows.'

'And yet you're employing Connection...'

He shrugged. 'Some things 'as to be done.'

10

Beth listened without speaking to what Luke was telling her about the issues Amanda Gilchrist had brought to their doorstep, and picked up the contract.

'I'll go through it carefully, Luke. I think she's right to be wary. This man wasn't sought, he simply appeared one day, and we need to know how he knew about her plans. Josiah Lightwood... I feel as if I know the name, but can't quite capture it. Okay, Luke, I'll forgive you, you were right to call me back in. It would have been too late to help her by Monday. I'll start by finding as much as I can about him. And let's hope it all works out for the best, because on the surface it looks as though it would give Amanda everything she needs to grow her tea shop. And I'd quite like a bistro in the village, anyway.'

'Thanks, Beth. I knew I was out of my depth when I realised it was about financial stuff. It's not about what you see on the surface, figures can be manipulated, it's what you read underneath and you're good at underneath reading.'

'Leave it with me. I presume we can contact Amanda anytime? You have her mobile number?'

He nodded. 'I do. Contract signed, small deposit left because

I figured super sleuth Walters wouldn't need long to work out if Lightwood was a bad 'un or a good 'un.'

Beth threw a paperclip at him. 'Get out of here and let me start work. Haven't you got a thief to catch with the lovely Tessa? You getting on well with her?'

'She's awesome. I liked her as a police officer, but now she can cut corners she's amazing.'

'Cut corners?'

'Don't ask. She's Beth Mark Two.'

A second paper clip followed the first, and Luke opened the door before saying, 'Oh, and if Fred tells you anything about me, don't believe it. He's stirring things.'

There was a look of puzzlement on her face as he closed the door. She picked up the first of her two doughnuts and bit into it. What did Fred know? She was head of a detective agency, and if she couldn't solve that little mystery, she shouldn't be in charge...

Beth rinsed her hands to get rid of the stickiness of the vanilla icing, and moved back to her desk. She pulled the notes towards her and stared at the name. Josiah Lightwood... why did she feel she knew him?

She opened up her computer and waited, hoping something would spring to life in her memory. It didn't, not until she typed in the name Josiah Lightwood. Then all the lightbulbs flashed at the same time.

The name Josiah had thrown her. That clearly his Sunday name, just as she always said Bethan was her Sunday name. During the week they used Joe and Beth. Joe Lightwood, recently retired both from the council and from his highly successful printing business.

Joe's retirement had forced a by-election, but he had simply said it was time to go. He had given thirty years of his life to his constituents, and it was time to hand over to a younger man. He left without a blemish to his name, and retired to his home in Bamford where he lived with his wife and two dogs. His children had all left home, and reading between the lines, Beth guessed he was bored. Retiring from both his position as CEO of his business, and the hustle and bustle of council meetings and surgeries meant he would have lots of time on his hands.

Beth would also lay odds on that his wife had encouraged him to find an interest, and thanks to his council connections he would have seen Amanda's planning application.

This all had to be put in a report for Amanda, and Beth began to type her initial findings. She sent a quick email off to Joe Lightwood asking for a meeting, preferably later that day, and then continued with her research on the internet about this man whose biggest crime seemed to be that he had retired from the council when nobody wanted him to retire.

But why a sleeping partner? She needed to confirm that was really his intention, so Amanda had all the facts, and the only way to do that was go to see the man himself. She worked for an hour at finding everything out she could about the popular councillor, then began to check through the contract.

The email arrived back from Lightwood, inviting her to his home at Bamford, saying he would be there at three that afternoon. She breathed a huge sigh, knowing he didn't have to see her, and feeling grateful she had his agreement.

She stood to grab a bottle of water and stretch her legs, and paused by her window. Oliver, the office cat, was jumping around on the grassed area behind the offices, and it occurred to her what a beautiful animal he was. Luke was his primary carer, saw that he was well fed, paid the vet's bills, and yet they all loved the dainty feline. She smiled as he jumped onto the small brick wall, and disappeared over the other side.

She took her water and left her office, stopping by Cheryl's desk. 'Everything okay?'

'Fine. It's been quiet, you all seem to be beavering away at whatever you're working on. You find your wedding venue?'

'I think so. I was going to go and look at a couple more today, but I was so impressed by yesterday's find, I'm pretty sure I'm going to book it. Joel said do it, and gave me his credit card, which wasn't such a smart move on his part. Has Fred said anything to you?'

'What about?'

'No idea. It was something Luke said, told me to ignore whatever Fred might say, it wasn't true.'

'Really? That probably means it was true. Leave it with me, I'll plague Fred until he tells me what's going on. I'll have to wait though, he's got a giant in with him at the moment.'

'A giant?'

'His name is Ken Freeman, and he seems huge. Not fat, solid and tall.'

'Okay, I'll leave it with you, Sherlock. I'm going out around half past two, to Bamford. I'll make sure you've the full address before I go, but I don't think you'll have to recover my dead body.'

'Oh good. Body recovery isn't really on my job description.'

'You got a job description?'

'No. I do everything that everybody else avoids.'

Beth laughed. 'That's okay then. As long as you know what you're doing. Tell you what, as a little reward. I'm on for afternoon tea for two at the tea shop in the village, so we'll go next week. That sound good?'

'Perfect. That's assuming you come back alive from this afternoon's jaunt.'

Beth held up a thumb and headed back into her office.

. . .

Luke began his list with the present employees currently working for John at Code Blue.

Dominic Acton, Ivan Newburg and Flora Robinson had all been head-hunted from Coates Electricals, and had all been at Coates Electricals when the Coates home had had the security system installed. The other two employees in the office had been brought in from John's team of beta testers, Kathy Easton and Brad Wells, but neither of these had ever had any connection to the workforce at Coates Electricals.

He added personal information to his list – addresses, phone numbers, relationship status, all of which he found on the files John had downloaded for them.

There was absolute silence in the office as both Tessa and Luke concentrated on their respective jobs, until Tessa spoke.

'He's still wearing the same North Face jacket. When he commits the crime in the winter months it's easier for him, he wears a black woolly hat as well which anchors his hood in place. And he wears black gloves. Driving gloves type, so nobody would query them. But what I don't understand is he's only done this five times in five years, where it's a high-end car. That's not enough to supplement his dole money, is it?'

Luke stared at her. 'You're right. He doesn't need the money. He does it because he can, for the kicks of getting away with it. Why doesn't he need the money? Because he's not on the dole. He's got a job, whether it's drug dealing or... anything else that springs to mind!'

'Or working in an IT company,' Tessa said quietly. 'We missed checking so much first time around with this case, it's unbelievable.'

'Was the main connection with the other five cases the MO?'

'It was. You've heard of HOLMES, where all info from every case is uploaded, and forces nationwide can access it?'

Luke nodded. 'That's what happened, and everybody agreed

it was the same, especially when we got CCTV images showing him buying the cars. There was never any doubt, but of course he was long gone by the time he had stolen the money back.'

'But that's something else. It's not only one person. He's not physically stealing his own money back, somebody else who's probably more adept at burglary is doing that. I suspect he's hovering somewhere with a car or a motorbike to whisk our burglar away to safety, and then they divvy up the rewards. They are a team. The Coates one went dramatically wrong, but he learnt from that. He found a partner. They're bloody clever at hiding themselves. I couldn't tell you from any of these CCTV films what the second man looks like, other than he's smaller than the one who buys the car.' Tessa sounded angry. 'It's so damn frustrating, but I'm no DI Mason, I'm not restricted by instructions to take it no further. Once we'd locked up Nathan Jacques and Robert Simpson it was treated as if it was game over. Well, it's not.'

'Do we know who installed the security systems at the other five places?'

'Yes, three of them were Coates Electricals, installed some time ago and never updated, and the other two were self-installations that didn't really work all that well, and certainly only had cameras on the outside of the house, nothing on the inside. Poor quality pictures for the self-installations didn't help, either.'

Tessa and Luke stared at each other across the table. 'Okay,' Luke said. 'I suggest we tear apart whoever worked at Coates in that security department, because I'm pretty damn sure that's where we going to find our next lead. Do you think John can get us in there?'

'I agree that's what's needed, but I understand John severed all ties with the new owners once he'd sold up. We forget everything that's supposedly been checked, because I'm sure it will have been sidestepped or ignored altogether, and go back to the beginning. I want to talk more in depth with Caroline and John, because they saw him face to face. Surely there's something they can bring to the fore that will help. I'm also going to tell Carl we're working on it, because you never know when we might need him. That sound like a plan?'

'It does. Shall we visit the Coates house tomorrow? I want to make a list of questions, because I want to talk to the three staff members who've left CE to move to Code Blue. I'll make it look like an informal chat, but it will be recorded. They hopefully will know something that they don't realise they know. We'll need to tell John what we're doing, but he'll go along with anything we do, he's desperate to get this sorted or he wouldn't have come to us.'

Tessa turned to her computer. 'I'll message him now, tell him what we want. Keep tomorrow free, this could take some time.'

11

———————

Joe Lightwood welcomed Beth with a smile and a handshake. 'Ms Walters. Thank you for your email. It all sounded very mysterious.'

Beth followed him through to a beautiful large lounge, and he introduced her to his wife.

'Shall I leave you?' Vera Lightwood asked.

'Not on my account,' Beth said firmly. 'I probably will only need five minutes of your husband's time, I need to confirm a couple of things for my client.'

'Client?' A slight frown appeared on Joe Lightwood's face.

'Amanda Gilchrist.'

'Amanda? But...'

Vera stood. 'I'll get us a pot of tea. Please, sit down, Ms Walters. Whatever issues Amanda has, I'm sure we can resolve them.'

'Please call me Beth. And a cup of tea would be lovely.'

Vera disappeared, and Joe indicated she should sit in an armchair. She did so with a smile.

'Please don't tell me Amanda is having second thoughts.'

'No but I think she's having a serious case of the

collywobbles. She has built up her business very successfully, and now is planning on sharing that success with someone else. It's a massive thing. She came to Connection and asked us to check you out before she signed the contract. Believe me, I know of your exemplary reputation, so this is a courtesy call, but one I have to make to justify the charges Amanda will be paying. They currently amount to the cost of afternoon tea for two, and will probably not rise beyond that.'

'You've checked me out?'

'Not really. I didn't have to, once I'd realised Josiah Lightwood was ex-Councillor Joe Lightwood. The Josiah threw me a bit, I must admit. That's something we have in common, neither of us use our full name.'

'You're Elizabeth?'

She shook her head. 'No, Bethan.' They turned as the door opened, and Vera joined them carrying a tea tray.

'We'll give it a couple of minutes to mash,' she said. 'Have you sorted out the problem?'

'We've talked a little,' Beth said, 'but I do have a couple of questions. Mr Lightwood...'

'Joe,' he said.

'Thank you, Joe. How did you find out about Amanda extending the premises?'

'My best friend is the senior officer in the planning department of the council. He knew I was looking to make a small investment in something, and I asked him to keep an eye open for a business where I wouldn't have to do anything except inject some cash. I don't want to work anymore, Beth, but I would like to see a small return for my money. I did some research on Amanda, went to see her and we got on really well. We're signing contracts on Monday – or at least I hope we are.'

Vera poured out the tea, handed Beth her cup and saucer and spoke. 'Can I have my little say now? Joe's retired, he wishes to invest, and he is doing it all for me, to give me some form of income when he dies. Because he is going to die. He has been diagnosed with cancer, terminal in about eighteen months so they say, and he is doing this for me, not for any nefarious reasons. He finished at the council as quickly as he could – only the council leader and the chief executive know his reasons for standing down – and while I have said many times that I don't need any form of income, he insisted on doing this. It will help this young woman and it will give Joe an interest.'

Beth sat in stunned silence. 'I'm so sorry, Joe,' she eventually managed to blurt out. 'I take it you didn't tell Amanda any of this?'

'She didn't need to know. I won't trouble her in any way, the contract stipulates my share of profits, and I've been very fair with her. I like her, and I like her work ethic. I hope she doesn't pull out because it seemed heaven sent when my friend told me about her. It was exactly what I was hoping for.'

'Please don't worry, Joe. My report will say she has nothing that should trouble her from joining forces with you. Fear of the unknown hit her like a ton of bricks, and here I am.'

'That's a relief,' he said with a smile. 'I didn't tell her about my other life as a councillor because it's all over, so she wouldn't have known anything about me. That was stupid of me. I didn't even tell her to call me Joe, I was so intent on keeping everything professional and business like, that I was Josiah to her.'

'Don't worry, I'll make sure she understands everything. This will be such a weight lifted from her, so thank you for being honest with me.'

Beth finished her tea and replaced the cup and saucer on the tray. 'You know, Amanda's food is amazing. The bistro will be a roaring success, I'm sure of it.'

Joe laughed. 'Oh, we've sampled it, don't worry. I did some research before I approached her.'

Beth stood. 'Thank you for your hospitality, and your understanding of why I had to see you.' She handed her card to Joe. 'If ever you need Connection services, please call me.'

She drove back to Connection at some speed, lost in her thoughts. She had thought it strange that one part of the contract was specific to where the money was to go in the event of his death, and now the reason was clear. She would ring Amanda as soon as she got in her office, and arrange to talk with her the following day.

She pulled up at traffic lights and slammed her hand onto the steering wheel. 'Damn bloody cancer,' she yelled. 'Damn it.'

Fred put the envelope containing the bank statements into his desk drawer and headed across the road to the Co-op, hoping Naomi hadn't finished her shift.

She had, but was standing talking to a customer in the doorway.

'Fred? You looking for me?'

'You, and a large bottle of diet Coke.'

'I'll wait here while you go and get one.'

She was alone when he returned, clutching a large bottle. 'I fancied a drink of something sharp,' he explained. 'It seems I can book tickets online for tonight, so have you given any thought to what you want to see?'

'I've heard *1917* is well worth watching, but if you don't like that type of film, I'm happy to follow your lead.'

'That would suit me, so I'll order our tickets when I get back in my office. I'll text you to say what time we need to be leaving here.'

'I'm really looking forward to it. My girls are amazed we're going on a second date, they said one would be enough for you.'

His laughter rang out. 'I hope there'll be many more. I have to confess, Naomi Taylor, you've hardly been off my mind since I met you outside Cheryl's.'

'That's good.' She grinned. 'I've got a bit of a soft spot for you.'

Fred drank half the glass of Coke in one go, and then took out the envelope to begin taking apart the bank statements.

They showed Joanne Freeman's current account, and he whistled at the amount in it. 'This much in a current account?' he said to himself. He slid the statement into his printer and took a copy – he decided it wouldn't be good practice to make notes on the original.

By the end of the first month of transactions he saw the pattern. Five thousand pounds was paid every week into her account, and at the end of every month she transferred a large chunk into her savings account. Regular utility payments were made, but no loans or mortgages. There was a monthly payment to Debra Burford, presumably for care fees, and as he checked further back he realised very little changed from month to month.

Occasionally a cash withdrawal would show, but the amounts were relatively small, obviously petty cash for incidentals she required in her life.

It was only when he reached a statement for her savings account that his breath caught in his throat. The woman had been seriously rich, and the throwaway figure of around a million that Ken Freeman had spoken of was a serious underestimation. And it seemed the weekly payment of five thousand pounds was the key to the vast amount of accrued wealth.

The only clue to the origin of the transaction was a number, 6218. It meant nothing, but he knew unless he identified exactly where the payments were from he couldn't begin to solve Ken's mystery.

And he knew a lady who could possibly, probably, help.

Beth walked back into Connection to be met by a smiling Fred.

'I'm suspicious when you smile, grumpy drawers,' she said.

'And so you should be. I only smile when I'm happy.'

'You're happy?'

'I'll be happier if you can do me a favour.'

'Oh Lord, will I end up in prison?'

'Hopefully not.'

'Come into my office, tell me what you need.'

They disappeared and Cheryl burst into laughter. How she loved working in this crazy atmosphere.

Fred waited until Beth had removed her coat, then sat down, patiently waiting for her to speak.

She pulled her keyboard towards her. 'Go on then, what do you need to know that you can't find by more conventional methods like asking somebody the answer?'

'This.' He pushed the copy statement across to her, with the transaction details circled. 'I need to know the originator of this incoming payment.'

She raised an eyebrow. 'You'll post bail?'

'Of course.'

'Leave it with me. I'll do my best. I might need some information from you in payment though.'

'Oh?'

'Yep. What have you got on Luke that the rest of us don't know about, and should do?'

'He'll have my guts for garters. He dropped Maria off at her home this morning, so that she could collect a clean uniform and her car before coming into work.'

'You mean...?'

He nodded. 'I'm sworn to secrecy.'

'Of course. I won't pass it on. My word, our Luke's growing up.'

It was relatively simple to track down the name of the person who had sent the weekly payment for so many years. It took longer to put in her own blocking to prevent anyone tracing who had been ferreting around inside bank accounts than it did to get the information she needed, and when she did get it, it caused a frown to appear on her face.

She double-checked her findings, swiftly wrote down the details, and went to find Fred.

Fred looked at his watch. 'That didn't take long!'

'Relatively easy. I'm a woman of many talents, and don't you forget it. It took me a bit longer because I double-checked it.'

She pushed the piece of paper across his desk. 'This is the person who's been paying your deceased lady five thousand pounds every week for almost forty years. Now you have to find out why. It's a lot of child support, especially as the child is now forty. Tread carefully, Fred, this man is no fly-by-night. You could be really opening Pandora's box, or anybody else's box, by outing this chap.'

'We've been asked to sort the mystery, so that's what I'm

doing. I can only give Ken the information – what he does with it is up to him.'

Fred pulled the small piece of paper closer and stared at the name.

'Shit,' he said. 'Shit.'

'Try not to let it hit the fan too much,' Beth said as she stood to leave him to his thoughts, knowing the internet would be his first port of call. His fingers would fly, typing in the name of Sir Henry Allbright.

12

Sir Henry Allbright. The man appeared to be a veritable god amongst all men, he had so many letters after his name. He was CEO of several companies, owned a house in Berkshire the size of two cathedrals and was born in nineteen forty to wealthy parents. He had no siblings, so inherited everything they left him, and he was as rich as Croesus. Probably richer, Fred mused. And probably, almost definitely, Ken's father. And probably a huge secret that had been kept for forty years. Three probables that were almost definitely correct.

He did some maths and saw that Joanne would have been twenty when she had her son, and twenty-two when she left him with her parents. They had to have been complicit in the deception, agreeing to tell the little boy his mother had died. Was the five thousand pounds weekly payment the price of silence?

Fred brought up a chronology of Henry Allbright's life, and found that in nineteen eighty he was the top man at several places, including the National Coal Board, the northern part of the railways system, alongside several smaller appointments. He could have met Joanne at any one of these places. Had he fallen in love?

Surely thousands and thousands of pounds was too high a price to pay to keep their secret from his wife? There had to be more to it than that. His wife was still the same smiling woman standing by his side at the moment as had been there back in the eighties, so Fred guessed she knew nothing about any child her husband may or may not have fathered. Fred delved further into their backgrounds and saw they were a childless couple. Or one of them was childless, and he didn't believe it was Sir Henry.

Fred jotted down his thoughts, recognising the need for a lot more investigation before he could take it all to Ken. And what would Ken do?

Even a blind man would be able to see that Ken wouldn't ignore it – he would want to meet the man he presumed was his father, would want to know more about the clandestine relationship in which his mother had been a major player; he would want honest answers. And Fred was under no illusions about the blunt Yorkshireman, there would be an 'or else' tagged on to anything he asked of Sir Henry.

Fred looked at the information he had garnered and put it into a file. This would be dynamite to a newspaper, so he took it through to Cheryl and requested it be put into the safe overnight.

'I've done enough on it for one day,' he explained, 'and I'd rather it be locked away.'

'Sensitive, is it?'

'I would say so. I'm going to see a film tonight, I hope I can concentrate on it and forget this for a couple of hours.'

'I'm sure Naomi will help you think of other things, and soothe your fevered brow.'

'Not so much a fevered brow, more a worried one. Seriously, Cheryl, if I'm right with this, and I think I am, this will be one hell of a scandal. It needs to be kept as far away from the media as is possible, but once our client finds out about it, I'm not sure I'll be able to stop him telling them.'

'The giant?'

'The giant. Ken Freeman.'

'Seems so nice, as well.'

'He is, but he's lived a lie for nearly forty years and when he finds out the true story, I'm not sure how he'll react. When I took on this job I thought it sounded interesting, bit of a puzzle, and I looked forward to solving it for Ken. It's morphed into something a little bit ominous, and it involves an octogenarian who probably thinks nothing can touch him, and he's got away with something for forty years. Anyway, I'm putting him in the safe, and I'm going home. I'll be in early tomorrow, because I need to start making cohesive notes, getting proof of my findings and suchlike. I can't go to Ken with half-baked theories, I've got to have proved everything I tell him, and if this involves me seeing this Sir Henry, then so be it.'

Beth rang Amanda and asked her to call in at the office the following day, and Amanda, her voice full of trepidation, said she would pop in around eleven, when all of her staff were on.

'Don't be scared, Amanda, there's nothing negative to report. In fact, I believe this deal is the best thing that could have happened to you, so sleep easy tonight. I'm preparing a full report on my findings, and I'll let you have it tomorrow. I don't want to go into details over the phone because some of it is confidential, but I'll certainly tell you everything face to face.'

'Thank you so much, Beth.' The trepidation had turned to relief. 'It suddenly hit me what I was doing, and it was mind-blowing and scary. When I saw Luke and Maria in the café, I knew I had to take it to Connection, and that it would be worth what it's going to cost. Thank you for ringing, and I'll see you tomorrow.'

Beth disconnected with a smile. She loved it when things went right, the business up in the North East had really jangled her nerves. And the investigation for Amanda had taken very little time, and had ended well.

Beth closed down her computer, and locked her office door.

'Has everybody gone?' she asked Cheryl, who was putting on her coat.

'Fred has, but Tessa and Luke are staying a bit longer. They're in the middle of something they need for tomorrow, a spreadsheet I think Luke said, so we're locking the door, and leaving the shutters for them to secure.'

'Good. It's felt like a really busy day for all of us – some days are like that, and other days we sit twiddling our thumbs. Have you noticed?'

'I have, but the twiddling thumb days are few and far between.' Cheryl laughed. 'I've picked up a new job for you today, but I've told them you're on holiday until Monday, and they're quite happy to wait until you ring them Monday morning.'

'So in theory, if I hadn't made an eleven o'clock appointment, I could have had tomorrow off.'

'In theory yes. But as you're going to be in, I'll email you the details of this new potential client, and you can decide when you want to contact them. You might get extra brownie points if you do it tomorrow.'

'You're all heart, Cheryl. I'm going home now to put my feet up for an hour or so, before Joel arrives. I might even ring Nan, I didn't get chance at the weekend with being in Middlesbrough. I hate her being in France, but she sounds so happy I know I'm wrong to feel like that.'

She picked up her briefcase and went out to her car. It was

bitterly cold, and she shivered as she climbed into the driver's seat. *Thank heaven for heated seats*, she thought.

Traffic was light and it seemed to take no time at all to get home to Little Mouse Cottage. She pulled up, put the car into park, and switched off the engine. A car pulled up behind her, and the passenger door opened immediately. She stood, a little unsure of what was happening, and then she saw her.

'Nan,' she said, and burst into tears.

Doris hugged her. 'Fleeting visit, sweetheart. We're on a plane from Manchester at nine tomorrow morning, so we're staying in an airport hotel tonight, but we couldn't go without seeing you. Alistair had a meeting in Leeds, and I wasn't sure if I was able to come until yesterday, but here we are.'

Fred collected Naomi, who was dressed to combat the icy cold in a sheepskin coat and boots, and they headed for the cinema in Chesterfield.

They chatted for the entire journey, completely at ease with each other, and as they settled into their reclining cinema seats carrying popcorn and drinks, he looked around him. 'This is a bit more luxurious than the last time I was in a cinema. This is more like a bed than a chair.'

'You've not been for a long time then?'

'Definitely not. Both Jane and I worked odd hours, so if we went out it was for a meal, rather than anything like this.' He looked around. 'I could get used to this carefree life.'

The lights dimmed and the advertisements began. By the time they ended Fred was struggling to keep his eyes open, but then the film started, and he became engrossed.

.   .   .

Walking back to the car, Fred finally spoke. 'That was truly amazing. I can't remember the last time a film captured me to that extent. Thank you for suggesting it, I'm sure it wouldn't have been your first choice.'

'Oh but it was, there's only so many times you can watch *Frozen* or *Peter Rabbit*. It was lovely to be an adult, and especially lovely as I was being an adult with you. You're a very special man, Fred Iveson. I thought it was an excellent film. Really enjoyed it.'

'Would you like to go for supper?' He felt slightly embarrassed, yet pleased, by her words.

She shook her head. 'No, it's so cold. Shall we head back to my place? I can make us a sandwich and a Horlicks, and we'll be warm.'

'Brilliant idea.' He put his arm around her shoulders, and held her tightly as they walked back to the car. It felt so good to be this close to her, and he knew he was feeling nervous yet happy at the prospect of getting to know this lovely woman so much better, maybe even the possibility of a future with her.

And so Thursday came to an end, with satisfaction on the faces of some of the Connection team, and troublesome frowns on others.

Luke and Tessa wore the troublesome frowns. They had watched endless hours of CCTV, and the only thing they had for definite was the buyer of the Lexus had teamed up with someone reliable to do his money recycling work. All the footage showed the same person doing the buying of the car, and another person doing the burglary. A highly successful two-man team. It became even clearer that the bungled attack at the Coates home had really been the practice run.

They had a list of ex and current employees formulated on a

spreadsheet, and both of them had taken a copy home with them to study it in depth – their plan of action was to go and see John Coates the following day and go through it with him, getting his own feelings about the list. But most of all they wanted to check out any employees who had remained at Coates Electricals after it had been sold on to its new owners. In view of the continuance of the system that began at the Coates place, and the fact that three of the subsequent burglaries had Coates systems installed, it seemed that the information was still being given out from the secure set-up boasted about by Coates.

Eventually Maria persuaded Luke into leaving the paperwork on the coffee table and laughed when he stood up immediately. He needed no persuading, and by midnight they were both asleep, spreadsheets and lists forgotten temporarily.

It wasn't the same at Tessa's house. She pored over the lists, considered looking at the CCTV from the last place that had been burgled, made herself some supper, had a glass of milk, and finally gave in to the sleep that was threatening to overcome her. She snuggled into the bed, wrapped her arms around Hannah's Harry Potter pyjamas, and drifted into a deep sleep. John and Caroline Coates were on the back burner, ready for the dawning of the next day.

13

Fred switched on the radio and the kettle simultaneously. He placed muesli into a bowl, removed the milk from the fridge and frowned. There wasn't much left and he needed to remember to get some. The frown changed to a smile. The Co-op sold milk. Naomi rang it through the till...

It had been a late night; he hadn't left Naomi until after one, and they had discussed, with some enthusiasm, going away for a couple of days. Fred said he would investigate hotels in the Lake District, and Naomi had been the one to say you only need to book one room.

He poured some milk into his mug and the rest into his bowl, then sat at the kitchen table, his thoughts drifting comfortably along. He hadn't been looking for a relationship, hadn't even known he wanted one, but suddenly there had been Naomi standing outside Cheryl's door, smiling at him. Making him smile in return. Now he felt as if he was smiling all the time. Smiley Fred Iveson, who would have ever thought that? He laughed aloud, and took his dishes to wash them before finding a warmer coat than the one he had worn the previous day. A light layer of snow generally promised a potential heavier fall later in the day.

He put the car into drive, and headed for Eyam. Today he would try to make arrangements to speak with Sir Henry, attempt to make some sense of what his brain was thinking was a straightforward case of denial of a child to the rest of the world, while accepting Ken was his and he would make suitable arrangements financially. The fallout would have to be dealt with once he had confirmed facts.

The eight o'clock news started as he pulled up outside Connection, and he left the engine running for a couple of minutes as he listened to the sombre tones of the newsreader talking about the coronavirus outbreak. The deaths in China were reaching alarming levels, and a man from Brighton had been diagnosed with it after contracting the virus in Singapore. It felt extremely far away, but as Fred switched off his engine and the radio became silent, he wondered how long it would take to land on the UK mainland, and what on earth they could do about it.

He opened the shutters, unlocked the front door, and went through to open the back door and entice Oliver in for breakfast. Oliver took no enticing. He came out of his cat shelter, sauntered towards the back door, and miaowed.

'And good morning to you too, young man. You want chicken or salmon today?'

Oliver made no further contribution to the discussion, merely waited patiently for something, anything edible, to be put in his bowl.

Fred poured a glass of orange juice and sat at his desk, opening up his computer. He logged on to the website that gave details of

Sir Henry Allbright, and wondered how best to contact him and get the end result he wanted – a face-to-face meeting.

He came across an email address and decided that could be his starting point, so he kept it short by asking for a meeting, and mentioned he had information for Sir Henry pertaining to the Freeman family. He included both his mobile and office number, and signed off with Connection Investigation Agency.

He sat back, sipped at his juice, and decided he would wait until lunchtime for a response, and if none was forthcoming by then, he would send off a second email with a little more detail.

Luke and Tessa arrived together, and were immediately ensconced in Luke's office. His desk was covered in paperwork; lists, spreadsheets, handwritten notes, and they began to work their way through them.

'I didn't play Code Blue last night because of this lot,' Luke grumbled.

'Sorry about that.' She grinned at his disgruntled face. 'I only lost sleep, not game-playing time.'

'I think I always knew it, but it struck me last night that it has to be considered a team of three, not only the bloke who we're looking for who buys the cars, not only the one who goes in that same night and steals back the money, but also the one who's giving them the security information about the property. That's splitting the profits three ways.'

'This has occurred to me. I think we're missing something somewhere. If they've only done half a dozen jobs since the Coates attack, that's not even going to keep them in aspirin, never mind their hard stuff. They're either into something else that pays well, or some of the stuff they're doing isn't being reported to the police. Do they have some other way of leaving threats when they do a job?' Tessa paused. 'We always felt there was some threat hanging over Jacques and Simpson, they absolutely wouldn't say a word about who he was. The only thing we got from them was they were paid five thousand pounds to be split between them, they didn't know who he was, and he approached them in a pub. How come everybody in the criminal world gets approached in a pub?'

Luke laughed. 'I've never been approached in a pub about anything other than to be told to drink up. The landlord wants to go to bed.'

'At two this morning I realised these car thefts are simply spending money for them, not serious earnings. Does that feel right with you? Would you agree?'

'I would,' Luke said with a nod. 'It's baffled me from the beginning. If it was something seriously lucrative they would step it up, but if they stepped it up the papers would get hold of it, and nobody would ever privately sell cars again on a Friday night.'

'Okay, we're going to chat to John, and then the people he has working for him at Code Blue. And maybe we'll get to see their little girl this time, fingers crossed.'

They began to sort the papers into some sort of order, merging both sets of thoughts and putting everything into a large file.

They went to the house first, and Tessa felt disappointed that Casey was once again having her morning nap. She hoped they would get to see her before they left, so after refusing a drink in the house they followed John through to the Code Blue premises.

Tessa had asked John not to warn anybody they were revisiting, and as they went through the door, all members of the staff looked up with some surprise at seeing the two investigators making a second visit.

John leaned against a desk at the front of the room, and all eyes swivelled towards him. They waited.

'Okay, everybody. As you can see, Tessa and Luke have joined us again, but this time they want to speak to you individually. I'm going to put them in the small office at the side of mine, so that whatever they say to you and you to them won't disrupt work being done by the rest of us. Please let me reassure you that nobody is under any sort of suspicion, this is more of a picture-building exercise so they can get a feel for how a business that is controlled by high security is run. So, this is the order they've requested. Dom, Ivan, Flora, Kathy and Brad. As the person in front of you comes out, please make your way to the office. Dom, I'll give you the nod when they're ready for you.'

There were no responses at all. Dom was the last to drop his head back down and return to whatever he had been doing before the boss had interrupted them, and Luke and Tessa followed John to the office he had set aside for them.

'Coffee machine needs switching on,' he said, 'and all the pods are in that drawer thing underneath. Caroline is doing us some lunch around half past twelve back in the house, so bear that in mind when you're working your way through the interviews.'

Tessa smiled at him. 'We don't normally get this sort of treatment, it's usually hostility all the way.'

'It could prove to be hostility,' John said. 'You've not spoken to them yet, and they may object to being questioned by somebody who isn't a police officer. Bet you get that all the time, don't you?'

'I'm pretty adept at blagging my way through it,' Tessa said with a laugh. 'I simply put my DI voice on.'

'Then I'll leave you to it. If you need anything, I'm only next door. Give Dom a shout when you're ready, I think it's probably better if I leave it completely in your hands now.'

'Thanks, John. We'll get a coffee and then bring him in.'

Dom Acton was a tall, attractive man who walked with slightly hunched shoulders, probably due to the years he had put in perfecting his computer skills and playing games. He sat down opposite Tessa and Luke with a brief 'Hi.'

Tessa spoke first. 'Hi, Dom. Thank you for talking to us. I'm Tessa Marsden, and this is Luke Taylor. We are partners in the Connection Detective Agency, and have been employed by John to check out some possible leaks in the security of certain things.'

Dom looked perplexed. 'With the games?'

'No, it's nothing to do with the games, it's to do with Coates Electricals.'

'Well, obviously I've left there.' His tone was turning icy.

Luke leaned forward. 'Calm down, Dom. Nobody here is being accused of anything, we wanted to talk to you as an ex-employee of Coates, because let's face it, three of you have transferred to here. John has complete faith in the three of you, we more want to check if any of you had concerns about anyone else you worked with at Coates.'

Finally Dom seemed to relax a little. 'Ah, I see. I'm sure John will have told you this, but the security at Coates was extreme, to say the least. We did really high-end security installations, both before John sold the business and after that time.'

'Surely you occasionally had to access the set-up of a client – they don't work for ever, do they? Or maybe they wanted an upgrade. What happened then?'

'Two of us had access codes. They had to be inputted within ten seconds of each other, so we had to be there at the same time to ensure we didn't lock everything down, and once both had been inputted, then key in his own code and we could access their systems. Nothing ever went wrong, and it always needed John and two others to get into the data.'

'So, there was you, and there was John. Who was the third while you were there?'

'Ivan, but with Flora as a backup if one of us was missing. You'll be chatting to her in a bit. Coates had to set up two new access code holders as we both left there on the same day. I've no idea who that was. They changed the codes we had to memorise, obviously.'

'So you, Ivan and the current owner of the company were the three code holders? I've got that right? Flora would be called in if one of you was missing for any reason?'

'Spot on. It was kind of a relief to lose that responsibility and to let somebody else have it.'

'Thank you, Dom. By the time we've finished talking to the others we may have a couple more questions. That okay with you?'

'It's fine, Luke. I'm not sure why you're questioning us, but if John wants us to play ball, then that's fine with all of us. He's a bit of a hero to his staff, is our John. Walk on hot coals for him, we would.'

'If that's a requirement for working here, count me out,' Tessa finished with a laugh.

14

Ivan stood, pushed his glasses back towards his face instead of balanced precariously on the end of his nose, and looked across towards Dom as he returned to his work area. Dom gave him a brief nod. Ivan picked up his water bottle, and strolled across the small office, wondering what the hell was going on, and why suddenly security seemed to be an issue at Code Blue. It didn't take him long to realise he had it wrong.

'I had a little to do with security there,' he explained, 'I stuck to working on smaller and better systems. John sold a really healthy business that soon became even healthier under the new owners. The company is easily twice the size now. They cover the whole of Europe – I went out to France twice in the last month I was there, to oversee two separate installations.'

'And presumably John knows of this massive expansion?'

'I imagine so. When he rang me to ask if I would be interested in coming to Code Blue – as if I wouldn't be – I was in France then. Believe me. It's multi-national now. The company is a world leader in the quality of the installations, whether they're for businesses or homes. I was in the home systems department, hence my trips to France. British people buy homes there, but then need security on them because they're not there most of the time.'

'And you don't regret leaving?'

Ivan shook his head. 'Not in the slightest. I could earn really big money by doing these overseas trips and I was good at my job, but once John sold up, it changed. It was inevitable I suppose, and because the pay was so good I stuck with it, but I didn't hesitate when John contacted me.'

Tessa glanced down at her notes. 'You live in a nice neighbourhood. Lived there long?'

'Twenty-seven years, and I have a full bedroom all to myself,' he answered with a laugh. 'I still live at home. Dad has MS and is in a wheelchair, so I've stayed. I'll move out one day, but that time isn't here yet.'

'No girlfriend?'

He shrugged. 'Kind of. Nothing too serious. We see each other when she's in Sheffield, but she's an air hostess so you can imagine she's not here too often. It works for us, and one day I may take my head out of my computer and grow up, but I don't think Lottie's counting on it.'

'And when you worked at Coates, you had nothing to do with the system that kept clients' details secure?'

'Only on a one of three basis. Obviously I had the details when I went to do installations, but as a bulk job of all installations, no I didn't. It was strictly on a need-to-know situation.'

Luke glanced at Tessa. 'Is there anything else?'

She shook her head and stood. 'Thank you, Ivan. I must confess I expected you to come in here speaking with a Russian accent.'

Ivan laughed. 'My mum's Russian. Some unpronounceable surname. We always say she married Dad to get rid of it. Shall I send Flora in?'

Tessa checked her watch. 'No, we'll start with Flora after lunch. We'll be back for half past one.'

He gave a quick salute and walked out of the door.

'I liked him.' Luke added something to his notes.

'Meaning you didn't like Dom?'

'Not sure. I felt he was holding something back. Or simply being a supervisor. Although it's not been said, I'm assuming he's second in command after John.'

'That's my impression. Could you do this job, given your love of gaming?'

Luke thought for a moment. 'Maybe for a week, then I'd be bored. I bet none of these have ever been driven off the road and nearly killed by a murderer, have they? Nope, it doesn't even begin to compare to my job.'

'When you put it like that...'

The pasta and salad prepared by Caroline was delicious, and suitably praised by her two guests.

'This is far better than cardboard Ryvitas,' Tessa said with a smile. 'You like cooking, Caroline?'

'I do. It's a skill that's developed since I married John. Before my marriage I was still at home with my mum and dad, so didn't have to cook, but I discovered I enjoyed it. John's the main beneficiary.'

'And now Casey. Is she still asleep?'

'She is. She's got a heavy cold, so I've given her Calpol and she's gone out like a light. I tried to keep her awake knowing you were coming through, but I couldn't. Babies don't follow rules.' She smiled.

'The last conversation Hannah and I had was about having a baby.' Tessa swallowed audibly. She couldn't believe what had burst from her mouth, her private thoughts never to be shared with anyone.

Luke reached towards her and squeezed her hand.

Tessa's face drained of all colour. 'Please... I'm sorry I said that. I know you're friends but I'm here in a professional capacity. It was because we were speaking of Casey...'

'Hey,' Caroline said, walking around the table to get to her. 'You can say anything here. You comforted me enough times after we lost our twins. Don't ever be afraid of speaking your thoughts aloud in front of us, especially when they're thoughts about Hannah. You two were perfect together, never forget that.'

'I don't,' Tessa responded quietly. 'It suddenly washed over me.' She picked up her glass of water and took a deep drink. 'I'm fine now, let's get back to what we need to discuss. Luke?'

Luke glanced at her as if checking she really was okay, then took out his notes. 'Before we go back in to Code Blue we wanted to go over again with the two of you exactly what happened that night the car was bought. In view of the fact that Tessa has questioned you in the past about this, we thought it might spark a different train of thought if I asked you. So, Caroline, what did he look like from where you were standing. And where were you standing?'

Caroline stood and walked a few feet away from the table. 'You have to remember we've had a new kitchen put in, but as far as I can remember I would have been stood about here. The old table was bigger, and now we have the island. We didn't have one before. So yes, I would have been about in this position. John went to the door when we heard the bell, and I sort of hovered, waiting for the man. I was surprised when they came straight in, he didn't even check out the car.'

'So he came straight through to the kitchen with John?'

'That's right.'

'Okay. Freeze your thought right there. Now I know this next bit may upset you, but if we're to find this man and let you sleep easier at night, we may have to be brutal. What can you see?'

'He was a weasel. He looked like a weasel. Sharp features, a winter weight North Face jacket, black, that seemed out of place because the weather was hot, summery, balmy, and until he stood in the kitchen his hood was up. He seemed to check out the place, but to explain that away he said, "What a beautiful home you have". Then he took down his hood and his hair was long, in a ponytail, long and greasy. Even with the padded jacket on he looked thin. I remember thinking he's wearing that to fatten him up, make him look older.'

'Make him look older?' Luke interrupted.

Caroline nodded, her eyes partly closed. 'Yes, he looked so young. Skinny black jeans, black trainers, and this puffed-up black North Face jacket. He explained he would be paying for the car in cash, and it was partly from his savings and the rest was a win on the horses. He'd been looking for a Lexus specifically, he only had fifteen thousand, and would I be prepared to accept that.'

'And did you?'

'I offered him a drink. He seemed in a rush and I wanted to slow it down. John was behind him, out of his immediate eyesight, and shaking his head at me to stop me being so welcoming, I think. Anyway he said no, he wanted to get the car home and sort out the insurance and stuff, and I said he could leave it until that was done, then come back and collect it, but he said he didn't have far to take it, and he would pay for it and drive it away. He'd take the risk.'

'Did he indicate how far he would be driving it?'

'No, but he did say he'd walked to our house, expecting and hoping to be driving back.'

'The money was in an envelope?'

'It was, but he insisted John count it. While John was

confirming it was all there, I did the DVLA stuff, and the address he gave didn't ring any alarm bells, but the postcode was S11, the next area that adjoins ours. I'm sorry, Luke, but I've tried and tried for the last five years to remember that address, but I can't.'

'Did he move anywhere else in the kitchen?'

'No. The camera in the corner didn't quite pick up all of him, and with hindsight we realise he must have known that, because he didn't move at all. As he went out with John to get the car, he put up his hood again. I'm assuming you've seen all the CCTV, Tessa?'

'I have. He does know where your cameras are, there's no doubt about that.'

'After that, of course, I never saw him again. We lost the car, and we had nothing to show for it. But we lost a hell of a lot more than a car, and while Jacques and Simpson are paying the price for that, he isn't.'

Tears ran down Caroline's cheeks, and John pulled her into his arms. 'They'll find him,' he whispered into her hair. 'Tessa and Luke will find him and give you some peace.'

'I feel like a piece of shit.' Tessa sat down at the desk, and waited while Luke made her a cup of coffee. 'Did we push her too hard?'

Luke handed her the cup, and sat by her side. 'No, I imagine she was pushed much more than that back at the beginning when they were actively looking for him, we're bringing it all up again. There were bound to be tears really. Don't beat yourself up about it, John won't blame us. He must have known we would have to ask the questions. He's paying us to do a job, and it's not the easiest job in the world. If Caroline wants results as much as she appears to want to know who he was, we have to make waves.'

Tessa nodded, knowing he was right. 'There's something else that's occurred to me. If sonny boy did have some hold over Jacques and Simpson, what was it? Maybe it's time now to talk to their families. Let's get some information on them, go and do a bit of pushing in that direction.'

Luke nodded. 'Is that my homework for tonight?'

'Too right it is. Their families are in the files. Neither of them had partners, but they did have mums and dads. Both had rough childhoods, but they appeared to love their parents. Especially Nathan Jacques. Maybe he's the one we should concentrate on. Get those fingers tip tapping on that computer, and let's see if they're still living at the same address. Perhaps they can tell us things now that they couldn't five years ago. In the meantime, we've three more people to talk to this afternoon, so I'll go and get Flora.'

'No problem,' he said, and laid his notebook and pen on the table, placing the recorder in the middle. 'Let the battle re-commence.'

15

———

The responding email came from a different address to the one Fred had used to initiate a conversation with Sir Henry, and he realised it was the man's personal email.

I'm sorry but I have no connection to anybody with the name Freeman. Good luck with your search.

Fred grinned. Let the battle commence.

My search has ended. I have bank statements in my possession that show a weekly payment of five thousand pounds to Joanne Freeman. My client is keen to talk to the person who has made these payments, but as yet is unaware of the name of the sender of the money. My investigation of paperwork belonging to the late Ms Freeman shows that person to be you. As a matter of courtesy, I will pass this

personal email on to my client, as I am sure
he will want to contact you.

Fred read through it twice – he didn't want Sir Henry to
think he was being set up for some blackmail scam, but he also
didn't want him thinking this was going to go away. He hit the
send button and sat back.

Five minutes later Sir Henry was on the line. He sounded
gruff, yet polite.

'I've checked out your agency,' he began, 'and realise you're
not into scamming people.'

'No, sir.'

'I'd like to speak with you. Is it possible you can visit me
here, at home? I would drive to you, but my wife absolutely
forbids me. I have to take my driver, but would rather keep this
between the two of us. Are you available tomorrow?'

'I am. I can be there for eleven. Am I likely to meet your
wife? I can prepare a cover story...'

'No, it's why I suggested tomorrow. She's off to London early
to do some shopping and take in a show, so we will be
undisturbed.' The gruffness was going from his voice as he
slowly accepted Fred was a genuine person. 'I'm sorry this has
come to light now, but enough of it at the moment, we can talk
tomorrow. I'll leave word at the gatehouse that you're to be
admitted. Thank you, Mr Iveson, I'll see you tomorrow at eleven.'

Fred disconnected and sat back, contemplating the way
things were evolving at speed with this case. He had no
intentions of passing anything on to Ken yet, that would have to
wait until he had met with Sir Henry, found out exactly what he
would be telling Ken, and arrived back home. By Monday the
facts would be clear.

In the meantime, he would tell Cheryl of his trip. No

reasons, only that he would be travelling the following day to a massive country house in Berkshire as part of his investigation, and he didn't anticipate her having to recover his dead body from said location.

Cheryl made a note of where he was going. 'Sounds posh,' she said.

'It is,' he replied, and said no more, quickly returning to his office before she started asking questions.

She watched him, and tapped her biro against her teeth, deep in thought. He had said he had to be there for eleven, so she decided she would send him a text at one on some pretext or other, and check he was still alive. She hoped the giant was going with him as she had logged Fred's journey to the Freeman case; hopefully her concern wasn't required.

Amanda was smiling. She confirmed the afternoon-tea-for-two deal, settled the final bill with Beth, and walked out feeling so much better than she had done three days earlier. It seemed her only worry was the health of her new partner, but she could now speak to him on the subject, let him know that when the time came she would welcome his wife to follow in his footsteps. The relief was immense that she now saw why she had picked up on unease on his part; she had read the situation incorrectly, and was truly grateful Beth had discovered the real Joe Lightwood.

She walked past the tea shop, now closed for the night, and stopped to look backwards towards it. The additional building would be around the side and the back, the front would change very little apart from a lick of paint and new signage saying The Eyam Bistro and Tea Shop, but at five o'clock every night the transformation would begin. The tea shop would lose its scones and jam image, candles would appear on tables throughout the old and new buildings, French music would play softly in the background, and the rustic charm would morph into French rustic charm. At half past six every day Eyam would become a French village.

She shivered with anticipation as she stood and saw her dream coming to life, and knew that the signing of the contract on Monday couldn't come fast enough. Stefan Patmore was ready to start work on Tuesday, although he had said it would be noisy. She anticipated many apologies being given out to her customers, but at least it wasn't the height of the season; it was locals and the hardiest of hikers who used her premises currently. In two months, when the tourist season really got under way, she hoped to have everything completed, with a French chef as part of the package.

She continued her walk home, her head full of future plans, and optimism very much to the fore. Her partner, Flora, was waiting for her, their meal prepared but not cooked.

'Hi,' Flora said, leaning towards her for a kiss. 'I was starting to worry, you're not usually late.'

'I had to nip down to Connection to see Beth. It's good news and bad news, but the good news is I can stop worrying about signing this contract, it's all above board.'

'I saw a couple from Connection today. Tessa and Luke?'

'Really? Why?'

'No idea. They asked all of us a load of questions, mainly about when we worked at Coates. She was surprised to see I lived at Eyam, but left it at that. I said I lived with my partner. Figured it was none of her business who I lived with.'

'Quite right too, it isn't. Luke's nice, isn't he?'

'He is. Smart too. A thinker.'

'Tessa used to call in for drinks when she was with the

police. She was a detective inspector, but then took a partnership at Connection.'

'I thought she seemed super-efficient. Luke was quiet, but then jumped in with a couple of questions that showed he'd been thinking. It felt like an uncomfortable half an hour, and I was glad to get back to my desk. They spoke to all of us.'

'Has it rattled you?'

'Not really. More puzzled. They seemed to think there was an issue with the security at Coates, and as Dom, Ivan and me to a limited extent were the code holders for the security file, alongside John Coates, the questions were fast and a bit relentless.' She shrugged. 'I kept saying I don't know, whether I did or not.'

'You still have the code?' Amanda's eyes widened.

'I still remember it, obviously, but it was of no further use from the second I handed in my notice. I lost that position, and somebody else was set in place. Same with Dom and Ivan. It wasn't all that secure anyway. I knew all three codes to unlock it, but before we put in our code we had to log our own personal three-digit code, so the computer knew who was registering what, and if it tied into that code.'

Amanda looked puzzled. 'What?'

'Okay – mine, for example, was ZX5296 for the code, and I could log in either first or second, but to be able to log in I had to choose and set three digits. Mine was J5c. So when required, I would put J5cZX5296. Dom chose his own three digits, as did John, but me with my photographic memory knew their codes anyway. I didn't know their personal three-digit bits.'

Amanda stared at her. 'My God, I'm glad I only run a café, and use a simple key and burglar alarm.'

Flora laughed. 'I explained all of that to Tessa and Luke, and they understood it. Guess they're smarter than you.'

'Probably, but they come to me for their scones with jam and cream. You feeding me or not?'

'I am. Chopped salad in the fridge, pizza in the oven. You want wine?'

'I most certainly do. I'll tell you all about my day while we eat.'

Flora smiled. 'And we'll talk about your woefully inadequate security system while we eat, as well. You're going to need much better equipment when the new place is up and running, so be prepared.'

Amanda groaned. 'More money, more money...'

Fred answered his phone as he walked through his door, inordinately pleased to see that it was Naomi on his screen.

'Hello, beautiful lady. I was going to ring you later. You okay?'

'I'm fine. Wondered what you were doing tomorrow.'

'Going to Berkshire at the crack of dawn. Should be home late afternoon.'

'Berkshire?' She said it as if it was the other side of the world.

'Where the Queen lives,' he said helpfully.

'You need company?'

'You're not working? I thought you worked Saturdays.'

'I've swapped next Friday for this Saturday. One of the girls needs next Friday off.'

'Then I would love company. But we'll have to be leaving by six, I've an appointment at eleven, and I'd planned on stopping for breakfast to break the journey. I'll have to leave you to walk round Windsor while I'm at the appointment, but it won't be a long talk, I'm sure. That okay with you?'

'It's brilliant. Think Her Majesty will be in? I've never been to Windsor.'

'Then I'll be happy to show it to you, we can discover it together. We could stay over…'

'We could. I'll check Mum has no plans for Saturday night, and get back to you. That okay?'

'It's more than okay. I'll check out hotels in and around Windsor. I'm sure they won't be full this time of year.'

'This is awesome. I only rang to suggest maybe you fancied a morning shopping in Sheffield, but you've topped that. I'll send you a thumbs up if everything's cool with Mum. Oh, and Fred, one room.'

He laughed as he disconnected. This woman made his heart sing, and put a whole new slant on his trip to Berkshire.

His phone pinged with a thumbs up two minutes later, and his smile widened. He would ring later with details of the whole trip, and then he could have an early night, ready for a dawn start.

He dished up his stew that had been in the slow cooker all day, then sat in front of the television for half an hour, planning in his head how the discussion would need to go with Sir Henry, and how to slide around how he knew Sir Henry was the sender of the money. He figured his best way was simply to say he'd found confirmation in the paperwork in Joanne's desk.

Fred took his tray into the kitchen, washed his few dishes, and went to stand at the back door for a few minutes, breathing in the fresh air and hoping that the few flakes of snow fluttering down wouldn't achieve anything more than the level they were currently maintaining. He wanted a nice easy run down the M1, not a battle against the elements. He locked everything up, went to bed and texted Naomi in comfort. They chatted via text for half an hour, said goodnight, and he quickly fell asleep, after setting his alarm for five.

The snow stopped snowing, and all was right in most people's worlds. Especially Fred's.

16

The motorway services served Fred and Naomi a passable breakfast along with an excellent coffee, and they sat and chatted for a few minutes after they finished eating. Naomi admitted to being a little nervous.

'Luke's father walked out when he decided he didn't like being a father or a partner – we were never married, never really spoke of it either. Suddenly I found myself left with three children. My mum was amazing. She moved in with us, which was a good idea anyway as she wasn't well at the time, and gave me the freedom to take a job to support our family. Since then I've had one date, and decided I never wanted to repeat that, and now there's you.'

Fred smiled at her. He had sensed her nervousness, a feeling that matched his own. He reached for her hand. 'I understand, you know. You're the first woman to wander into my life since I lost Jane, and you took me by surprise. You smiled. That smile that makes your eyes laugh, and my first thought was *Oh hell, this is Luke's mother*. And now the thought that truly scares me is if I had remained with Playters and not moved to Connection, I would probably have never met you. I promise I'll never intentionally hurt you, Naomi, and I'm looking forward to getting this interview over and done with so we can enjoy seeing Windsor together.' He stood. 'Come on, let's get the next part of the trip over. We're making good time, so we might be able to grab a coffee in Windsor before I have to leave you for an hour or so.'

Naomi laughed. 'Don't worry about me. I've brought my credit card. I can amuse myself very easily.'

Sir Henry Allbright was a tall man with a good head of pure white hair, despite his eighty years. His eyes were the brightest of blues, and it occurred to Fred that if Sir Henry still looked this smart at such an advanced age, he must have swept Joanne Freeman off her feet as a young and probably naïve twenty-year-old. And the blue eyes of this octogenarian perfectly matched the blue eyes of Ken Freeman.

They shook hands, and Sir Henry led him through to his library. Tea was served to them by a black-suited man, who disappeared as silently as he had arrived.

'So,' Sir Henry began, 'are you here to wreck my carefully manufactured life?'

Fred smiled. 'I hope not, sir. Connection was approached by a man called Kenneth Freeman, who, despite having been told his mother had died when he was two, suddenly inherited money and property from her following her recent death. I was allocated the case, went out to visit him and he told me the story. He wants to know why he's basically lived a lie, so he's tasked me with finding out the truth. He's now moved into his mother's cottage in Bradwell, in Derbyshire, and I removed the contents of a bureau, with his permission. He said he wouldn't understand the stuff anyway, he's not mathematically minded, so asked me to go through it. The bank statements revealed the weekly payments, and other documents revealed the sender of the payments.'

Sir Henry sipped at his drink and stared into the fire. A log fell, and sparks drifted up the chimney. 'I loved her,' he said. 'She applied for a job as my PA. She was far too young, but her confidence carried her through. My wife and I, who I love deeply, had discovered we couldn't have children. They cured her cervical cancer, but only by doing a hysterectomy. Joanne blew into my life and has been in it for the last forty years, albeit from afar. We have managed to meet on several occasions and she took the decision to send the child to live with her parents. We realised that as he got older he would start to add two and two together and work out who I was, so to spare my wife, Joanne sent our son to live with Joanne's parents ten miles away. She had contact with her parents, knew how he was getting on, but we all conspired to keep everything from him.'

'The payments into her account have now stopped. You knew she had died?'

'I did. I knew her death was approaching, and she wrote several letters to people she knew, ready to be posted after her death. She arranged with Debra, her carer, to post them on the day of her death. I think I always knew it would eventually come to light, and now it has I'm going to have to tell my wife the whole story.'

Fred too stared into the mesmerising flames. 'Don't do anything in a rush, Sir Henry. Ken knows nothing of this yet, although I will have to meet with him on Monday. I think your first step is to see him. Joanne never met anyone else?'

Sir Henry shook his head. 'No. Maybe if one of us had died we could have moved on, but while ever the two of us inhabited this earth we only wanted each other. It was that deep a love from the first moment we spoke together. That won't change now she's gone, and yet when I tell my wife it will hurt both of us so much. I love her too, but it's not the same.'

'And the payments to Joanne have continued all these years?'

'I'm an extraordinarily rich man, Mr Iveson. I made sure my lover and our son were well provided for. I didn't send money directly to Joanne's parents, but I know that Joanne did. He lacked for nothing, and I provided Joanne, and now our son, with the cottage at Bradwell. She loved her home, and now I'm sure our son will be happy there as well.'

'Ken, he's called Ken.'

There was silence for a moment. 'He's okay?'

'He is. He's a really nice man, very tall like you, your blue eyes, and with the broadest Yorkshire accent you'll ever hear. When you meet, and I think you will, take a Yorkshire dictionary. He's bewildered by what has happened to him, and is eagerly awaiting my report, but I want that report to be complete before I pass it on to him. Do you have a private number where I can reach you, in case I need to know anything else? I don't want to cause any disruption while you're making decisions about what to do next. However, this much I feel pretty safe in saying. I don't think Ken will cause you any worries. I suspect he will want to meet you, but he will understand your wife knows nothing about the situation. Don't tell her anything yet unless you feel you have to.'

Sir Henry handed him a card. 'This is my personal mobile number. I would like to meet Kenneth, but I'm not sure I can visit the cottage again. The memories…'

'We can facilitate the meeting at Connection, or you can even meet halfway along the M1, but meeting in a service station may be a bit public. I'll leave you to think about it. I really am sorry for your loss of Joanne, Sir Henry. I too lost someone I loved very much in the Twin Towers terrorist attack, and it takes a long time to recover. Love is wonderful until you experience loss.'

The two men stood and Sir Henry walked with Fred to the imposing double front doors. They shook hands. 'You'll be in touch?'

'As soon as possible. You have my mobile number if you need to speak with me, and I'm spending the weekend in Windsor, if you should need me for anything before I head back to Derbyshire Sunday evening.'

Fred found Naomi sitting in a park eating a sausage roll and drinking from a can of Coke. There were several shopping bags by her side, on the bench. She smiled as she saw him approaching.

'That's lunch?'

'It is. They looked so good in the shop window. I brought you one.' She fished around in one of the carrier bags and produced a paper bag and a second can.

'Thank you.' He sat by her side, still a little lost in thoughts caused by the meeting. He put his arm around her shoulders and pulled her close. 'Thank you for coming with me. I can't really talk about the meeting because I was there on behalf of a client, but I've met a man who truly knows the meaning of the word love. It's been an enlightening meeting.'

Sausage rolls finished and rubbish tipped into a waste bin, they spent the next hour strolling around Windsor, staring up at the castle and making the decision to visit it the following day when they would have the entire time to dedicate to being sightseers.

They booked into the hotel and Naomi giggled at being called Mrs Iveson. She also giggled when she took a phone call from Luke, who was trying to persuade his mother to do a Saturday night curry.

'I'm not there.'

'What do you mean?'

'I'm not there. Can't Maria do you a curry?'

'We like your curries.'

'Your nan might do you one. Ring her and ask her.'

There was a pause. 'So where are you?'

'Windsor.'

'Windsor? As in Windsor Castle? Where the Queen lives?'

'That's the place. It's very pretty.'

'But...'

'Luke, sort out a curry for tonight, and let me go. We're about to get in a lift and we'll lose the signal anyway. Love you. Bye.'

'That was Luke?'

'He wants me to make a curry for tonight.'

'He's going to be a very disappointed young man.'

'I want to be a fly on the wall when Mum tells him where I am, and who I'm with.' Her laughter rang around the lift.

'Will I have to avoid him Monday morning?'

'He may have some questions...'

The lift opened on their floor, and they checked out the room numbers on the wall. They turned right, and reached their room. Naomi inserted her card, and pushed open the door before turning to Fred. 'Come here,' she said, and pulled him towards her, walking backwards into the room while kissing him.

He heard the door close with a slight phhht behind them, but his concentration was all on what was happening inside the room.

They landed on the bed together, and the kiss deepened.

.   .   .

When Luke rang for a second time, having spoken to his nan, it went ignored. It was only later, when their room service meal had been delivered and set up by the waiters, did Naomi contact her son. She sent him a picture of the meal, and captioned it 'hope your curry is as good as this'.

Fred and Naomi simultaneously switched off their phones. 'We'll join the world again in the morning after breakfast. These next few hours are ours, so let's make the most of them.' Fred reached across the exquisitely set dining table and grasped her hand. 'Thank you for travelling all this way with me, and for temporarily being Mrs Iveson. I know this weekend will end, but I don't want it to. I promise I'll talk properly to Luke on Monday, he has to know I'm serious about seeing you.'

She laughed. 'As Luke seems to now be living with Maria, he's no room to talk.'

'You know?'

She nodded. 'His landlady told me, assuming I already knew. I haven't said anything, he's old enough to know what he's doing, and they do seem right for each other. Twenty twenty seems to be starting off okay for everybody, let's hope it finishes in the same way. For the record, Fred, I'm pretty serious about you as well.'

17

The body lay undiscovered in Ecclesall Woods for the best part of Sunday, and then a child, walking with his father as the daylight began to fade, stumbled across it as he ran giggling in an attempt at getting Daddy to race after him.

'Daddy!' he shrieked. 'Man.'

And Daddy really did race after him.

The area was soon fenced off by crime scene tape and the police team from Sheffield began their coverage of the surrounding ground. Lights were set up and the whole place became floodlit. The forensics team confirmed it was a male, deceased at some time in the previous twenty-four hours, estimated age between twenty and thirty years, no obvious cause of death. Post-mortem at seven next morning, they were told, and that was where it had to be left until the world woke up to a new week.

The puncture wound was immediately apparent to pathologist Harry Phillipson. 'I think we'll find out this was our cause of death... but he was no regular user. There are no other marks at all, on either arm or anywhere else on his body. In fact, I would say this is one very fit young man. Muscles well defined, I suspect he works out regularly. He's not on our fingerprint database so I can't help with identification. I've sent bloods off for analysis to see what was in the syringe that went into his neck, but I suspect heroin. He'd obviously upset somebody.'

DI Eileen Haughton listened to the pathologist's words concerning cause of death, then tried to switch off as she realised the body was about to be cut open. She leaned forward and spoke into the microphone. 'Let me have the full report as soon as it's available, will you, Harry? I'll go and put things in motion to try to find out who he is.'

Phillipson held up a thumb, and Eileen got out of the viewing area as fast as she could. She headed towards her office and sat down, opening up her computer. There had been nothing on the body, no wallet, no identification of any kind, and even the missing persons list didn't suggest anything that could even vaguely match the body currently lying in the morgue.

John Coates kissed his wife and daughter and walked along the corridor towards his office in Code Blue. It seemed quiet, and he guessed his staff members were engrossed. He decided not to interrupt, and walked through the main room and into his own office.

He went through the fifty-three emails he had managed to accrue overnight, replying to the ones who merited or needed replies, and deleting the others. He liked a clean and empty inbox. Once that job was done, he pulled Ice White up, and went directly to the part of the game that was giving him cause for concern. He worked on it for an hour, and then looked up as his office door opened.

'Sorry to trouble you, John, but is Ivan poorly?'

'What? Sorry, Flora, what do you mean?'

'He's not in yet, and we were working on something together on Friday. I could do with him being here, or at least speaking to him, but if he's poorly, I don't want to ring him.'

John stood. 'Nobody's heard from him?'

Flora shook her head. 'No, I've already asked them, but we all assumed he would have let you know if he was ill, or had an appointment or something.'

'Strange. I'd best ring him, check he's okay. His mum will know.'

He dialled Ivan's mobile number but there was no response. He looked up the landline number for Ivan's home, and felt relief when it was answered.

'Hi, it's John Coates. Is Ivan there?'

'Oh, hello, Mr Coates. No, I'm sorry he isn't. I'm not sure where he is, he didn't say Lottie was in town, but he didn't come home last night. I assumed he was with her, and had gone straight to work from her place.'

'He's not here.' John felt cold. 'If he arrives at home, can you ask him to give me a ring, please?'

'Now you've got me worried. I'll ring Lottie's mobile number and see if she answers. If there's no answer it means she's flying so won't be able to help us. I'll ring you back, Mr Coates.'

'John?'

'Hi, Tessa. I have hairs standing up on the back of my neck.'

'So that's not simply a cliché?'

'No, it's not. It's actually happening. Ivan's gone AWOL, and

I'm not sure whether to ignore it, or do something about it, so I thought I'd ring you.'

Her mind switched to the conversation on the typed-up transcript she had read only ten minutes earlier. 'You've presumably checked with his mum?'

'Yes. It seems if Lottie, his girlfriend, is home, he stays with her, so it's not ringing alarm bells with Mrs Newburg. I think it is now I've contacted her. She's going to try to get in touch with Lottie, but if there's no answer it will mean Lottie is flying. I imagine his mum will then go into proper panic, because this isn't what Ivan does. If he's not with Lottie, he's with his mum helping take care of his dad. He's never done this before, not even for an emergency. He once had to go to the dentist but he rang to tell me.'

'That was the impression I got from our chat. Leave it with me, John. I'll get back to you as soon as I can.'

Luke looked at her from his side of the desk. 'Problem?'

'Ivan's missing. Totally out of character. Could we have spooked him?'

Luke frowned. 'Or has he told somebody about our conversation with him?'

'We're missing something here. He's definitely not the man we've been hired to find, because either John or Caroline would have recognised him. Is he connected in some other way?'

'I don't know. What do we do next?'

'I'm ringing Carl.'

'You have any strangers under lock and key you can't identify?'

'Not that I know of. Problem?'

'Somebody we interviewed has now gone missing, and his boss is concerned. His name's Ivan Newburg, late twenties.'

'The name doesn't ring a bell, but the ones in the drunk tank tend to be our regulars. They'll be going home this morning. Hang on a minute...'

'There was silence that felt longer than a minute, and Tessa tapped her biro on the desk while she waited.

'You there?'

'I am. You found him?'

'I'm not sure, but you need to contact DI Eileen Haughton at West Bar. We had a notification in the last quarter of an hour from Sheffield – they recovered a body in Ecclesall Woods last night. PM going on at the moment. No ID, it says. Give me five minutes to tell her you're ringing, but I'm sure you'll know her anyway.'

Tessa laughed. 'Oh I do. We've got drunk together several times. I'll ring her in five minutes.'

'Tessa, good to hear from you. You've heard about our body?'

'I have, but I'm hoping I'm not giving you the ID on it. We have somebody who appears to have gone missing, lives in Ecclesall. Carl said you found your body in Ecclesall Woods?'

'We did. Tell me about your misper.'

'Twenty-seven, called Ivan Newburg, still lives at home with his parents because his mum needs help with his dad who has MS. Ivan's a nice chap. If I told you he had a tattoo on the inside of each wrist would you be interested?'

'I would if the tattoos say Blue Code.'

Tessa felt her face drain of colour. 'It's the other way round. It's Code Blue. He was one of the developers of the game.'

There was a momentary silence. 'Then I guess we have our ID,' Eileen said quietly. 'Tessa, can you email me his full details, please? I'll go and talk to his parents. Sometimes this job can be really shitty. I'll need to talk to you again once we've got a firm ID on him, but I'll give you a ring.'

'I'm going to call his employer now and tell him what you've told me. I'll ask John not to contact his parents yet, so will you let me know as soon as you've spoken to them? I'm sure he'll want to go see them.'

'John? Would that be John Coates? Little things are clicking in my mind now you've mentioned the words Code Blue. His company distributes the game, doesn't it?'

'It does and it would be him. I'll probably have to tell you the full story, but my first allegiance is to John. Don't forget I'm in the private sector now, and he pays my wages.'

'We could make the chat over a drink?'

'Too right we could. Let me know when you've notified Mr and Mrs Newburg.'

The shock was written on Luke's face. 'Ivan's dead?'

'It seems so.' Tessa stood and walked to the window, staring down at the garden below, bereft of any colour other than green. She leaned her forehead against the window pane, then thumped the wall to her left viciously.

Luke stood and put his arm around her. 'Hey, don't destroy my office. Come and sit down, I'll make us a fresh drink. I wanted to hit something as well... sheer frustration. But a wall isn't sensible.'

He led her around to her chair, and she sat down with a thud. 'Have we brought this about, Luke? Of the five people we interviewed, I liked him the best. Dom Acton and Flora Robinson were playing silly buggers with us, and not telling us anything unless we asked the direct question, and everything seemed to be above the heads of Kathy Easton and Brad Wells.

That was possibly because they were beta testers and didn't transfer from Coates. But Ivan was different, perhaps because he freely admitted to still being at home, living with his parents because his dad was poorly. What the hell has led to him being found in Ecclesall Woods, dead?'

'And why now? There has to be a link to our asking questions. What's going on? Who did we rattle that made them do this to Ivan?'

'That's the point,' Tessa said, speaking slowly. 'We haven't really got started yet, the only ones we've interviewed are the employees at Code Blue.'

'And John and Caroline Coates.'

'Surely you don't think...'

'No, I don't, but we have to include them in the list. We have interviewed them. And it would be easy for somebody working in the Code Blue premises to install equipment in the Coates house, wouldn't it? They'd certainly have the technical knowledge, they could probably make the equipment, and they'd only have to walk through that corridor that links the two houses.'

'For what reason?' Luke was clearly piquing Tessa's interest.

'To listen in on conversations?' Luke said. 'But I don't doubt we'll find out if that supposition proves to be correct.'

'You've a quick mind, Luke Taylor. Not only quick but devious.'

'Hattie Pearson taught me well. I believed everything she said, until I realised she was the one who'd killed her daughter.' His reference to the elderly lady who had featured at the forefront of his previous case brought a smile to his face. She'd had him fooled for quite some time.

'One avenue I'm beginning to follow is that I no longer think this is only about stealing posh cars and then getting the money back, I think it's much much bigger, but I think it's all about knowing the weaknesses in the security systems, or having some weakness programmed into them ready for any potential burglars to walk in and help themselves. There are so many burglaries that go unsolved, and this would go a long way to explaining most of them, I reckon.'

18

Fred drove out to Bradwell, feeling quite happy with the news he was about to pass on to Ken Freeman. He was feeling happy in general; the weekend with Naomi had been all that he could have asked for, and he felt not only refreshed, but rejuvenated.

They had laughed all the time – Naomi had a dry sense of humour that constantly surprised him – and had been suitably impressed by Windsor Castle. On the drive back home they had stopped for a meal, lingering over it a little too long, as they both realised the weekend was nearly over.

And then it was.

He pulled up outside Whitelilac Cottage and sat for a moment, still enjoying his thoughts of the weekend, then picked up his folder and got out. Ken came out to meet him, and they walked into the cottage together.

'Tha's got summat?'

Fred nodded. 'Indeed I have. Plenty to talk about, so we might need a pot of tea.'

'No problem.' Ken clicked on the kettle. 'Sit down. You had breakfast?'

'I have, thanks, only need a drink.'

Fred opened up his folder and shuffled the pages into a sensible order. After saying goodnight to Naomi, the following hour and a half had been spent writing up the weekend's meeting with Sir Henry, and trying to work out in his head the best way of explaining things to Ken.

The subject of his thoughts placed a mug of tea in front of him, and sat down next to him.

'Okay, we can talk now. Am I royalty?'

Fred laughed. 'Not quite, but almost.'

'Well, as long as I'm not the next king, that's fine.'

'Okay, I'm going to start at the beginning. If you've a question, stop me.'

Ken briefly closed his eyes, then opened them, the blue gaze he turned towards Fred an exact copy of the gaze Sir Henry had used. 'My father's still alive, isn't he?'

'He is, but don't jump the gun.'

'Understood.'

'Your mother applied for a job working as PA to your father. That was their first meeting, and from what he says, it was an instant connection between them, totally wrong because he was already married, twenty years older than her, and yet they fell in love.'

'Shit...' Ken mumbled.

'On top of that, your father's wife had had to have a hysterectomy following the discovery that she had cervical cancer that had spread, so they removed everything, meaning, of course, that they couldn't have children. He started to see Joanne, and soon they were lovers, both realising it could never go anywhere because of the recovering wife. And then Joanne discovered she was pregnant with you.'

Fred took a sip of his hot tea and winced as it burnt his tongue.

'It's Yorkshire tea,' Ken said, as if that explained why it was so hot. Fred nodded, knowing exactly what he meant.

'One thing I want to stress, Ken, is that your father is a good man. He told me he's only ever loved two women in his life, his wife, and Joanne. He's not a serial philanderer, as he put it, but circumstances meant he couldn't leave his wife and live with Joanne. And she fully understood. They have always managed to meet up at least a couple of times a year after she left his employ, and of course you know he has supported her financially, and now you in what she has left to you. He met you several times until you reached the age of two, and then they had to take the heartbreaking decision to place you with your nan and granddad. They were fully aware of the situation, knew of the circumstances with your father and what would happen if the newspapers found out about the affair, and they agreed to bring you up. It was agreed to tell you she had died, and although she saw you sporadically, it was from a distance. She saw you play football a couple of times, but your father never did. He lives some distance away, but Joanne made sure she remained close. What I'm really trying to say is that you were loved by everybody, but exceptional circumstances forced all of them to do the best they could to please the innocent one, your father's wife. Even at this stage, that has happened. I went to see him on Saturday, because his wife had gone into London for the weekend to see a show, and he could see me in safety without her asking questions.'

'Where does he live?'

'Just outside Windsor.'

'I am nearly royalty then.'

'You'd think you were if you saw his house.'

'That's never going to happen, is it?'

'Not during the lifetime of his wife. I think you'll like him, and he does want to meet you. He's not convinced he can come to this cottage, it holds too many memories for him. I have offered our offices to facilitate the meeting, or I suggested meeting at a services on the motorway, but either way if you want me there I will be.'

'Does he have a name?'

Fred hesitated, then pushed Sir Henry's card across the table. 'That's your father.'

Ken picked up the card and studied it, then lifted his eyes to Fred. 'Fuck me.'

'That's one way of expressing shock, I suppose. You know of him?'

'Only what I've read in t'papers. Charity work and stuff. Good God... and he wants to meet me?'

Fred nodded. 'Yes he does. It has to continue to be a secret, but if you feel you can't allow that to happen, he is prepared to tell his wife and take the consequences. It's your call, Ken, but you know what I'm going to advise, don't you?'

'Yeah.' Ken laughed. 'Keep your mouth shut and don't rock a boat that's been in calm waters for all these years.'

'And?'

'I'm telling nobody. He doesn't need ter worry. What's he like?'

'I enjoyed chatting to him. He's like you; tall, same blueness of eye colour, quite fit for his age, and a damn good conversationalist. Doesn't speak Yorkshire though, but I'm sure you can teach him.'

Ken looked down at the card still clutched in his hands. 'They should teach it in schools.'

'Could be a new career for you.'

'Seriously though, Fred, I'm a bit different to him, aren't I?'

'What's a dialect, Ken? I imagine your mum probably had a

twang to her voice. He didn't strike me as being the sort of man who would bother about something like that. I spoke to him for quite some time, and my Derbyshire accent can come across a bit strong.'

'Did he say when we could meet? Presumably he's retired now?'

'He's certainly retired from what we think of as work, but he does do a lot of charity stuff. He seems to be on a fair number of boards, so I think he'll have to sort out a meeting date. What about you?'

'I'm going nowhere. Going to start decorating the cottage, I like doing that. And let him decide where.'

Fred picked up his drink again, this time a little more wary of the scalding liquid. 'I'll email him later and tell him you now know the story, and ask him to suggest a date. I think he was keen to see you again after all these years, I guess you've changed since you were two.'

'Slightly. I've grown a bit. It's a bit scary, all this surfacing now. I feel as if I don't know who I am anymore. All them years...'

'He's a good man, Ken. Don't be afraid to meet him, and I think there's plenty of years to get to know him better. Is there anything else you want to ask? I've written everything down in here.' Fred patted the buff folder. 'Read through it all with another pot of tea, and I'm always available.'

'There's probably loads more I want to know, but I can't think at the moment.'

'One thing I'll tell you. He lives in a massive house, and he took me through to his library. Awesome room, as you can imagine. Thought I'd mention that, because I can see you like books.' He glanced around at the piles waiting to be sorted.

'I'm going to fit some proper bookshelves, there wasn't room at Nan's house but here I've plenty of space to do things like that.

And you're reight, I do read a lot. The wood is coming this afternoon, so I'm looking forward to getting stuck into that.'

'What really amused me, after we sat down in leather armchairs in front of this great big fire, a butler turned up with a tea trolley. I've never been served tea by a butler before.'

Ken laughed. 'Well, if he comes here he'll get it like I've made it for you. I'll have to be t'butler.'

Fred went over the conversation as he drove back to Eyam. Ken seemed to have taken it all very well, and his own opinion was that the father and son should meet at Whitelilac Cottage, where they could relax and get to know each other. He knew he would have to persuade Sir Henry, but he also knew he had to try.

Fred drove down through Bradwell and arrived at a queue of traffic just before the tiny bridge that was the only way out of the village. He sat waiting patiently for the huge lorry that was trying to get into the village to sort itself out, and all the car drivers tried to squeeze over another couple of inches to give the lorry driver a little extra wiggle room.

Eventually the traffic began to move again, and he smiled as he reached the T-junction at the end of the road. Another large truck was indicating to turn onto the road that he'd just come down...

He pulled out and headed back towards Eyam, but not before calling in at the flower shop in Hope. Naomi had asked him if he'd like to go for his evening meal, and he didn't intend going empty-handed.

Amanda Gilchrist reached the Connection door at the same time as Fred, and he held the door open for her.

'Two gentlemen in one day,' she said, smiling at him.

'There are some of us still knocking about.'

'Clearly. But I've had two in one morning. Is Beth in?'

Fred looked at Cheryl, and she confirmed that Beth was in, but on a call. 'You want a cup of coffee while you wait?' Cheryl said.

'No, I'm good thanks. I'll hang on a couple of minutes, I wanted to tell her some good news. After all this stuff on the television about this coronavirus, it's nice to hear something exciting.'

'Certainly is.' She glanced at her little switchboard. 'She's off now. Let me check she doesn't have to go back on, and then you should be able to go in.'

Cheryl pressed the internal line, and confirmed that Beth was indeed free to speak to Amanda.

Amanda took the seat Beth offered. 'I wanted you to know that I've done it, I've signed on the dotted line, met Joe's wife, and all is hunky-dory. He apologised for not giving me the whole story, and his wife told him he was an utter idiot. Quite funny really, but I feel so much happier, and I wanted to thank you for making this a good day, and not a potential bad one.'

'You're very welcome. And don't forget Cheryl and I are coming up tomorrow for our afternoon tea. We're looking forward to it. Crunching numbers all day can be a bit stressful, so it will be a lovely break for us. You off out to celebrate tonight?'

'We were, but Flora rang about ten minutes ago to say one of her colleagues has been killed, and she's upset. I guess we'll probably stay in and have a bottle of wine or something. She liked Ivan a lot, was working with him on some project or other – it's really knocked her for six.'

19

Beth walked Amanda to the door and waited until she climbed into her car before asking Cheryl if Tessa and/or Luke were in.

'They both are. They're in Luke's office.'

'I'll go up.'

It was quiet. Both Tessa and Luke were heads down and working on their laptops, and Beth slowly slid her head around the door.

'No biscuits, no doughnuts? What's this all about then?'

Luke stood. 'Hey, welcome, big boss. Can do a bit of creeping and go and fetch some if you want doughnuts.'

'No, I'm good, I was only joking. I'll settle for a coffee though. I have a bit of information to pass on to you.'

'Information is good.' Luke walked to the coffee pot and poured a cup for her.

'Thanks, Luke.' She sat by the side of Tessa, and leaned back. 'Your deceased man from this morning... it turns out Amanda Gilchrist's partner works with him.'

'Who's Amanda's partner?'

'Flora. I don't know her surname.'

'Robinson. Small world, isn't it?'

'It is. I asked Amanda if they were going out to celebrate her tea shop's expansion, and she said probably not because a work colleague of Flora had been killed. Then she mentioned the name Ivan, and my mathematical brain added two and two together. I thought I'd better mention it in case you needed to know.'

'Thank you. Flora and Ivan were working on something together. Don't know what it was, but she was the one who alerted John to Ivan's absence. It seems there was something she wanted to change but didn't want to do it without backup from Ivan.'

'Any further news on it?'

'Bits and bobs. John has been to see Ivan's parents who are distraught. They rely heavily on him, so John is arranging for carers to go in and help with his father's care. They've also managed to get news to his girlfriend's employers who will tell her when she lands. She's on her way back to Doncaster airport from... Poland, I think John said. In the meantime, I'm waiting to hear from DI Haughton – she'll ring me as soon as she knows cause of death, but she said the pathologist suspected a heroin injection.' Tessa frowned. 'Horrible way to go, and definitely premeditated. You don't accidentally kill somebody by heroin injection.'

'You didn't suspect him of anything prior to this happening?'

'Not really. We're still at the asking questions stage. I can't see this being a quick case. We're making a list of relatives of the two men currently in prison for the original attack on Caroline Coates, we intend going to visit one or two.'

'You go together.'

Luke nodded. 'Panic not, we will.'

'Okay, I'll leave you to it.' Beth picked up her coffee. 'I'll return the cup when I've finished with it. Maybe.'

Quietness descended once more, but neither went back to their laptops.

'What's going on?'

Tessa shrugged. 'No idea. We seem to be going round in circles. Did Flora mention she had a partner?'

'Yes, and she said she lived outside Eyam but no further details. All of them seemed reluctant to speak freely. You think it's because we're private detectives and not police detectives?'

'I'm sure of it.' Tessa scowled. 'I may have to start being a bit more bullying, and less of the Mrs Nice Guy. Woman. Whatever.'

'I agree. And I'm going to stop sitting down, become a prowler, stand behind them, make them feel intimidated.'

'You think we've hit on the answer?'

Luke laughed. 'No, but I'll enjoy trying.'

They put their heads down, and continued to search the internet for family members, people they intended intimidating and coercing – after they'd tried being nice.

Fred emailed Sir Henry Allbright with details of his morning meeting with Ken, and offered his suggestion of a meeting at the cottage, saying it would be more informal and less threatening to both parties. Fred wrote at length of the work Ken was planning at the cottage, and then clicked send after crossing his fingers that he had done enough to convince the elderly man that it made sense to meet there.

Fred then made notes on his computer, bringing his report up to date, although not finalising it. That wouldn't be done until after he had facilitated that first meeting between father and son. Fred hadn't known what to expect when he had entered that huge house on Saturday morning, and had been pleasantly surprised to be treated as an honoured guest, and made to feel very welcome. He had half-expected some hostility, but then he hadn't known the full story of the life-long love that had been between Sir Henry and the younger Joanne.

Fred was considering calling it a day and heading off home when the reply came. It seemed Sir Henry had had a change of heart, and the cottage would, after due consideration, be the best place to meet. He offered a choice of dates, stating that he would be free for all of them, and he would happily work with Ken's choice. He would book a hotel somewhere close to Bradwell, and stay overnight, as his driver shouldn't be asked to do two long journeys in one day.

Fred smiled as he read the email. He did wonder how he was going to explain swanning off to Derbyshire for a couple of days, but then realised Sir Henry probably already had a good reason set up to do such a thing; he had had years of practising subterfuge.

He rang Ken, read him the message and organised for the coming Friday to be the day most suitable.

'My wood's 'ere,' Ken said. 'I've made a start, so I'm 'oping it will be all smart and tidy by Friday. In 'ere, anyway.'

'You don't hang about, do you?'

'I like DIY. Actually, it's more I like wood. When I've done this I'm going to work on t'smaller bedroom. There's an alcove in there, screamin' out for built-in wardrobes. Not done one before, but I reckon I can. Been chatting to a neighbour while t'wood were being delivered, and she were well impressed.'

'Glad you're starting to meet people, Ken. Reight, lad, I'm going to message thi' dad back now, and get 'im 'ere for Friday. How's that for a bit of Yorkshire?'

'It'll do,' Ken growled, 'but it's not as reight as mine.'

Fred laughed as he disconnected, and pulled his laptop towards him. He sent off a quick email suggesting Friday, and received an equally quick one back saying yes.

Naomi loved the flowers, and immediately disappeared to put them in water, leaving Fred with Rosie and Imogen, and their grandmother Geraldine who made a quick introduction, and the two girls hesitantly approached him.

'You work with Luke?'

'I do. Smart young man, your brother.'

'I've got his room,' Imogen said. 'He left me his desk.'

'No he didn't,' Geraldine interrupted. 'You moved all your art stuff into it, so he couldn't really take it.'

Fred laughed. 'Then you're a smart young woman as well as him being a smart young man.'

'I thought so as well,' Imogen said with a smile. 'He had to buy a new one.'

Rosie joined her sister. 'And I've got my own room all to myself now. We miss Luke loads, but we don't want him to come home again.'

'Rosie!' Naomi caught the tail-end of the conversation. 'Don't be awful. He's our Luke, and if he ever wants to come home, he can.'

Rosie giggled. 'He'll have to sleep in a tent in the back garden if he does, because there's no bedrooms left now.'

Naomi turned to Fred. 'I do apologise for my evil daughters, Fred. They're truly horrible towards Luke.'

'That's okay, I had a sister who was like these two. She couldn't wait to get rid of me.'

'Okay, girls,' Naomi said, 'your punishment for dissing your brother is you can go and set the table.'

There were initial signs of mutiny but eventually they disappeared into the dining room, and Fred, Naomi and Geraldine were left to enjoy the peace.

'Lovely kids,' Geraldine said, 'but it is nice when they've gone to bed.'

Flora and Amanda shared a bottle of wine, and toasted the signing of the contract. 'I'm so pleased for you, Amanda, you deserve this. Is it still all starting tomorrow?'

'It is. Stefan will be there early, but I've given him a key. We've discussed how it's going to be done to help me keep the business open, so I'm hoping there's nothing unforeseen on the horizon that will change those plans. But enough of that. Tell me about Ivan.'

'I can't really. I don't know very much, and I want to cry anyway. It's strange without him, he was a friend. It seems he was found in Ecclesall Woods late on Sunday, but he'd no identification on him so nobody knew who he was. I've no idea how they did ID him, but it seems it is him. Why would anyone want to kill Ivan? He was so nice, helped me no end, and we were working together on this new game. It was going so well, and now I feel lost. Lottie is going to be devastated.'

'Lottie?'

'His girlfriend. She'll know by now. They were meeting her plane to tell her. She's an air hostess.'

Amanda pulled Flora closer. 'I'm so sorry. How did he die?'

'Not sure, but John suggested he was injected with something.'

'That's awful. Look, the fire needs another log putting on. What say we don't bother, we take this wine up to bed, and close today down?'

'Brilliant idea. Not sure I'll be able to sleep, but we'll be comfier there. Thank you, Mands, for being here for me.'

'No problem. You didn't tell Tessa we were together?'

'No. Should I have?'

Amanda shrugged. 'Not necessarily. I told Beth without thinking, so I imagine Tessa and Luke will know now. It won't be a problem, will it?'

'No, I only didn't tell her because we'd all made a bit of a pact that we'd tell them the very minimum we could get away with it. They're not the police when all's said and done, they're private investigators.'

'Licenced private investigators, not simply nosy sods. They're asking questions for a reason. Might be an idea to be a bit more forthcoming if they talk to you again. Come on, let's head upstairs. Busy day tomorrow, probably for both of us. And if you need me, ring me. Yes?'

Flora looked at the woman who was such a big part of her life. 'Yes. I promise.'

Fred drove home feeling tired, well fed, and happy. The girls had been in bed by eight, although giggles and voices had been heard until about nine, but spending time with Naomi and Geraldine had been really enjoyable. Geraldine took herself off to bed around nine, clutching her Kindle and a glass of water, and finally they were alone.

They talked of general things, with Fred keeping clear of anything connected with work, and eventually he stood and took her in his arms. The kiss was deep and satisfying. 'I have to go home, and I know you start early. I don't want to go but...'

'Then stay.'

He shook his head. 'Not until your girls know me a bit better.

This weekend was magical, lovely lady, I can live with that for a while. You make me very happy, Naomi.'

'And you make me smile all the time,' she responded, before pulling his head down to kiss her again. 'Will you join us tomorrow for our evening meal? Please?'

'If we can have a takeaway. I don't want you to feel you have to keep feeding me, that's not fair. Do you *all* like Chinese?'

She laughed. 'Just a little bit. Like... immensely.'

'Then Chinese it is. I'll come straight here from work instead of going home first, and we'll sort it out with the girls.' He kissed her again, and closed the door gently behind him, a huge smile on his face.

20

Amanda slept with the stillness of the dead, so Flora slipped quietly out of bed and headed for the bathroom clutching her phone. She locked the door, sat on the toilet seat and began to type.

We need to talk. Those PIs now know I live with A. Can we go out for lunch tomorrow instead of taking sarnies? Feel so upset about I.

The reply came quickly.

Yes. Stop worrying. You told A anything?

Very little. She knows I'm upset. See you in morning.

Flora flushed the toilet in case Amanda was awake, and left the bathroom. She headed downstairs and poured herself a glass of milk before sitting at the kitchen table. She got on well with Dom, but Ivan had been her rock, guiding her through the intricacies of game development, being so patient with her until she grasped what he was showing her, and she didn't want to imagine how life would be at work now he was gone.

And there was the issue of his parents... how would they cope without him? She knew she had to visit them, but had no earthly idea what she would say. She drank the milk and went back to bed, then tossed and turned for most of the night, her thoughts in turmoil. What was deeply concerning was that she couldn't tell Amanda everything in her mind, and that didn't sit right with her.

Tessa and Luke arrived within a minute of each other, surprised to see Cheryl already there.

'Couldn't sleep?' Luke asked.

'Don't be cheeky, young Luke. The kids had to be in school early so I took them instead of them catching the school bus. Hence I'm here fifteen minutes early. I won't ask for overtime pay,' she said with a laugh.

The doorbell pinged and Tessa joined them. 'Thought I'd be first in,' she said.

'Actually, none of us were first in, Fred was already here when I arrived.' Cheryl pointed to the light board, and Fred's light was glowing amber. 'If you need him for anything, grab him now. He was on the phone a few seconds ago, but he's off now.'

Fred looked up as his door opened and he smiled.

'Don't smile at me,' Luke said. 'You didn't smile when you started here, and now you do and I know why.'

Fred changed his smile to a laugh. 'Got out of the wrong side of the bed, did you? Was it yours or Maria's side?'

Luke felt the blush starting and said no more on the subject.

'Can I intervene?' Tessa grinned at both of them. 'Fred, we might need your input. Are you off out, or can you join us in Luke's office?'

'Give me ten minutes to finish bringing this report up to date, and I'll be with you.'

'Cut Fred some slack.' Tessa's tone was sharp. 'I know you think you're protecting your mother, but honestly Naomi doesn't need protecting from him. I've known him a fair few years, and he's a solid, dependable bloke who would never hurt her, or let her down. And your mum deserves some happiness, she's had twenty years of bringing up a snarky son. So pack it in, let them enjoy this new friendship, let them enjoy going out together. And let them enjoy sleeping together if that's what they want to do, it's hardly any business of yours. You're not Naomi's father, Luke, you're her son.'

Luke looked down at the floor. 'I know.' He lifted his head. 'My mum fell apart when Dad left, and it made me really protective. I'll back off, but if he hurts her...'

'He'll not hurt her,' Tessa scoffed. 'He's a big softy, is our Fred, and I think he's fallen pretty hard for your mum. So leave them to get on with it. Okay?'

'Okay. I'll apologise to him. I know I'm being stupid, but I never want to see Mum in that state again.'

Fred walked through the door and Luke held out his hand. 'Sorry, Fred. I was being the protective son.' They shook hands.

'As if I'd hurt her. For somebody to understand me so much that they buy me a sausage roll and a can of Coke for lunch is a true miracle. I'm not letting her go, I give you warning now. We're not rushing anything, I promise you, but I really like your mum, and nothing you say will alter that.'

Luke gave a brief nod, and sat down. 'Glad that's out of the way, perhaps Maria will get back to talking to me now.'

Tessa clapped her hands. 'So we've called a truce? Right, on to the Coates situation.'

'Where are we?' Fred picked up the tea that was waiting for him, and took a drink of it.

'We want to interview members of the two thugs' families. Things like this simply weren't covered once we'd got them in custody, as you know. In fact, also as you know, this whole case was a shambles. The conviction was based purely on CCTV evidence. I'm not saying that evidence was wrong, it wasn't, but we didn't take it far enough. Jacques and Simpson pretended they didn't know the man who'd paid them to get his money back, but they knew him, I'm sure of that. There's either something waiting for them when they're released, or he had some hold over them and they daren't say his name. So we need to talk to their mothers. Neither of them have a father at home, and their families are still at the same addresses. Nathan Jacques, who was the smarter of the two, has two younger sisters, Molly, sixteen, and Paula who is twelve. The mother is Wendy Jacques, and that's her maiden name, so presumably she's never been married.'

Tessa paused to glance down at her notes. 'Robert Simpson did have a father present at the time of his conviction but he's since died of Motor Neurone Disease. Tanya Simpson, the mother, lives at home with her remaining son, Andrew, who's now eighteen. Both families live close to each other, on Woodseats Road in Sheffield, so I'm proposing that Fred goes to chat to the Simpsons, and Luke and I to the Jacques family.'

She looked at her two colleagues, and they nodded in agreement.

'You expect some trouble from the Jacques family?' Luke asked.

'Not really, but there are two teenage girls there who might respond to the charm and good looks of Luke Taylor. If Andrew Simpson is home, I suspect he'll appreciate Fred's authority. If not, he can charm Tanya.'

Fred laughed aloud. 'It's been a few years since I charmed anybody, but I'll give it a go. Are we going this morning?'

'After lunch. I've done a bit of work on these two families, so I need you both to read through these reports before we go, and fix everything in your minds. You may be able to drop some little nugget out that will push them into talking. For instance, Fred, Andrew Simpson is in his first year at uni. He's stayed in Sheffield, and is doing Politics, History and French. He seems to be a much smarter kid than his older brother. Get him chatting, you never know what will come out. I remember the mother, Tanya, being a bit of a mouse, totally bewildered by her lad going for a long stretch in prison, and unable to believe he had actually kicked a woman hard enough that she aborted her two babies.'

Fred took his mind back to that awful time before speaking. 'Little woman, the family never had any money because of the poorly husband. She couldn't go out to work because she was his carer, and she looked downtrodden and ill all the time. I think Robert going to prison took the life out of her.'

'Did you interview her at the time?'

'Kind of. It was more a visit than an interview because she sobbed all the way through it. I suspect she might remember me because I tried to comfort her. Young Andrew never left her side. I'll be honest, I couldn't wait to get out. I felt as though I was intruding, and Alex Mason had told me not to put too much effort into the visit.'

Tessa frowned. 'I'm seriously considering going to see him.'

'Mason? Not without somebody by your side recording every word he utters. Nobody trusted him, Tessa, and when he left straight after this case was finished, we all breathed a sigh of relief, remember? And when they made you up to DI, there was a massive round of applause because we knew from then on results would be genuine.'

Tessa felt a blush suffuse her skin. 'Well thank you, kind sir. I wish they hadn't classed it as cold by the time I took over, but right at the beginning of my career as a DI wasn't the time to start making waves. It's why I'm determined to sort stuff now, to do what I can for John and Caroline.'

Fred picked up the report on the two families. 'I'll read these in my office. What time are we going?'

'About two. Take a recorder and make sure they know we're using it.'

Fred walked across the road to the Co-op. He was surprised at the minimal traffic – it was a nice day, if a little cold, but a bit of sunshine always brought the visitors to Eyam, many of them repeat visitors because they couldn't get enough of the plague story. He wondered if the stories of the coronavirus that had started spreading to other countries including the United Kingdom was putting people off going out and about, and he smiled at the thought of everyone mimicking China and walking around with masks on all the time, once outside the home environment.

Naomi was standing by a till, obviously training a new employee.

'I won't distract you,' Fred said quietly. 'I wanted you to know I've spoken to Luke about us, and I think I've eased things.'

'Thank goodness for that,' she said equally quietly. 'Are we still okay for tonight?'

'We are. I'm out this afternoon, but I should be back by four at the latest.'

'No,' she said to the trainee. 'It's that button for fresh bread, that one's for pre-packaged.' The woman held up a hand in acknowledgement.

'I'll leave you to get on with it. See you tonight.'

'Thank you for talking to him, he's only looking out for me.'

Fred gave a brief nod, and headed back across the traffic-free road. He could see Stefan Patmore's truck and van further up the road, and realised today was the day for the start of the building work at the tea rooms. An evening opening bistro in the village would be very welcome, and he for one couldn't wait for it to happen. He was whistling to himself as he returned to his office. Life felt pretty good.

21

Woodseats Road was a long steep road, with terraced houses built for Sheffield's steel workers in the early nineteen hundreds. Over the years they had been privately bought with many then rented anew to Sheffield's burgeoning multi-national residents. It was a close-knit community, and when Tessa pulled up outside the Jacques home she felt eyes on them from surrounding houses.

'Wouldn't like to live on this road when it snows,' Luke said.

'It's worse where you live.' Tessa smiled. 'This road is a main bus route, so it's one of the first to be gritted. Eyam simply dies, it's so cut off. It's the house with the red door. I'm sure it wasn't red last time I was here. Looks very smart.'

She locked the car and they walked towards the terraced property. Luke noticed that Fred's car was parked outside a house six doors further down the steep road, and he mentioned it to Tessa.

'Thought he might be here first. That's the Simpson home. His car is superb for this job. I'm thinking about getting a new one. When I move to Eyam I'll definitely need a four-by-four that can handle snow.'

'You're moving to Eyam?'

'Could be,' she said as she lifted her hand to knock with the shiny brass owl doorknocker.

The door opened slightly, a chain preventing it opening fully.

'Mrs Jacques? Sorry to trouble you, we have met before. You knew me then as DS Tessa Marsden.'

Wendy Jacques seemed to hesitate, then nodded. 'Yes, I remember you. What do you want?'

'A quick chat. It's nothing to worry about, I promise you.'

The door closed and the chain was removed. 'You'd best come in then.'

They stepped directly from the front door into the lounge, and Wendy stared pointedly at their feet. They both removed their shoes and placed them on the shoe stand by the door.

'What can I do for you? He's still inside, you know.'

'I know,' Tessa said. 'We wanted a chat. First of all, I am no longer DS Marsden.'

'I heard they made you up to DI when they got rid of that other one.'

Tessa smiled. 'He retired. No, I meant I'm no longer with the police and haven't been for about six weeks now.' She handed her card to Wendy, who stared at it.

'Connection? You're a private investigator now?'

'I am. And this is my colleague Luke Taylor. We'd like to record this conversation if it's okay with you, because we believe when your son was sentenced, and it was right that he was, there was something wrong. The information in front of the judge led him to give both Nathan and Robert the maximum sentence that the law allowed.'

Luke switched on the recorder; he figured she hadn't said no.

She stared at them for a moment, before indicating the settee. 'Please sit down. I'll get Molly. She's not in school today.'

She walked across to the bottom of the stairs and called her daughter's name.

Molly Jacques joined them a minute later, a frown on her face. 'Who are you?'

Tessa explained once again, and Molly sat by her mum's side on the smaller of the two settees.

Tessa took a deep breath. She recognised the importance of not antagonising the two people facing her, but the tension in the air was palpable.

'We are trying to trace the man who involved Nathan and Robert in this criminal activity. Our client has given us all the information he has, but I believe you and your son were let down by the system, and not enough was done to investigate and track down the man who was behind it all, the one they said they met in a pub and they didn't know his name.'

There was a brief nod from Wendy, but she remained silent.

'It's a standard phrase from criminals, the man they met in a pub, and I'm afraid judges discount it completely. If they had given even one smidgeon of a clue as to who the man was, I believe their sentences would have been halved, and Nathan would be home with you now, but they didn't.'

'He didn't know him...'

'I don't believe that, and I think you probably don't either. Since Nathan has been inside have you received any threats from anybody, veiled or otherwise? You see, we think he either blackmailed the two lads into helping him, or he had some other hold over them such as a threat to their families while they were inside.'

Luke fixed his gaze on Molly. 'Molly? Has Nathan spoken to you of anything? Did he give you any reason for their actions?'

Molly clutched her mother's hand. 'He gave them drugs.'

'Molly,' her mother said.

'Please, Mrs Jacques. Help us find some reason for what these two lads did, and why they've remained silent.'

Wendy Jacques took a deep breath. 'Nathan didn't use drugs. I don't think Robert did either. The first time I spoke to Nathan after he was arrested, he cried. He said that man had given them some drugs about a week before they went to the Coates house, and kept giving them to him and Robert all that week. On the Saturday morning they met him and he gave them their instructions to get the money back, and some more drugs. He said if they took the special tablets they'd have no worries.'

'Why didn't you tell the police?'

'I did. I told that DI. Sorry, I can't remember his name. He said he'd pass the information on.'

'It never cropped up in court. The lads had high levels of whatever they took on that Saturday still in their system on the Sunday, so they must have been absolutely stoned. And two babies died as a result. We need to know everything you know, Mrs Jacques.'

'I don't know anything else.' She brushed away a tear. 'And what good will it do?'

'I'm not making any false promises, but this case can go to appeal, on the grounds of additional evidence that wasn't there first time around. But without producing the person who recruited them...'

'Whether they know the name or not, they won't say.' Molly spoke quietly, still clinging tightly to her mother's hand. 'You're right, he did threaten them. If they had breathed one word of his name, and they do know it, he would have made sure I was offered drugs, and so would Paula and Andrew. If Nathan and Rob didn't accept his terms, the drugs would be forcibly given to us. They've made a pact never to reveal it, they'll do the time.'

'Nathan told you this?'

Molly nodded. 'He did. Mum went to get us all a coffee one

day, and he told me. It was to warn me, to protect me.' She turned to her mum. 'Sorry, Mum. He asked me not to worry you by telling you, he wanted me on my guard. And looking out for Paula.'

'Do you know who he is?' Tessa spoke softly, deliberately trying to lessen the tension.

'No, I don't. And Mum came back with the drinks before I'd chance to ask him. I honestly don't think he'll ever tell anybody; he's scared to death of whoever it is. The only thing he did say, as Mum walked back up the room, was never trust a man with blonde hair. I thought it a bit strange because the man they were supposed to be looking for had longish dark hair, but I couldn't talk any more about it because the coffee arrived.' She smiled at Wendy. 'Stop worrying, Mum. Nobody has ever approached me, and I'm pretty sure they haven't tried selling or giving drugs to Paula and Andrew. We wouldn't have them anyway.'

'That's good to hear, Molly. Have Andrew and Paula ever said anything? That maybe they were scared, or they were being followed?'

'They've never said anything to me, and... well... Andrew's my boyfriend. I'm sure he would have mentioned anything strange that was happening.'

Tessa stood, and Luke leaned forward to collect the recorder from the coffee table. 'Thank you for your help. If you think of anything else at all, please ring me. We're trying to get proper justice here, because something's definitely off kilter.'

They put on their shoes, and stepped back onto the street, Wendy's parting words staying in the air around them. 'At last I feel a little bit of hope.'

Fred enjoyed the cup of tea Tanya Simpson made for him, and found Andrew Simpson to be a pleasant young man, but that was all he got from his visit. Andrew had had a fair amount of contact with his older brother, but no information had come his way. He said Robert repeatedly told him to watch out for the girls, back at the beginning, but now his conversation was sporadic, and the last time they had been to see him he had suggested they might want to make their visits every two months instead of monthly.

Fred switched off the recorder, thanked them for their time, and handed his card to them.

'Anything, anything at all that you can think of, please give me a call. We believe this man has made a career out of burglary and robbery, and we don't want his next job to be a murder. We also believe he used Nathan and Robert as guinea pigs. The Coates job was his starter for ten, so to speak. When you next visit Robert, please try to get him talking. Anything he can remember about the man, any mannerisms, anything he might have let slip, that's the sort of information that will eventually catch him.'

'Mr Iveson, it's not a time for talking when we visit Robert. He's very withdrawn now, not the son I remember from his teenage years. We'll do our best, but don't expect anything.'

They met up back at the office and discussed the afternoon's developments.

'Don't trust a blonde man?'

'That's what Molly told us Nathan said. It puzzled us as well. Both John and Caroline described him as having longish dark hair.'

'A wig?'

'In view of what Nathan has said to his sister, I'm leaning towards that. Maybe we need to talk to John again.'

'I can draw,' Luke said.

Tessa and Fred looked at him, Tessa clicking on immediately to what he meant. Fred was a little slower.

'Stick men?' Fred asked.

'No. I meant I'll take home that identikit picture of this chap with his long greasy hair in its ponytail and replace it with blonde hair in a couple of styles. Then we'll decide what we can do with them.'

Fred gave a low whistle. 'I'm impressed. You can draw that well?'

'I'll give it a go. I've always drawn, so we'll see what happens. I must admit I've never done anything like this before so it probably won't work, but we won't lose anything by trying.'

'Then let's call it a day. This is a damn frustrating case, and I for one want to go home, read a book and forget it. An early night would be more than welcome as well.'

'Good idea. I'm off for a Chinese with Naomi and the girls.'

Tessa's phone rang and she glanced at her screen before answering it. 'Hi, Eileen. You okay?' She remained silent for a few seconds, then said thanks before disconnecting. 'It seems Ivan died from a massive overdose of heroin. He would have died quickly. What a crap end to anybody's life.'

22

Luke felt Maria lean against his back, her arms creeping around his neck.

'You okay? You want a drink or anything?'

'No thanks, I'm good. Maybe we'll have one before bed if I'm happy with this.' He tapped his pencil on the sketch pad.

'I'll leave you to get on with it. I'm going to jump in the shower, put on my pjs and do some studying. It's only two weeks to my exam. Shout out if you want anything.'

He gently squeezed her hands, and switched his thoughts away from sharing the shower.

He studied the face of the man described by John and Caroline, filtered him carefully into his brain and made the first tentative stroke on the pristine paper. He worked steadily for an hour, discarding his first attempt but knowing he'd got it with the second one.

It was simply the face. No hair, nothing below the neck, and eyes that seemed too small for the face. He knew that perception would change once he began to add hair. He took the finished version to his printer and copied it several times, then returned to the kitchen table. He began to carefully sketch blonde hair, taking his time replacing the dark shoulder-length style seen by the Coateses.

The difference it made caused a gasp from Luke. It was astounding and he knew nobody would recognise the two drawings as being the same man. He drew five different hairstyles, never deviating from blonde locks, then pulled all five pictures towards him. He knew he was too close to the pictures and wouldn't recognise anyone from them without taking time out from the sketches, but he hoped others would be able to see something, anything, in the portraits. As a final flourish he drew the last print as a bald man, then spread them all out before calling Maria's name.

Maria looked tired, but she was keen to see what had kept Luke away from her all evening. She touched each sheet, then stared at Luke. 'These are amazing. You certainly have a talent with a pencil.'

'Thank you. I've always enjoyed drawing, but don't get much time to do it now. I need Tessa to cast her eyes over these tomorrow – Fred as well, because something may click with them. If it doesn't, we haven't lost anything, and I've enjoyed the drawing session.' He smiled at Maria. 'You want a glass of wine?'

She shook her head. 'No thanks. Would you think I was daft if I asked for a hot chocolate and then an early night?'

'Awesome idea. I'll make the drinks, and you sort out your stuff.' He gave her a gentle kiss, and slipped the pictures into a cardboard file before turning towards the cooker. He poured milk into the pan and stared into the white liquid as he gently swirled it around. Pulling the glass cups towards him, it hit him with a flash. Glasses. Glasses changed an appearance completely.

He made the hot chocolates, then took a couple more copies of the original portrait. He handed Maria her drink along with a kiss, and explained he had more work to do. An early night was looking less likely with every passing second.

Wednesday morning blew in with a heck of a gale. Maria had already left for work by the time Luke's alarm informed him he had to get up – the cockerel sound was certainly the most irritating on the planet, but by far the most effective.

He sat on the edge of the bed allowing his brain to catch up with his body for a moment, and thought back to the previous evening's work. He now had twelve pictures to show Tessa and Fred, and in an ideal world one of them would say I know who that is, it's Joe Bloggs from Attercliffe. In his world his expectation was that they would say they couldn't connect to any of the faces.

He showered, popped a bagel in the toaster and had a glass of milk before picking up his briefcase and heading out of the door. He waved to Jenny, his landlady, and jumped in his car, holding on to the door as a gust of wind tried to snatch it out of his hands. He set the heater to work at full blast, and a smile crossed his face as he thought back to Doris Lester's grumbles at his old car for only having intermittent warmth, before a maniac had caused Luke to write it off.

Luke was first in the office, but closely followed by both Tessa and Fred. All three assembled in Luke's office, and he handed round coffees before they became immersed in their discussions.

He placed his folder on the desk and took out all the pictures.

'I was up late last night,' he said. 'This is the result.'

He laid out the pictures, and Fred and Tessa's eyes moved to each one as it was placed meticulously by the side of the previous one.

Tessa leaned back and said 'Wow. I'm impressed. Different hairstyles, different blonde shades – and even some with glasses. This is a fantastic job, Luke. Did you sleep at all?'

'About four hours. I didn't even hear Maria get up, she had a six o'clock start this morning for a biggish dog operation, but I must have been dead to the world. I didn't notice time passing when I was working on them, I like drawing, but when that pesky cockerel started this morning I could have thrown it through the window.'

'You have a cockerel in the bedroom?' Tessa asked.

'I do. Mum bought me an alarm clock years ago to get me up for school. It's a very loud cockerel noise. I left it behind when I moved out, but Imogen brought it to me last week. Said she knew I would want it. Maria, of course, loves it, but she's not had it blaring out every morning for the last eight years or so. It's got to go.'

Tessa reached across the table and pulled a picture towards her. The hair was a light shade of blonde, and he wore dark-framed glasses.

'You know him?' Fred asked.

'There's something...'

Both men waited expectantly.

'Luke, have you got blanks of them?'

'I took copies of each one at various stages. Tell me what you want.'

'I want this one but with a darker blonde – I think the style is right. And let's try metal-framed glasses as opposed to dark plastic. Maybe it will shock my brain into gear.'

Luke pulled out the much-fuller folder of staged drawings, and rifled through them until he found the one he needed. He picked up his pencil, and began to darken the hair. The drawing bore no glasses, so once he was satisfied the picture would now be classed as a dark-blonde male, he began to work on the eyewear.

Luke was as engrossed in getting it right as he had been the previous night, and he was suddenly aware of Tessa's face appearing into his space.

'Keep going,' was her terse comment, as he hesitated. 'Just keep going.'

He did, and eventually sat back. 'Job done.'

Tessa pulled the paper towards her. 'Are you too close to see it?' she asked Luke.

He laughed. 'Last night I thought one of them looked like Rod Stewart, and that was the point when I realised I would be no good at this stage, that it was down to you and Fred to see things I couldn't. Believe me, after drawing this lot, they all start to look at bit Rod-ish. Tell me what you're seeing.'

'I'm seeing, quite clearly, Ivan Newburg.'

Luke stared at her, then opened up his laptop. He quickly found the Code Blue website, picked out Ivan's picture and enlarged it to full screen. He spun the laptop around, and heard Fred whistle.

'Too right it's him. Not sure I understand what's going on, but it's him all right.' Fred held the two pictures side by side. 'But how the hell has he managed to fool John Coates all this time?'

'He changed his appearance. If I'm remembering correctly, the Coates both said he had a slight Cockney accent, but anybody can mimic another accent so we don't tend to place much credence on voices. They both agreed on the appearance though, which he had clearly altered if this is indeed Ivan Newburg.'

'So what do we do now?' Luke looked and sounded perplexed. 'It doesn't really make sense to me. Why did he risk everything by going to work for John?'

Tessa gave a slight laugh. 'Cockiness. He knew John hadn't recognised him when he bought the car, despite being one of his key workers at Coates, and that was doubly confirmed when John offered him the job of game developer at Code Blue. And really this explains why we thought this method of stealing money by buying cars for cash, then stealing the money back wasn't particularly lucrative in the long term. It didn't need to be. He did it for fun. For pocket money. To show he could. He earned a healthy salary, bonuses, pension pot – there was simply a crooked side to him, I'm guessing. And he upset somebody.'

'So where do we go from here? If this truly is Ivan, we have to let John and Caroline know, then case closed.' Luke frowned. 'It feels as though we're missing out on something.'

'We're missing out on finding Ivan's killer,' Tessa said, 'but our first priority is to John Coates. He employed us. Then I can tell, and show, what we've come up with to DI Haughton. I'll ring John, tell him we need to see him this morning, and to make sure Caroline is there as well. This is really all about her, not so much John. I suspect he's come to terms with what happened, but Caroline certainly hasn't.'

Oliver miaowed in agreement and jumped down from Luke's knee, before heading round to the other side of the desk and seeking out Fred's lap.

After some discussion it was left to Fred to hold the fort at Connection – Beth and Simon had an unscheduled day trip to Middlesbrough thrown into the pot. Tessa and Luke left for a nine thirty meeting with John and Caroline Coates, leaving Fred without the worry of having to get back for his eleven o'clock appointment.

Cheryl watched them set off with the warning to stay safe in this bloody gale ringing in their ears, and Luke was the one wrestling with the steering wheel all the way to the Coates' home.

John came out to meet them. His smile was welcoming. 'Bit breezy,' he said. 'Bet it was bad coming over the tops.'

'Muscle-building exercise keeping the car on the road,' Luke agreed with a smile. He held out his hand and John shook it.

'Come inside, I'm sure a cuppa will be welcome.'

They followed him through to the kitchen, and Caroline waved a teapot at them.

They thanked her and she busied herself making the tea, while they sat at the kitchen table. Luke took out his folder of drawings, but kept them in front of him.

John let his eyes rest on the folder. 'In your phone call you said you believed you had some news for us, not confirmative but potential.'

Tessa nodded. 'We do. I want you to look at what we have to show you, keeping an open mind. We had one piece of information to go on that at best wasn't unhelpful, but it was a very scrappy comment we were given. It was that the man who employed Jacques and Simpson was possibly blonde.'

23

'I'm finding it hard to take in.' John ran his hand through his hair, by now beginning to resemble hedgehog spines. 'There was I, drinking whisky and meeting distributors for the new game in a hotel in London, and some clever sod is doing the job I've longed to do, and bumping him off here in Sheffield.'

'We're taking these pictures to DI Haughton after this, leaving it all with her, but I think she will agree with our conclusion.'

'You know, it's strange now with hindsight, but when he came in to our kitchen to hand over the money I saw something, a resemblance to something or somebody that instantly disappeared. Maybe that was my subconscious recognising a part of Ivan that I knew, but that he'd tried to hide. And he did it very successfully. Even now, when I can see it in black and white, I'm finding it hard to accept. He was part of my main security team at Coates, I trusted him absolutely. Here at Code Blue he had a high level of trust that was equal to Dom's. Everybody liked him, everybody got on well with him. Yet it seems he had another side that nobody knew anything about.'

'Somebody did,' Tessa said slowly. 'Somebody knew because

he was injected with a massive dose of heroin between twelve and two on Sunday afternoon. But that's not our concern, that's for Eileen Haughton to sort. I believe our job has come to an end as far as your employment of Connection goes, but I'd like to keep the file open until we have confirmation that Ivan Newburg really was the man who destroyed your lives. Unofficially I believe we're right, and I feel you especially, Caroline, can now start to put it behind you. I hope so.'

Caroline had been silent during the explanation of the pictures, and had simply stared at the portraits. Now she pulled the one resembling Ivan towards her. 'I liked him. He was always polite. He came through from Code Blue last week to bring a letter that had been delivered there instead of here, and he was so nice. He played with Casey for a couple of minutes before heading back down the corridor. And now you're saying he was the reason my babies died!'

'Oh, Caroline, I know it must be hard for you. But it had to be somebody who had expert knowledge of your security in your home. Three people did – Dom, Ivan and John.'

'Ivan actually worked with me to design it,' John said quietly. 'I trusted him completely, and he was my first choice when I was bringing people over from Coates to Code Blue. I wanted him to be the supervisor, but he turned that role down, saying he had too much responsibility at home with his father, so couldn't give everything to what would be required in that position. I believed everything he said. And he's done the same con with other people?'

Tessa nodded. 'Oh yes. There are around five that we are sure about, and maybe a couple more that could be him. The police are baffled. Wherever he's been caught on CCTV he's had the dark hair, he matched with your description perfectly. If somebody else has clicked on to who he is, they've certainly made him pay the price. I suggest you don't tell the others yet, I think the police have to prove everything first. They can do that with facial recognition, and I'm pretty sure it will confirm what we're now saying. If it doesn't, we're back to square one, and we carry on looking. Personally, I believe it was Ivan. Facial recognition is no good if the suspect doesn't have a criminal record, and clearly Ivan didn't. But they can do it with pictures of his face, and the pictures from the CCTV.'

Caroline reached for John's hand, and he gently squeezed her fingers. 'We're getting there, sweetheart. He's dead now, thank God.'

Eileen Haughton had listened carefully to their story, had been impressed by Luke's drawing skills, and had confirmed that facial recognition could now be used as they had a corpse in the morgue who potentially could be linked to a figure on CCTV. She promised to let them know the results as soon as they were available, and they departed for Eyam feeling a sense of relief.

The wind hadn't lessened in any way, and Luke drove carefully. The skies were filled with dark grey clouds, and the rain began as light spatters as they crossed the moors, but within five minutes was torrential. He could feel the tension in his muscles as he pulled up outside Connection, and they ran the few steps to get in the door.

'The wanderers return,' Cheryl said with a smile. 'It's been a bit lonely in here today. Beth and Simon are still over in Middlesbrough because they've been asked to stay for a second meeting tomorrow. It's going to be too lucrative for Connection for them to turn it down, and then Fred went out to follow some woman or other after his eleven o'clock was finished, so I've read about a hundred pages of my book.'

'Busy day then,' Luke said.

'Intensely busy. And Fred says can you give him a ring later and let him know how you got on.'

'I'll do it,' Tessa said. 'Everything's been churning around my head all the way back. I think I'm feeling a bit puzzled, but I'm not sure why yet. Whatever's niggling away through my brain will eventually become clear, and it could easily be Fred who triggers the thought.'

'Well, I'm going to feed Oliver, then I'm going home unless you need me for anything, Tessa.' Luke ran his hand through his hair, trying to ease a troublesome headache that he knew had been caused by the intensity of concentration on the drive home. And lack of sleep.

'No, Luke. Go home. Take it easy, and no drawing tonight. You did a brilliant job, and hopefully it's resolved the case. I think it'll be tomorrow before we hear from Eileen, so forget about it all for tonight, and relax.'

He headed into the kitchen, and Tessa and Cheryl smiled simultaneously as they heard the rattle of the cat food box.

'He loves that cat,' Cheryl said.

'Certainly does,' Tessa agreed, 'but right now he needs to go home. He was up till the early hours of the morning drawing portraits, and of course he couldn't spread it over two nights. He had to get it all done last night.'

'He's an amazing artist. He drew a portrait of Keith for me, a couple of months after he died. Luke also had it framed; it's on the wall in my lounge. It's superb.'

'Last night he took a face drawn by a police artist, and left off the long dark hair that was evident on the original suspect. He then replaced it with several different styles of blonde hair, one picture after another, and if that wasn't enough, he started again and gave them all different types of glasses. As a result, he got very little sleep, and now he's got a headache.'

'Silly boy,' Cheryl said. 'The first aid box is in the kitchen, he can take some tablets.'

Tessa laughed. 'I'll tell him. He'll not have thought about that for one minute.' She walked through to the kitchen to find Luke sitting on the floor, Oliver on his knee, and play fighting with the little black cat.

'Cheryl says painkillers are in the first aid box, so take some. It was a direct instruction, so don't ignore it,' she said.

'Didn't know we had any.' He lifted Oliver and placed him on the floor. 'Go away, pal, I've to be medicated.'

Climbing to his feet with a degree of stiffness, Luke reached for the small green box and took out two tablets. He washed them down with water, and leaned against the sink. 'Have we got this right?' he asked.

'I have no idea. My feelings are that yes we have, but I've no proof of that. We'll know soon enough. And Caroline will want to shake the hand of the man who's injected that heroin, I'm sure. She might have little Casey now, but she'll never get over the loss of her twins.'

'Perfect couple, aren't they?'

'I always thought so. He never left her side after the attack other than to go home for a quick shower, then he was back again. Absolutely idolised her. Nobody expected her to survive, but he talked constantly to her, held her hand, kissed her. He brought her back to life far more than the treatment she was getting, because that was mainly rest following the operation to remove most of her reproductive system. He brought her soul back to her.'

'Then let's hope this gives them closure. And if it does, it was all down to that tiny bit of info that he could possibly be blonde. Maybe Jacques and Simpson will now feel able to confirm his name, if we truly have got it right.'

'Let's hope so. Now go home, Luke, and try to have a nap to clear that headache. I'll see you in the morning.'

'Thanks, Tessa. Drive carefully when you set off.'

She heard him say goodnight to Cheryl, then went out into reception. 'It took him six months to start calling me Tessa. It was DI Marsden all the time. Even Hannah was DS Granger to him. Such a polite lad. And so easy then to make him blush. He's grown up a lot since I first met him.'

'Smart kid. I've known him from birth really. His dad was a bit of a pain in the arse, but once he'd gone it seemed like Luke came into his own. I think he was scared of his dad, scared to upset him in case he took it out on Naomi. This job was perfect for him, and now look at him. A partner, no less.'

'He was brilliant with Doris. She taught him loads, set up the courses he was to take, went on surveillance with him, mentored him in general. I think he felt a bit lost when she told everyone she was leaving, but she'd left him in a good place with qualifications, and I don't doubt she still keeps in touch with him.'

Tessa reached across and picked up Cheryl's cup. 'I'll go wash this, and then we'll lock up for the night. I know we're early, but have you seen the weather? We need to get home and batten down whatever hatches we've got and ride this one out.'

Cheryl gave a thumbs up, and started her closing-down routine. She sent a text to Fred to say they were closing early, and he speedily returned the message with an okay.

The night drew to a close with everyone praying that the wind would have dropped by morning light, and the UK's weather returned to some form of normality without an accompanying howling gale.

John Coates heard a thud from the front of his house and

stepped outside to investigate. The large tubbed lilac tree had blown over, and landed by the front door, so he heaved it upright, leaving it until the morning to return it to its correct place.

He paused for a moment, taking in the driveway and any other tubs, but there was no further damage. He wished he could say that about his beautiful wife. Turning, he went back inside and gently closed the door on the storms of the night.

24

Thursday the thirteenth of February dawned with some sunshine trying to break through, although bitterly cold. The wind had died to occasional gusts, and Luke felt energised by the deep sleep he had enjoyed. His headache had gone, and he was looking forward to Tessa hearing from DI Haughton with the facial recognition results.

He dropped Maria at the vets, intent on finishing at the same time as her and then collecting her to drive to her parents' house, where they would be fed. He knew Maria was missing Buddy, her little dog, but they had mutually agreed that it was better for Buddy to remain with her mum and dad, to ensure he wasn't left on his own all day. It didn't stop her missing him though.

'Bring Oliver over for nine,' she warned Luke, as she reached to kiss him.

He shrugged. 'You sure we have to do this?'

She was firm. 'Stop being such a wimp, Luke Taylor. Of course he needs to be done. He'll be a better, more settled cat, and he'll not be wanting to leave you and go find some other mug to take care of him.'

'Okay, okay! I'll make sure he's there for nine.' Luke gave in, knowing she was the expert, whereas he was simply the cat lover.

He watched as she sprinted to the other side of the road, then raised the shutters at Connection and went to work. Oliver was waiting for him, but was only given a drink of water much to his obvious disgust. They played for ten minutes, then Luke helped him inside the cat carrier.

Cheryl had arrived, and she looked inside the carrier. 'Good luck, baby,' she said. 'We're all rooting for you.'

Fred sat in his car with the camera easily reachable on the passenger seat. The green Toyota Avensis parked outside number twenty-seven had been featured on the last few pictures taken by him, and its owner, Owain Ratcliffe, had been snapped going to the house three times so far over the previous three days, arriving each day around eleven.

Investigation had shown him that the owners of the house were Cameron and David Goodwright, and Fred waited patiently hoping that today would be the day when Cameron appeared on her own doorstep as she waved goodbye to Owain. Proof that the car was at the house wasn't enough for Fred's client, she wanted a photograph of the two of them together, preferably in a clinch.

Fred opened his sandwich box and took out a ham sandwich. He took a bite and then slammed it back down as the front door of number twenty-seven opened. Owain stepped outside, then looked backwards, into the house.

The camera was already resting on the steering wheel, and Fred had set the zoom exactly right. He waited.

Seconds later a man stepped out, and they kissed each other before hugging.

'Shit,' Fred muttered. 'This isn't going to go down well when Mrs Ratcliffe sees what Mr Ratcliffe has been doing.' He continued to snap pictures, and then for the first time heard Owain Ratcliffe speak.

'Cam!' he called as he reached his car. 'Ring me after ten, she'll be in bed by then.'

Cam? Fred almost laughed aloud. He had assumed Cameron would be in line with the sex of Cameron Diaz, and that the man Owain was busy smooching with was David.

Fred watched as the Avensis pulled away, and waited for 'Cam' to disappear back inside before starting his engine. He drove to a nearby river and pulled into the parking area, where he finished off the contents of his sandwich box, and poured himself a drink from his flask.

It was clear he had all the evidence he needed, he simply had to write up his report. He suspected there would be words of profanity when the report was read, and he was almost looking forward to delivering it. Just not yet. He would write everything up and print off the pictures later, and make an early appointment for the following day.

He took out his book and settled down for a half-hour read, but thoughts of 'Cam' being a man kept intruding into his brain. How wrong can someone be, by using assumption as a tool of choice. *Lesson learnt, Fred*, he thought.

He heard patters of rain on his windscreen, so replaced his bookmark in the new Stephen King, and readjusted his driving seat before starting the engine. He drove back to Eyam, all the way his brain working out how to write the report. Owain's wife had known nothing, other than her husband kept disappearing and giving her silly excuses for not being available on his phone.

Mae Ratcliffe would have her answers shortly, and Fred guessed all hell would break loose once she did have those answers.

.   .   .

Maria returned Oliver to the care of Luke, who immediately stopped everything. He was shocked by the plastic cone around Oliver's head, but Maria warned him not to give in to Oliver's demands for it to be removed.

'It's important he can't get to lick his wound, so no being a softie, Luke Taylor,' she warned. 'We'll take him home with us for tonight, so I can keep an eye on him, but he'll be okay here after that.'

Oliver didn't make a sound, simply batted at the cone with a front paw then drifted back to sleep.

It took Fred some time to put all the facts together in a cohesive way, and then he printed off the pictures. They all showed dates and times, and when he'd finished he gathered everything into a cardboard file ready for seeing Mae Ratcliffe the following morning. She had been agreeable to an appointment at ten when he had explained he had somewhere to be for eleven, and she had tried to ferret information from him, but he had explained he had photographs to show her, and he would prefer not to give confidential facts over the phone. It didn't seem to occur to her that the confidential facts were confidential to her.

Fred closed the file happy that everything was done and clearly explained, then left his office to talk to Cheryl.

'Hey, fount of all knowledge,' he began. 'If I said to you someone was called Cameron, tell me how you would see them in your head without actually having met them.'

Cheryl leaned back and looked at him. 'How old?'

'Oh, between thirty and forty I would say.'

'Okay. Smart, classy dresser, dark shoulder-length hair with a bit of a curl at the end, still quite slim although starting to put on a bit of weight round the middle. Am I anywhere near?'

He slid the photo across Cheryl's desk of the clinch between the two men. 'That one is Cameron,' and he placed his finger on the jean-clad figure.

'It's a man!'

'I was as surprised as you. It seems two people own the property in the background, David and Cameron Goodwright. I didn't think much of it when I took this, because I assumed I'd discounted David without any good reason, and this was David. My client's husband was having an affair with a man, not a woman. Which meant Cameron would eventually have to find out her husband was playing away with a man. Except it didn't work out like that. This is Cameron. Or Cam, as Owain Ratcliffe called him.'

Cheryl looked at the picture for a few seconds more, then lifted her head. 'She's not going to be best chuffed, is she?'

'Nope.' Fred grinned. 'And I've got the pleasure of explaining it all tomorrow morning.'

'It's confirmed,' Tessa said, only her head showing around Luke's office door.

'It's him?'

She nodded. 'No doubt at all, according to Eileen. That coffee still hot?'

'It is. You want one?'

'We should celebrate our artist extraordinaire. Coffee and biscuits could do it.'

'You'll have to be quiet,' Luke warned. 'Oliver's asleep.'

'Oh God, I forgot it's his operation day. He's okay?'

'Sleeping it off.' Luke stood to pour the coffee. 'Tell me what Eileen said.'

Tessa closed the door and sat down opposite him. 'She didn't really say much. They can finally close the Coates case, that's for sure. The facial recognition is as exact as it could be. Eileen is off to see his parents this afternoon, and then she's going to see John and Caroline tomorrow. However, although I didn't point this out to her as she's a good friend and handy to have onside, the Coates are our clients and without John coming to us, I dare say none of this would have emerged. So I'm going to set up a FaceTime chat with them, and I think we should both be on this end. That okay with you?'

'That's fine. I'm picking Maria up at five, and we're taking Oliver home with us tonight so that she can keep an eye on him, but I've nothing that can't be delayed.'

'Okay. I'll message John and ask if they can be available on screen at four. We'll only need ten minutes at the most.'

She took out her phone and quickly sent the message, then picked up the biscuits that had magically appeared on the table. 'Chocolate cookies,' she said thoughtfully. 'They're new.'

'They're also mine.'

'And you are a truly generous person, Luke Taylor, to share them with me. I love you for it.'

'You're flannelling me. My mother warned me about women like you.'

'She did?'

'No, but she would have if she'd thought about it.'

John and Caroline appeared side by side at the kitchen table. Caroline looked drawn, her face pale and with dark circles under her eyes. Tessa wanted to reach through the PC screen and hug her.

'Are you both okay?'

John nodded. 'We are. You have news for us?'

'I do. It has been confirmed by facial recognition that Ivan was the person responsible for the series of car cons – they can link him to five definitely, with a further two possibilities. However, his death has closed cases, obviously, and they now consider yours no longer a cold case, but a closed one. The murder of Ivan is a new case altogether, and no doubt at some point they will talk to you about it, as his employer. Tomorrow I believe DI Haughton is coming to see you about this confirmation, but as our clients, I wanted to pass the news on.'

Tessa could see Caroline's tears. 'Caroline,' she said gently, 'it's finally over. I'm sure you'll sleep more easily, knowing you don't have to stare at everybody to see if it's him, and hopefully he will soon be out of your nightmares.'

Caroline's head dropped, and Tessa heard a muffled, 'Thank you, Tessa. Thank you for everything.'

'I'm happy I could help, that we managed to get this case resurrected. He deserved to be punished, and he would have served a considerable sentence. He didn't deserve to die, but somebody obviously thought he did. I'm sure DI Haughton will track that person down – oh and there's a strong possibility Jacques and Simpson will now start being a bit more forthcoming. It was Ivan they were terrified of, him and his threats against their families. I'm sure DI Haughton will be talking to them as well, and they'll realise they no longer need to be silent.'

John joined in. 'You'll send me your final invoice?'

'I will. I'll do all the sums tomorrow, and email it to you. It goes without saying that it's been a pleasure to meet up with you again, even if I haven't had even a glimpse of Casey. Don't be strangers, John. Keep in touch.'

'I can't thank you enough, Tessa. And Luke, when Ice White

is launched, you'll be getting a complimentary copy in the mail. Signed.'

Luke punched the air. 'Awesome. Thank you so much, John. It will be treasured.'

25

Friday was a day of red roses. Maria had hers delivered directly to the vets, Joel brought his home ready for the return of Beth from her trip to the North East, and Naomi's were delivered to her home.

Luke had woken Maria at seven with a kiss, and a 'Happy Valentine's Day', as he carried in a tray with toast and coffee for the two of them, and a small gift on it.

She smiled. 'Oh, this is lovely. Thank you so much.'

He carefully slid back into bed, and handed her the box. 'Will you be my Valentine?'

'Might do.' She smiled at him, then reached behind her to take an equally small packet from her bedside drawer. 'Will you be mine?'

'Might do,' he replied.

'Do we eat toast first, or unwrap?'

'The toast is hot...'

'Toast,' she said.

. . .

Maria's box contained a thin gold chain with a tiny gold heart on it, and he helped fasten it around her neck. 'It's beautiful,' she said, touching it lightly with her fingers. 'Did you choose it?'

'It chose me.' He laughed. 'Remember me saying I needed to get something for Mum's birthday at some point because it was coming up? I went to look for some earrings for her, and saw this. I knew who it was perfect for. And it is.'

'It is. Now open yours.'

By the time he had undone the third bow he was laughing. 'Three bows?'

'Security.'

He removed the paper and saw a fourth bow tied around a white box.

'More security?'

She nodded. 'Of course.'

The pen that lay nestled inside was hallmarked silver, and was inscribed *Maria loves Luke.* He held it in his hand, carefully balancing it along his fingers. 'Wow.'

Maria laughed. 'I'm glad it got a wow. A partner in a business should have a good pen, and now you do. Underneath the pad it was fastened to are three refills, so save the box.'

He leaned over to kiss her, and their undrunk coffees went cold.

Fred was at the Ratcliffe home by ten, and definitely not looking forward to the conversation. The sunshine was bright and he had lowered his sun visor, but lifted it when he arrived in order to survey the property.

It was a large detached house, set on the outskirts of the village of Baslow. He needed to ensure the green Avensis wasn't anywhere around, and he had to cross his fingers and hope it wasn't in the garage. He sat for a couple of minutes, then opened his car door, picking up his briefcase as he did so. The front door opened and Mae Ratcliffe beckoned him in.

'I thought it was you,' she said with a smile. 'Owain's gone, so we can talk.'

He followed her through to a large room, a lounge that was lined with bookshelves, and held no television.

'Tea?' she asked, and he thanked her.

He wandered around the room, interested in her choice of books. There were many classics, but also a vast collection of crime and horror novels. He spotted a copy of the new Stephen King he was currently reading, complete with a bookmark halfway through it. *A plus point*, Fred thought, *she uses bookmarks*.

She came in carrying a tray, and placed it on the coffee table. 'Sugar?'

He shook his head. 'No thanks. Only milk.'

She handed him his drink, and they sat in opposite seats.

'A lovely room,' he began. 'One day this is what I will do with mine. I've got lots of random bookcases, but nothing that resembles this.'

'I read a lot. Owain built this.' She swept her arm to encompass all the walls. 'I told him what I needed, and he drew up a plan and built it. I'm going to miss his DIY skills. Because that's going to happen, isn't it?' She narrowed her eyes as she asked the question.

Fred sighed. The time had come. 'Possibly. I do have pictures. The first two days of surveillance showed your husband driving to an address, but I only captured him going in and coming out. What does he do for a living?'

'We have a car dealership. He works flexible hours, so I really wouldn't have suspected anything by any changes in him going to work, but *he's* changed. And he gets text messages which are quickly deleted. Phone calls where he suddenly has to go, because a customer wants to talk to him – why? There are plenty more sales people at work. He's the owner, the boss. I knew there had to be somebody else, and you've confirmed it.'

Fred took out the pictures. 'This is the house he's been visiting. Do you recognise it? It's in Chesterfield.'

Mae stared at it for some time. 'I don't think so. Who lives there?'

'David and Cameron Goodwright.'

'Never heard of them. Is she pretty, this Cameron woman? Younger than me?'

Fred took a deep breath. 'She's a man. Your husband calls him Cam.' He handed over the photograph of the two men kissing as Owain left the property. 'This was taken yesterday as you can see from the date and time stamp.'

'But...' She stared at the picture, a look of horror on her face. 'A man? My husband of twenty years is homosexual?'

'He's certainly in some sort of relationship, of that there's no doubt. He called out to Cameron Goodwright as he reached the Avensis yesterday, and asked him to text after ten because you would be in bed.'

Mae was clearly struggling to find words. Eventually she spoke. 'A man.'

Fred sipped at his tea and waited. He didn't want her to ask him which would be the best weapon with which to kill Owain, but he suspected that conversation was probably in her head.

'I can't have him back in this house,' were the words she finally managed to say. 'I need to ring our son. He'll know what to do.'

'He lives nearby?'

'Close enough. He's in student accommodation in Sheffield. He'll help me through this nightmare.' She stood abruptly. 'Thank you for your help.'

'No problem. Everything is in here.' He handed the file to her.

'And your bill?'

'All in there. And if you need anything further, don't hesitate to contact me. I've put in my card.'

Fred walked towards the door and paused. 'I'm sorry it ended like this, really I am.'

'It's only ended for him, it's a new beginning for me.'

Whitelilac Cottage in Bradwell was bathed in winter sunlight when Fred arrived. It didn't seem as if Sir Henry was there yet, so Fred parked up and walked towards the front door. Ken was busy putting compost into a window box.

''Ey up, Fred,' he said. 'Keepin' busy cos I'm nervous. I made this yesterday from what was left of t'bookshelf wood. Looks all reight, I think.'

'Looks brilliant. You got plants for it?'

'Some winter pansies I picked up in t'supermarket. They'll brighten t'place up till t'weather warms.'

They both turned at the sound of an engine, to see a Bentley pull in behind Fred's car. Ken put his trowel into the window box, wiped his hands on a cloth, and walked to the garden gate. The tension in Ken had suddenly increased, and Fred touched his arm.

'Everything will be fine,' he said quietly.

Ken gave a short nod, and they waited for the Bentley to pull away, and Sir Henry to reach them.

'He'll come back and get me when I ring him,' Henry explained, then held out his hand. 'Hello, Ken. I'm your father.'

Fred was stunned by the transformation in what Ken now referred to as his library. He had coloured the wood with a dark stain, filled up several of the shelves with his books and used his mother's pretty ornaments to stand where there were no books. The fire was lit, and Ken asked them both to sit down before disappearing into the kitchen to make them a drink.

'These are the bookcases you said he was building?' Sir Henry asked.

'They certainly are. Can you remember how this room was?'

'I can. Pretty, cottagey, the chesterfield sofas are the same but the... the ambience is so different. I was afraid to come to this house, Fred, I really was, but it is now different, and my memories can remain where they should be, in my memory. His mother would have loved what he has done to it. She was an avid reader, and when he ventures into the loft I'm sure he'll find even more books.'

Ken returned with a tray. 'Heard you mention the loft. There's boxes of books that will all come down 'ere, but I'll set a week aside to tackle that. Thinking of puttin' a train set up there.'

Henry's eyes lit up. 'I've got one. I had an empty room, so I bought a starter set. It's grown now, but my wife constantly grumbles about it. She wanted the room for something or other, so while she was at her sister's home for a couple of days I commandeered it.'

'Did Mum ever see it?'

'No, we could never take the risk. When you reached the age of two, we made certain decisions. One was to place you with your grandparents so that you would never be able to inadvertently let it slip who I was, and the other was to always keep our relationship to Bradwell and never to let it impinge on my home. I've loved her all these years, Ken, unconditionally. When she told me about the cancer we knew our time of keeping things from you was drawing to an end. In a way, it's a relief. My life is now in your hands, Ken. You know the facts.'

Ken laughed. 'I'm no tittle-tattle. It goes nowhere else but these four walls. I'm pleased to have met you, pleased to see how alike we are, and tha'll always be welcome here. I won't run to t'papers or owt, but tha might have to learn Yorkshire.'

Henry picked up his drink. 'Happy to do that. This is a reight good cup o' tea.'

Fred drove back to Connection with a huge smile on his face. Valentine's Day wasn't only for lovers, he decided, it was for fathers and sons as well. He'd left the two men arranging to have a meal that evening at the hotel where Henry was staying, but had declined their invitation to join them. He had plans of his own for the evening.

He was to collect Naomi at seven to take her for a meal. He hadn't told her the meal was at his home, and that Geraldine already knew Naomi would be staying over. The old lady had packed a bag for her daughter, and it was now sitting in Fred's car boot.

He entered reception and blew a kiss towards Cheryl. 'Happy Valentine's Day, lovely lady.'

'And to you, Fred,' she replied. 'There's a message on your desk.'

He walked into his office and saw a single red rose. The note with it was simple. *Thank you for coming into my life. N xxx*

Fred took a glass from the kitchen cupboard, filled it with water, and returned to his office. The rose was stood in it, and put safely out of harm's way on his shelf.

He decided to make a start on the final bill and the full report for Ken while it was still fresh in his mind, but halfway through it he realised he'd had enough. He had things to do at home, some shopping to pick up, a fire to light – what on earth was he doing hanging around the office?

He closed his door behind him, and Cheryl looked up, startled. 'Off out again, Fred?'

'No, I'm done for the day. Naomi's coming to mine for a meal, although she doesn't know so don't say anything. I want to make sure my place is warm and welcoming, so I'm heading home early.'

'Say no more,' Cheryl said, 'say no more.'

26

After a very leisurely breakfast and a check-in with Geraldine that the house hadn't burnt down and the girls hadn't left home, Fred and Naomi opted to go for a walk. It was a beautiful crisp morning, so they drove into the car park at Chatsworth and simply walked, no pre-determined direction, no pre-determined ideas.

They strolled along the banks of the Derwent holding hands, and Fred knew he hadn't felt so happy in such a long time. The previous evening Naomi had confessed that she had never had a Valentine card until Fred's – she had met her ex when they were fourteen and he had never bought her one. When he walked away there hadn't even been love, never mind a card. Fred had felt saddened. At least he had known an all-encompassing love for Jane, although he now admitted that what he felt for Naomi was definitely comparable.

His happiness when in her company kept a smile on his face that had been missing for far too long. He squeezed her hand a little tighter and she responded in kind.

'Shall we head up there and get us a coffee?' He pointed towards the tea rooms.

'That would be lovely. It feels really strange being an adult doing things with another adult. Normally when I go for a coffee I go with the girls and Mum, this feels almost illegal.' Her laughter rang out. 'Come on, I'll treat us to this illegal coffee.'

'Not on your life. Today I treat you. You're my special lady, and that's not only for today.'

They headed up the incline and into the tea rooms where the scones were too delicious to resist.

Half an hour later they were returning to the car, Fred clutching a huge house plant. Unfortunately the tea rooms had been part of the garden centre, and Naomi had fallen for the plant that she said would look spectacular in the corner of the lounge.

The back of the car resembled a jungle by the time it was strapped into a seat belt, and Fred drove home using his side mirrors only – the view from the interior mirror was of greenery.

'We should talk,' Maria said solemnly.

Luke put down his game controller and looked at her. 'We should. We should?'

'Yes. I seem to have accidentally moved in with you.'

Luke tried not to laugh, she looked so serious. 'You have. If I'm remembering correctly, you said I'm staying tonight.'

'Don't laugh at me, Luke Taylor, I've been thinking this through. I might start spending more time at Mum and Dad's house.'

'What? Why?' He felt a slight edge of panic and knew it showed in his voice.

'Well... I really did intend only staying for that one night and then I thought we would talk about where we went from there, but where we went from there was back into bed.'

'And that's wrong? It's not as good for you as it is for me?'

'Of course. I simply felt I gave you no choice in anything.'

And the laughter finally escaped. 'Come here,' he said, standing up. He pulled her into his arms. 'For the first, and probably the last, time in this relationship I'm going to take the lead. I don't want you to go anywhere, I love living with you, I fell for you the first time I saw you in the vets. Please don't leave me, Maria. Let's put this on a proper footing – this is your home now as much as it is mine.'

Maria laid her head against his chest. She had been building up to the conversation since the early hours of the morning and now she felt relief wash over her.

'Can we go buy a lamp table then, I hate that cardboard box in the corner.'

'Your wish is my command. I'll close down Code Blue and I'm ready. Oliver's okay?' The cat was still living with them, but almost back to his normal self, albeit with a big plastic cone around his neck.

'He's fine, eating and drinking normally. You can take him back to the office on Monday.'

'That's good news. We're all missing him. So are we okay? We're a proper grown-up living-together sort of couple?'

She smiled, her eyes lighting up. 'Seems like it. It was playing on my mind...'

'You should have said. I'm not telepathic even though I'm amazingly brilliant.'

'I'll bear that in mind.'

Tessa felt idle. The closure of the Ivan Newburg case had, in the end, taken her by surprise. She did briefly wonder if they would ever have discovered the identity of Caroline's attacker without

Luke's drawing skills, because the Ivan of lank dark greasy hair didn't in any way resemble the smart-looking man with blonde hair who she had met in the Code Blue office.

She felt that Ivan must have continued with his criminal lifestyle – who had he upset enough to bring them after him with a syringe full of heroin? She read through her notes once more, sighed, and popped them back in her briefcase. They would go back to the office on Monday, report fully written, and be filed properly. It was over.

So why did she feel so uncomfortable about it?

Sir Henry walked carefully between the headstones, following his son's footsteps. Ken held the small map showing the location of the grave, and he stopped suddenly.

'It doesn't have a headstone.'

'Not yet. She did everything else – chose this plot, paid for the funeral, asked for burial rather than cremation so you would have somewhere to visit if that was what you wanted to do, and she made sure I had this little map so I could visit anytime. She was a remarkable woman, was Joanne.'

'I'll organise having one put on now I know where she is. Those flowers look fresh.'

'I have a fresh delivery made every week. The florists shop in the village is very good about it, I explained Joanne was my sister.'

Ken gave a brief nod of acknowledgement, and laid his own flowers by the side of Sir Henry's.

'I'll look after it always, so nay worries about that. You'll visit again?'

'Of course, and as often as I can without giving my wife cause for suspicion. Now I'm retired I can't suddenly disappear as I used to do, but I intend keeping close contact with you if you're agreeable to that.'

'Then there'll be no more staying at t'hotel. I have a spare bedroom that is my next project, tha'll stay with me. We can muddle along together without magnificent steak meals, can't we?' As Ken spoke his mind switched to the mouth-watering food he had enjoyed the previous night.

'Thank you, Ken.' Henry couldn't say any more. Loving Joanne had cost both of them sharing in the upbringing of her precious child, and it suddenly hit him how much he had missed.

'And I'll listen ter t'folks in village and try to talk better.'

Henry grabbed hold of his son's arm and spun him round. 'No!' He was adamant. 'Keep your heritage, Ken. I can't change the way I speak, and you mustn't change the way you speak. My God, I can almost understand it now!'

They laughed together, and Ken bent down to touch the earth covering his mother.

'Bye, Mum. We'll see you soon.'

They walked out of Bradwell churchyard and back down to Whitelilac Cottage, enjoying the crispness of the air. Sir Henry's driver was waiting inside the car, and he got out to open the door.

Ken shook hands with his father. 'Don't be a stranger. I'm off to build you a wardrobe, so 'appen you'll want to see it sometime.'

'Too reight I will.' Henry smiled and climbed into the back seat.

Ken leaned inside. 'Ring or text when you're home. Take care.' He closed the door and watched as the big car slid slowly away and down the road.

'Bye, Dad,' he said, and entered the cottage feeling a little sad. He picked up his phone and texted Fred.

Thank you.

Eileen Haughton wasn't having a good weekend. This was always a problem with her when she had information come in on a Friday, but it wasn't so urgent that she needed to bring her team in on a Saturday to follow up that information. Okay, so Ivan Newburg was the thief who had caused such devastation in the Coates family, but he was dead. The information that had come in confirming that didn't give any leads as to his killer and she knew work would start on that Monday morning, but now she was twiddling her thumbs for two days.

Tessa. Maybe talking it over with her would help. She picked up her phone.

'Morning, Marsden.'

'Morning, Haughton.'

'You busy?'

'You about to make me busy?'

'Thought you might fancy a coffee at that little café in Baslow.'

'The one with the delicious scones, jam and cream? Too right I might.'

'Eleven?'

'Brilliant. Is this classed as work?'

'Erm... no, don't think so.'

'Oh good. I don't have to tell Cheryl.'

'Cheryl?'

'Our receptionist. She insists on knowing where we are at all times in case she has to recover our dead bodies.'

'If I promise not to kill you, will that suffice?'

'Certainly will, see you at eleven.'

. . .

Eileen was waiting for Tessa inside the café, and the waitress brought them a menu as soon as Tessa sat down.

They decided to go with scones and coffee, and once they'd given their order, Tessa sat back.

'So?'

Eileen hesitated. 'So... I don't know.'

'It is work, then. I knew I should have told Cheryl.'

'She scary?'

'She is on this subject. We're all very well trained now. I'll have to say I met you accidentally if it slips out I saw you this morning.'

Eileen laughed. 'I need to meet this dragon. I could do with her controlling my lot.'

'You can't have her. She's awesome. So what are we here to discuss?'

'I have absolutely no idea. I simply feel uneasy. Yes, it's confirmed that we've closed quite a few cases in one fell swoop, but it's left us with who killed Newburg. I've got different people heading out to interview his family and friends, and I've allocated DC Aalia Khatri to go with me to talk to John and Caroline. I think that's where I'm struggling. It feels as though they aren't telling me everything. You think either of them remembered something they're reluctant to mention?'

Tessa frowned. 'I don't think so. They've always been open with me. The whole situation of the death of their babies has made her very protective of Casey, but that's not a crime. I've not met the baby yet – in fact she's a toddler now. Mentally Caroline hasn't been in a good place for the last five years, and I know John hoped adopting a baby would bring some form of closure for her, but that didn't happen. It's why he came to Connection for help. He knew she wouldn't rest until he was locked up, the chap who came for the car in the first place.'

The scones and drinks arrived, and both women busied

themselves with the art of 'jam first or cream first', before sitting back and enjoying each other's company and the scones.

As they walked back to their cars, Tessa touched Eileen's arm. 'Ring me after you've spoken to them?'

'I will. And when you're writing up your report for your files, if there's any tiny little thing you think I might need to know, tell me, will you?'

'Of course. Eileen – ask about the baby, will you?'

27

Monday initially was a bit of an anti-climax. Beth and Simon were confident they wouldn't have to make any further journeys to the North East, Luke and Tessa believed their case to be over with Tessa about to devote her morning to completing the report on it before submission of their final bill to John Coates, Fred was looking forward to ringing Ken for an update on his weekend with Sir Henry, and Cheryl was happy that everybody was filling in the diary online at last.

Oliver was returned to his rightful home at the office and spent the morning trying to persuade everybody in turn to take off his cone, but while they all stroked and petted and played with him, nobody fell for his requests.

His last hope was Cheryl. He jumped onto her knee, and she laughed. 'It's difficult to answer the phone with a cone in front of me. You're going to have to get down, Ollie.' She attempted to lift him without touching the operation site and he dug in his claws.

'You little ...' she said, rubbing her leg. 'Luke, take this tiger up to your office and teach him some manners. That hurt.'

'Aw, Ollie, come on, we know when we're not wanted, don't

we?' The cat miaowed as Luke gently picked him up, and they disappeared into the lift.

And so peace descended as everyone checked their own personal diaries for what they needed to prepare for the coming week.

Tessa moved on to writing up the report in full for John Coates, and to annotate the number of hours allocated to the job. It was fairly convoluted as three of them had worked on it, and she had to ensure all hours for Luke and Fred were included. She got to the end and breathed a sigh of relief. The invoice was substantial and she stared at it for a moment before leaving her upstairs office and heading downstairs to Beth's.

'Is Beth free?' she asked Cheryl, who checked her lights before saying yes.

Tessa knocked and opened Beth's door. 'You got a minute?'

'I have. I'm trying to unwind, it's been a hell of a job, this North East one. Simon's been a godsend, believe me. We were more than ready to come home. You got a problem?'

'Not really, I want you to check I've not missed anything from this final bill for the Coates.'

'No problem. You want to pour us a coffee while I look through it?'

Beth checked, taking several minutes to do so, then picked up her cup. 'I can't see anything that could be queried. Quite a lot of hours went into it, but it was never going to be easy, was it? There's no doubt that dead body was the same chap then?'

'No doubt at all. Luke did an amazing job with the drawings. He drew the face, without giving it any hair, then began to draw different blonde hairstyles, some light some dark, because all we had to go on was a warning passed on to one of Nathan Jacques' sisters not to get involved with a blonde-haired man trying to get them to try drugs. Up to that point we'd only seen a dark-haired man. When Luke had finished doing the hairstyles, he started again and tried different glasses frames in case he wore glasses. It was a long night for him.' She laughed. 'By this time the pictures were all merging into one, and he wouldn't have recognised the man even if he'd been Prince Charles, so he brought them to me and I saw it straight away. The pictures were that good. Then we found out Ivan Newburg was dead. Strange case, full of twists and turns, and...'

She stopped, unsure whether to go on.

'And...?'

Tessa shrugged. 'I don't know. Gut instinct says something's out of kilter. But it's not our problem. We've done what we were asked to do and brought that to a successful conclusion. If there is more to this, I'm sure DI Haughton will sort it. She's interviewing the Coates this morning, and she said she'll ring me later.'

DI Eileen Haughton and DC Aalia Khatri were welcomed into the Coates home, and Caroline disappeared to the kitchen to make drinks.

John showed them into the lounge, and the two policewomen took the armchairs. Aalia took out her notebook, her slender frame poised and still as she sat quietly. They had agreed Eileen would do the talking, Aalia the observing and note-taking.

Eileen looked up and smiled as Caroline walked through carrying a tray of coffees. 'Thank you, Caroline.'

They waited until they all had a drink in front of them, and then Eileen began.

'I understand, Caroline, that you saw Ivan the Friday afternoon before his body was discovered on the Sunday?'

'I did. A letter for me had been delivered to Code Blue, so he came through with it. I was in the kitchen, and I heard him call out my name, so I told him where I was. We chatted for a couple of minutes, and he went back through to the office. And that's it.'

'And John. Presumably you were still in the office?'

'No, I left Friday lunchtime for a weekend in London. We had a convention of game developers. The post hadn't been when I left, or else I would have brought this random letter through to my wife, but presumably Ivan thought it might be important so brought it through here. Despite now finding out who Ivan is, or was, we absolutely trusted him, you know.'

'So, London. When did you arrive home?'

'About ten, last Monday morning. I left straight after breakfast, because I'd all sorts of ideas and plans I wanted to talk over with the team as soon as possible, before I forgot anything. It had been a busy weekend, I met lots of people, and in particular a smallish company who we could potentially merge with, opening up a much bigger share of the market for Code Blue.'

'So to clarify, you left Friday lunchtime, arrived home Monday morning. Can we have a couple of names of people at the convention for proof of alibi, please, John?'

He looked shocked. 'I'm under suspicion?'

'No, of course not, but I wouldn't be doing my job properly if I didn't check. You're an intelligent man, you know I have to do that. We believe Ivan was killed between twelve and two, even though he wasn't found until after dark. If your alibi holds up, you clearly didn't do it, and you'll be the first person of interest crossed off our list.'

He gave a slight nod and spoke directly to the note-taking DC. 'I have several cards in my wallet of people who were there. I'll photocopy them for you before you leave because they have their contact numbers and companies on them. It will be easier than writing them down.'

'Thank you, sir. Much appreciated.'

Eileen sipped at her drink, and looked around the room. 'This is a lovely lounge. Is Casey not around?'

'She's asleep,' was Caroline's sharp response. 'It's morning nap time. I like to keep to her routine.'

Eileen smiled. 'You're very lucky if you can do that. I have two children, both in their teens now, and I too liked a routine when they were tiny. Naps at a certain time, bed by seven at the latest following a bath, up at a reasonable hour – unfortunately they didn't agree with me and my routines. Casey must be a special little girl if she sleeps when you put her in her cot, without arguments and tantrums.'

'She is a special little girl.' For the first time Caroline started to bend. A smile crossed her face. 'She's very bright, and loving. She made such a difference to our lives when the adoption agency rang to say they had a newborn little girl for us.'

'How does it work? You jumped in the car, nipped down to the agency and were handed a baby?'

Caroline laughed. 'Pretty much that. I did it on my own because John was in America when the call came. We'd signed all the papers because we knew the baby we were going to get, and we thought she was due a couple of weeks after she was actually born. She arrived early and John was still in the States, selling Code Blue. I collected her, and she's the best thing that ever happened to us. He came home to be plunged straight into being a daddy.'

'I don't see enough of her,' John admitted. 'Caroline sees to everything. I've never changed a nappy, although I don't doubt I could if push comes to shove, but we love walking in the park, playing on the swings and slide, and I reckon I get the best part of this parenting thing, I get to play. Caroline sees to food, hygiene and bedtime. No hassle for me.' His eyes sparkled when he spoke of his daughter.

'You sound like my ex. He liked playtime, but none of the other stuff. So I won't get to meet Casey then? Perk of the job, meeting the kids. So, Caroline, where were you Sunday afternoon?'

The question was abrupt and Caroline visibly flinched. 'What do you mean?'

'I need to know where you were Sunday afternoon, say from eleven onwards, until about two. I don't doubt John's alibi will hold up to scrutiny, but that leaves you at this present moment without one.'

'I was here. With Casey.'

'Nobody else?'

'No. We went to the park in the morning and she fell asleep in her pram as we walked home so I put her straight into her cot, made myself some lunch and watched TV until Casey woke. That would have been around one. I made us some lunch, and then we read a bit, did a couple of Peppa Pig jigsaws and John rang at three for a chat. We were on the phone for about half an hour.'

'She had to stop the conversation because our beautiful daughter was starting to eat the Peppa Pig jigsaw pieces, so we said bye, and that was it until I arrived home Monday morning,' John concluded.

'Can I see your phone, please, Caroline, to confirm that?'

'My phone? I don't know where it is...'

John stood. 'It's on the kitchen window sill. I'll get it.'

'No,' Eileen said. 'DC Khatri will get it.'

Aalia stood and disappeared in the general direction of a

kitchen. She returned quickly with the phone and handed it to Eileen, who asked Caroline to open it up.

Eileen viewed all calls and saw the one from John at a couple of minutes before three, then glanced at calls either side of that for a few numbers. There was one at three minutes past eleven to Ivan Newburg.

'You rang Ivan?'

Caroline hesitated. 'I did. I was having a bit of an issue with our security system. It was beeping and I couldn't make it stop. He said he was out with a couple of friends but he would call round later and look at it. He didn't call, so in the end I changed the code, more in hope than anything because it was really starting to annoy me, and it worked. I didn't call him to cancel because I couldn't believe I'd cured it, I expected it to start again, but he never did arrive. Now I know why. Can I say, DI Haughton, I really don't like you questioning me like this. I don't have to answer any questions actually. If you'll excuse me...' She stood, moving towards the door.

Eileen put down her drink. 'I'm sorry, Mrs Coates, but I'm going to have to ask you to accompany me to the station. There are inconsistencies, and we need to double check everything and make sure your statement is accurate. And believe me when I tell you this. If I ask you questions in a murder enquiry, you damn well do have to answer. Get your coat, please.'

'What? But... Casey...'

'I'm sure your husband can manage. You should be home by this evening.'

Terror crossed Caroline's face. 'I can't leave Casey!'

John put his arm around her. 'If you need a solicitor for anything, ring Thomas, he'll sort you out, but you're only going to give a statement. You'll be back here in no time, and I'm more than capable of looking after Casey.'

. . .

Caroline cried all the way to West Bar. John could have cried when he lifted Casey from her cot and caught the not so fragrant and unmistakable baby smell.

28

Flora laughed as she heard John's voice ask her if she'd ever changed a baby's nappy.

'Certainly have. One of my sisters has three kids, the other one has two, so I'm well-skilled in child care. You got problems?'

'The smell tells me I have. Can you come through?'

'Two minutes and I'll be there.'

Flora closed down her computer, spoke to Dom as she passed by his desk, and laughed as he said, 'Well, that's a shitty job you've won for yourself.'

She walked quickly down the connecting corridor, wondering where Caroline was – she had never left her husband in charge of Casey before. Flora heard John call out for her to go in, and she saw him in the lounge, with Casey standing in front of him, holding on to his knees. Still a little unsteady on her feet, she was taking advantage of a sitting-down daddy with knees to cling to.

'She whiffs,' John said. 'The changing stuff is up in her bedroom, and that's as much as I know.'

Flora bent to Casey's level and scooped up the little girl. 'Phew,' she said as Casey clung to her, 'stinky Casey. Come on, baby girl, let's go get you changed so you smell nice and sweet again for Daddy.'

'It's first door on the right at the top of the stairs,' John said, relieved his first nappy change wasn't going to be a smelly one, surely no child could do two in a day that were as fragrant as that.

He watched Flora disappear upstairs and sat back on the sofa. His thoughts swiftly flew to Caroline, who he knew would be terrified at being in an interview room at the police station. He was angry with Eileen Haughton, thought that taking Caroline with her was out of order, and utterly unnecessary. He took out his phone to ring Carlo's Italian restaurant. He could book a table for around six, and all three of them could go for a meal, bring normality back. If Casey fell asleep, that would be fine, they'd cope.

He heard Flora's voice calling his name and he crossed to the bottom of the stairs. 'Everything okay?'

'I... I don't know. Can you come up?'

He took the stairs two at a time, filled with dread but had no idea why. Casey was laid quietly on the changing mat, playing with a teddy Flora had handed her to distract her while she cleaned her up.

'You okay?'

'I don't know...Oh my God, John, she's a boy.'

John knew he was in panic mode. Flora had agreed to say nothing, and to stay with him for the rest of the working day while he tried to sort out the mess that was suddenly his life.

Casey was smelling much fresher, and sitting playing with

an assortment of toys in the lounge, while John and Flora watched on, both wondering what the next step was.

'What does it say on her birth certificate?' Flora finally asked, not knowing how to handle the situation at all.

'We don't get a birth certificate, it's an adoption certificate, and I've never actually seen it. I was in America when the baby became available, and Caroline had to collect her on her own. It was a chaotic nightmare when I returned home, and we got stuck into the parenting thing. She said she'd put all the paperwork in the safe, and that was it. We were never checked on, we got on with life figuring they would probably turn up out of the blue one day and check everything was okay with Casey. That never happened, and now...'

'You want a suggestion?'

He looked up at Flora. 'A suggestion?'

'Get the adoption certificate out of the safe, and do it now before Caroline comes home.'

'God, Flora, she's my wife. I've never gone behind her back before.'

'I don't see you have a choice. If everything is okay, you can return it to the safe and she'll be none the wiser. But how can it be okay? She's told everybody it's a girl, and suddenly it's a boy. Maybe she never got over losing her girls, and wanted a little girl to replace them. It could be something that simple. She can be helped through that with counselling.'

'You're right of course. I'll go and get it now.'

Flora was on the rug with Casey when John returned. His face was ashen. 'There's nothing in there except some money, our passports and the house insurance documents. Nothing at all.'

'You want some advice?'

'I'm not sure what I want.'

'Connection. Get Tessa Marsden here. She'll know where to turn. Your only other alternative is to ring this DI woman who took your Caroline away. But if you do, Caroline won't be back with you tonight.'

He picked up his phone, scrolled to T and rang Tessa.

The gates were open and Tessa and Luke drove up to the front door. 'Let's allow him time to talk. I couldn't make much sense of what he was saying, but he was... distraught.'

Tessa was surprised to see Flora happily playing with Casey on the floor, as she followed John into the lounge. Luke was a couple of feet behind her, carrying his briefcase.

'So this is Casey!' she said. 'Good to finally meet you, little lady, I was beginning to think you didn't exist.'

John and Flora exchanged a quick glance.

'What's going on?' Tessa asked. 'If there's a problem we can sort it.'

After listening to John and Flora tell the story, Tessa sat back, a frown creasing her forehead. 'The adoption was done officially through the council, you say?'

'Yes, and we knew we were having a little girl, and the due date of the birth. The birth mother was a known drug addict and the baby would have been taken from her at birth, so she asked that it be adopted. It was her second child dealt with in this way, so they said.'

'When did you get Casey?'

'According to Caro, her birthdate is the first of November, twenty eighteen, but we got her on the seventh. I returned home on the twentieth of November. Caro was really well organised, the perfect mother, as she has been ever since. I don't know why she's said all along the baby was a girl...'

'John, I think you're in real trouble here,' Tessa said quietly. 'Do you still have information on the contact at the Children's Department who was orchestrating the adoption?'

'It will be on my computer.'

'Can you email her, and tell her you and your wife would like to adopt a second child now that your first child is growing up?'

'Give me two minutes.'

He disappeared, and Luke had joined Flora on the floor as they did the Peppa Pig jigsaws. 'Some of these pieces are a bit chewed,' Luke grumbled. 'Casey did you do this?'

The child gave a huge smile which Luke took to mean yes.

John returned, the worried look still etched into his face. 'I've sent off the email, but God knows what will come of it.'

Tessa took hold of his hand. 'Listen to me or don't listen to me, it doesn't matter, but I think you may have to prepare yourself for losing Casey. I think his real name is Billy Vanton. I don't know the exact date he was stolen, but I do know it was pre-Christmas because I remember his mother pleading with the unknown woman who had taken him to give him back to her so she could have Christmas with her child. The father wasn't capable of speaking, he was so distraught. This wasn't one of Derbyshire's cases, he was stolen from the maternity unit here in Sheffield so it was a South Yorkshire case, but everyone was put on the alert to find the child.'

'No...'

'What do you want me to do?'

There was silence that seemed to stretch into eternity. Finally he spoke. 'Can you speak to DI Haughton? Instead of waiting for a reply to my email, I'm going to ring the woman who was our contact at Children's Services. I have to know why we haven't got the little girl we thought we were getting.'

The conversation Tessa had with Eileen was difficult; Caroline had been taken in for questioning because she had no alibi at all for the time Ivan Newburg was killed. It seemed there may be a crime of a different sort in the offing, and Eileen agreed she needed to re-visit John Coates immediately.

Tessa disconnected, and leaving the baby with Luke and Flora, she went in search of John. He was in the kitchen, and she backed out when she realised he was in the middle of a telephone conversation. He waved her in, and she sat at the table, waiting until he'd finished.

'So we were never down for a baby?'

He listened to the response which was confirmation of his question. 'Thank you for your help. Bye.'

John sat and stared at his phone for a while before speaking. 'Shit. It seems Caro lied to me. We didn't get an acceptance, so God knows what I signed, they weren't happy with Caroline's state of mind, recommended she have counselling and re-apply in twelve months.'

'You said you were in America when Caroline collected Casey?'

He nodded. 'I was. She timed everything to perfection, didn't she? The baby was two weeks old by the time I saw her, and it never occurred to me to query anything, because as far as I knew, we were having a baby. She explained it away by saying it was an earlier-than-planned arrival. And she was so sweet saying she would take all the pressure of having a baby away from me, I could concentrate on the business, I would never be expected to so much as change a nappy, my interaction with

Casey would be playtime. What on earth would she have done as the baby got older? Chopped off his penis? For fuck's sake, Tessa, this is such a bloody mess.'

'I know, and if the little boy is Billy Vanton, he will be returned to his real parents. But they've also taken Caroline in because she has no alibi for the time the police believe Ivan Newburg died. Is there any way she could have guessed Ivan was the mystery man?'

John shook his head. 'I would have said no, but she's suddenly become a complete mystery to me. I'm telling you, Tessa, I don't know what I'll say to her when I do get to see her.'

'I don't think you'll be seeing her for quite some time. Kidnap carries a heavy sentence. They'll investigate it fully, but while they're doing that she will be remanded in custody. She's a danger to the public – once she knows she's lost her Casey, if she was loose on the streets she could very easily help herself to another baby.'

'How the hell did she get Casey? Sorry, Billy.'

'She simply walked into the hospital, to the units where the mums have had a difficult birth and are in a room of their own, and she waited until the new mum went for a wee. She walked in, picked up the baby, dropped him into a holdall, and walked out. She took advantage of the fact that the mother, when she went to the toilet, began to haemorrhage badly, and pulled the cord for assistance. They dealt with her, got her back on the bed, and then realised the baby had gone. It was all captured on CCTV, but I can tell you here and now, the woman looked nothing like Caroline. Scruffy looking with short black hair, ripped jeans, chunky black jacket and a tatty holdall, not a named brand. Nothing like Caroline,' she repeated. 'But she's got away with it for fifteen months.'

29

Eileen spent a considerable amount of time talking to John. She had arrived with a member of the forensics team who had taken a swab from inside Casey's mouth and was then despatched immediately to expedite a DNA test.

John told Eileen as much as he knew of the acquisition of their baby, explaining his absence for the beginning of her life in the Coates family, and that he never for one minute queried the baby's arrival because they were expecting to be collecting a little girl. Yes, she had arrived earlier than expected, but pregnancies didn't always go the full forty weeks. He had seen no reason to query it, and they had been thrown headfirst into parenthood.

'I am ninety per cent sure it's Billy Vanton,' Eileen said quietly. 'Mrs Vanton gave us one piece of information about the missing baby, a small birthmark on the back of his neck shaped like a crescent moon. That birthmark is there. We obviously have to double check with a DNA test, but I believe Billy will be back with his real parents very soon. Immediately the results of that test confirm what we believe to be the truth, Caroline will be charged.'

John leaned forward, resting his elbows on his knees. 'I feel as if I don't know her at all. We've been together for the best part of ten years now, and the woman I've loved for all of that time has disappeared. It's as if somebody else has taken her place.'

'She's certainly become very skilled at keeping secrets,' Eileen agreed. 'I shall be temporarily shelving the questioning concerning Ivan Newburg – I only wanted a full statement from her anyway, because she seemed to think it wasn't a serious matter – until we sort out this mess. I have to go from here to warn the Vantons that there have been developments, and I expect to have to handle tears. They never believed their son was dead and always hoped he was being loved and cared for, but I don't think they ever gave up hope of getting him back. Mrs Vanton called in to see me about three months ago. She told me she was pregnant, she didn't want to know what sex the baby was because he or she wasn't being seen as a replacement for Billy, but a younger sibling for him when he came back to them, and she was definitely having a home birth. That woman's faith in her son coming home was quite inspirational, I'm telling you, and it seems she was right.

'I had to admit to her we were no nearer finding Billy, and I remember the smile that lit up her face. "You will," she said to me. When she'd gone I felt like shit. That somebody could have so much trust in me was galling enough, but for me to have nowhere else to turn to find this child, that was devastating. So telling her what I now have to tell her will be a two-edged sword, I'm afraid. I can see both sides. I can see the Vantons, always having only memories of their one-day-old son, and I can see Caroline, her twin daughters kicked out of her body and never drawing breath. Caroline needs help and will get it, but that's some way down the line still.'

'Caroline's had help,' John said. It came out almost as a growl. 'It was the first thing I did when she came home from hospital. She was in a hell of a state mentally as you can imagine. She'd been told she would never have another child naturally, and no matter how many times I told her that didn't matter she refused to believe me. It was after a year of counselling that she started to come round to the idea of adoption.

'This was at the same time as I began work on Code Blue, and started to set up the business, so she dealt with the adoption people. I had to attend a couple of meetings with her, but basically she did everything else. According to our liaison officer in Children's Services, that was the point where we were told we couldn't be considered at that time as it was felt Caroline wasn't sufficiently recovered mentally from the assault, but to apply again in a year.

'This was all news to me, because Caro told me we had been accepted, and we needed to sign on the dotted line. She produced a form requiring both our signatures, which I'm now assuming she put together – that was part of her job when she worked for me, and she was excellent at doing it. I signed it, and I kept getting updates. Eventually we had the news about the little girl we would be getting, due towards the end of November. I felt I was safe doing the big American trip, but she phoned me to say the baby had been born early, was a good weight and she was picking her up the following day. And that was it. Casey was here when I got back and we have loved her so much. Was I naïve? I don't think so. I had no reason to doubt Caroline's words.' He slumped forward again. 'I feel so bereft now.'

A soft-bodied Peppa Pig hit him on the forehead, and the little boy said, 'Daddy.'

Flora headed back along the corridor into the office, but John asked Tessa and Luke if they would mind staying. Eileen spoke to Children's Services after going into the kitchen, and came back to them to ask that a small bag be packed for Billy, as he was going to be collected in the next hour. No matter the outcome of the DNA test as to parentage, the little boy would be kept *in loco parentis* by Social Services until the whole situation could be resolved.

'Shall I do it?' Tessa asked quietly, and John thanked her. She headed up to the nursery, and picked out a couple of pairs of dungarees, with three plain white T-shirts. She found three random Babygros that were fine for either sex, and added a pack of nappies. She realised that she too felt like Eileen – torn between feeling sorry for the Vantons and feeling sorry for the Coates. It briefly occurred to her that she was being completely irrational.

Tessa carried the holdall downstairs and left it in the hallway. 'I've packed some unisex things, that will get Billy through the next couple of days. We should probably get together some favourite toys as well.'

John stared at Tessa and Eileen. 'I can't believe we're all being so matter of fact about this. I've loved this child for fifteen months now, and yet I'm expected to stand back and watch while she... he... is taken away by a stranger and I'll be expected to cope with it all. I won't even have Caro by my side while all this is going on.'

The peal of the doorbell interrupted them, and Eileen left to admit the two women from Children's Services.

The little boy was strapped into a child seat in the back of the Range Rover, his eyes wide. He was clutching his Peppa Pig, a bewildered expression on his face. He said 'Daddy' a couple of times, reaching out with his hand, but John had said his goodbyes and knew if he went anywhere near he would completely lose the plot. They had to take him, and take him quickly.

One of the women sat in the back with the little boy, and the other climbed into the driving seat. They began to move, to pull out of the gates, and John crumpled. Luke stepped forward and took the older man's full weight, helping him back inside the house. John reached the settee and collapsed.

'I'll make a drink,' Tessa said, and went towards the kitchen. She searched around until she found a brandy, made them all a strong coffee, and topped John's up with a slosh of alcohol.

She stood in front of the man who had become her friend, and handed him the drink. 'There's brandy in it, John, it will help.'

He was crying without having any idea it was happening. The tears flowed freely down his face. 'God, Tess, what do I do now?'

Eileen, returned to being DI Haughton, promised John she would check in with him via telephone later, and contacted Aalia Khatri on the way out, asking her to meet her at the Vanton home.

The two police officers arrived almost together, and Eileen waited while Aalia locked her squad car and came to join her.

'Okay, the Vantons have no idea why we're here. We have to play this gently, and I suggest you find the kitchen and make a pot of tea. They're going to need it. Don't forget we have an advanced pregnancy to deal with, and I for one never saw myself as a midwife.'

Aalia grinned. 'Okay, boss.'

.   .   .

Kelly Vanton answered the door, and Mitch, her husband who fortunately worked from home and rarely left her side, followed closely behind her. Kelly was magnificently huge, and she smiled as she saw who was on the other side of the door.

'Eileen Haughton, we are blessed. Come in.'

Eileen stepped through the doorway, and Aalia held out her hand. 'DC Aalia Khatri,' she said. 'Good to meet you.'

They all went through to the lounge and Kelly eased herself down into the armchair; Eileen hoped she would be able to lever herself back out of it.

'You're huge,' Eileen said, smiling at the obviously relaxed woman.

'You're telling me, and it's only one, so they say.'

Mitch hadn't sat, had remained standing in the doorway.

'Come and sit down, Mitch,' Eileen said. 'We have things to tell you before you're inundated with press tomorrow.'

Mitch looked at his wife, and walked across to her. He perched himself on the arm of her chair. They turned frightened faces towards each other.

'Is he... is he dead?' The question was expelled in a rush from the back of Kelly's throat.

Eileen nodded towards Aalia, who immediately stood.

'Before I tell you anything, I'm going to ask Aalia to make us all a drink of tea. And you, Kelly, have to remain calm. We don't want any early deliveries. I don't mind delivering letters, but babies I can't do.'

There was a brief flicker of a smile from Mitch, but Kelly's face was stony.

'For fuck's sake, Eileen, what's going on? Why are you here?'

Eileen waited until she heard the sounds of a kettle being filled, before speaking. 'Today I called Children's Services in to remove a little boy from a house, and to place him in a safe home for the night. The little boy has been really well look-after, he's in perfect health, and I've already had a DNA swab taken. If the DNA test proves him to be your Billy, he should be home with you very shortly.'

There was a brief moment of silence while Kelly and Mitch took in and digested Eileen's words, then Kelly said, 'Whoop, whoop' very softly, before screaming the same words out loud.

Mitch pressed his hands on her shoulders as she tried to get up. 'Sit down, crazy woman,' he said, a smile widening across his face.

'I told you, I told you, I told you,' Kelly screamed. 'I knew one day this would happen. Oh my God, Eileen, thank you so much.' She paused and leaned back into her husband, giving up on the idea of getting her bulk out of the chair for the moment. 'Does he have the birthmark?'

Eileen smiled. 'He does. He's a beautiful child. But there are things I have to tell you.'

30

'You've arrested her?' Kelly couldn't have looked more puzzled. 'But surely it's help she needs, rather than locking up. She's obviously had a terrible time, losing her own two babies.'

'You're being very generous, Kelly,' Eileen said quietly. 'She kidnapped your little boy. She brought him up as a girl, and she's been a very caring and loving woman towards him, but she wasn't his mother. Children's Services deemed her not yet stable enough for motherhood, so she helped herself to Billy.'

Mitch seemed much more sensible. 'What if she comes looking for him, even if it's only to see him again, once she's released?'

'That's a long way into the future,' Eileen said. 'It won't be a short sentence. But she will be released and told she can't see Billy or you under any circumstances.'

'We could move, but there's always ways of finding somebody...' Mitch was clearly looking to the future and scaring himself in the process.

'If you're happy here, and you have room for two children, then don't let her force you out.'

'What about her husband? Didn't he realise?'

'That the baby was a boy? No, he didn't. His wife saw to all the bathing and nappy changing, he was kind of an entertainments manager, did the nice side, the playing, the trips to the park. The first time he knew the baby was a boy was this morning. Since then his life has definitely gone pear-shaped. We took his wife in for questioning on a different matter, one in which I don't believe she's involved, but it left him alone with the baby for the first time. She was truly in a blue funk, I can tell you. It soon became clear the baby needed changing, so he asked one of his employees if she would do it. She did, but called him to the nursery as soon as she realised the baby wasn't a girl.'

'So how soon will it be before Billy is back with us?'

Eileen smiled. 'I've already said we have to have everything corroborated with DNA, but if that is a positive match with you two, then it could be as soon as tomorrow.'

There was a small squeak that came from Kelly as she drew in a breath. 'Tomorrow? Oh my God, if you saw the amount of rubbish we've stored in the spare bedroom you'd die. Mitch, cancel anything else you've booked in for tomorrow, we've got to get ready for our baby to come home.'

Caroline sat on the small bed in the holding cell and stared at the McDonald's Happy Meal they'd provided for her. She'd refused everything at first, but their insistence that she have something to eat, and their threat to bring her a Big Mac if she didn't make her own choice, forced her hand and she ordered a cheeseburger Happy Meal. She pulled out a chip and nibbled on it, marvelling at how anyone could take a potato, cut it up, and make it absolutely tasteless.

She had never been brave enough to take Casey into a

McDonald's, but once she got out of this place, she surely would find the courage to walk through the doors with Casey. Wouldn't she? Pictures flashed across her mind of standing in front of the ordering machine, Casey by her side in the pushchair watching everything her mummy was doing, and not knowing that in a few moments she would experience chicken McNuggets for the very first time. A slight giggle escaped from her lips, and she picked up a second chip.

She ate it, then re-folded the top of the box that seemed to have some connection with Minions before pushing it to one side. She really didn't want anything to eat, but she could kill for a cup of tea. Kill.

She put the McDonald's detritus on the floor and swung up her legs. She was finding it hard to believe she was still here, she still hadn't given the statement that was supposed to be the reason she was here. She was beginning to wonder if she had been smart to refuse a solicitor, maybe he would have got her out of here, even if it was only overnight. Now she was stuck in this pokey little room, unable to communicate with anybody, and Casey would be crying for her mummy. Daddy wouldn't know how to handle her... and would Daddy have changed her nappy?

She shivered at the thought. Maybe he wouldn't bother, maybe he didn't know how, maybe he wouldn't call in somebody else to help him. Or maybe he'd already seen the penis on the little boy he had believed to be a little girl. Maybe that's why she was still here...

Tessa sat with Luke and Maria swapping and sharing pizza slices. The day had been distressing, and Luke had insisted she didn't drive home, persuading her to stay and have pizza with them and spend the night on the sofa bed.

Maria had managed half a glass of wine before admitting defeat, but Luke and Tessa were on their second bottle.

'Be grateful you deal with sweet pretty animals,' Tessa said wearily to Maria. 'I don't seem to find anything sweet or pretty in my job, unless it's that little girl Casey, and she turned out to be a boy.' She gave a deep sigh. 'Lord help us, I have no idea how this will go when it gets to court, but it could be some time before John sees Caroline again.' Tessa picked up a slice of the pepperoni pizza, and stared at it for a moment before biting into it. 'Funny name, pepperoni. Anyway, why do you think she called Billy Casey? Reckon it's because Casey can be for either sex?'

Luke thought for a moment, biting into his chicken and mushroom topped slice. 'I think that was her idea, yes, but how would that help? Whatever she called the child, it's still a boy, and without physically chopping it off, he'll always be a boy. Oh my God... you don't think she had that in her mind?'

'No, of course not.' Tessa grinned at the pained expression on his face. She picked up her glass. 'This is a nice wine.'

'Fred brought me half a dozen bottles. He's got a bit of a wine cellar thing under his house, and now I seem to be the son-in-law sort of, I reckon he's buying my friendship.'

'Good grief, you really don't know Fred, do you?' Tessa laughed and reached for the bottle to top up her wine. 'He's given them to you because he actually likes you, not because he wants you to like him. In Fred's world, the only person he'll want to like him is your mum, and I think that's already a done deal.'

'She really does like him. We had a bit of a chat...'

'Tell me you didn't try to put her off!'

'No, I said I liked him, and if she was happy it was fine with me.'

Maria laughed. 'He came out with all the cliches and platitudes, then when we got outside he gave this huge sigh and said "Well, it looks as though I'm going to have a stepdad, doesn't it?" I creased up with laughter.'

They finished the remaining pizza slices, and Maria carried the empty wine bottles and glasses into the kitchen before wishing them goodnight. She handed Tessa a pile of pretty lemon bedding, and Luke opened up the sofa bed for her. He added his goodnights, and left her to make up the bed.

Tessa was the first to wake, but stayed in bed, unwilling to get up yet. As she'd nodded off to sleep she'd had almost a premonition that the following day would bring a degree of unhappiness, and she briefly remembered that feeling as she surfaced to face a new morning of sunshine and blue skies, but guessing there would be no warmth in the winter sun.

She heard the pitter-patter of feet and then the lounge door opened, with Maria waving a cup at her.

'Coffee or tea?'

'Coffee, please. I need something to counteract the alcohol. I must remember to congratulate Fred on his excellent taste in wines.'

'Stay in bed for a bit, wait while the central heating takes the chill off. You want some toast?'

'You're spoiling me. That would be lovely. My morning toast is usually eaten in the car on the way in to the office.'

'You're the first guest we've had stay overnight, although I know the girls are itching to come and stay. Rosie and Imogen adore Luke, and he treats them like princesses. It's really funny to watch.'

Maria disappeared to make the breakfasts for all three of them, although Luke looked none too healthy when he popped his head around the door to wish Tessa good morning.

Tessa frowned. 'You look rough.'

'I always look like this when I get up before the heating kicks in properly. It's freezing out there. Don't be fooled by the sunshine.'

'Luke, it's mid-February. Nobody in this country would ever be fooled by mid-February sunshine. Get out for a run, that'll warm you up.'

'Yeah, right,' he muttered, as he left her still huddled under the duvet, toasty warm.

Everybody was in work by half past nine, and although it was only Tuesday morning, Tessa thought she should call the weekly meeting a day early. Fortunately everybody agreed they could attend, and ten o'clock saw them sitting around Beth's desk, with the main telephone line switched to Cheryl's mobile phone. There was no way she was missing out on a weekly meeting for the sake of a possible call.

Beth opened the meeting by confirming what had happened in the North East and she added that they were satisfied it was now all down to the police to proceed with the prosecution. She also confirmed two new accounts definitely on the books, and a third one still thinking about it.

Fred gave his report on the Ken Freeman case, and answered any questions that seemed to fly over the desk towards him. Beth finished his section with a 'Well done, Fred,' and he wished he had a halo to straighten.

Tessa and Luke took it in turns to report on the Ivor Newburg case, taking it slowly in view of the strange twist that had happened as a result of Eileen Haughton getting antsy with Caroline Coates and taking her in to West Bar to sign a statement.

'The baby girl is a boy?' Beth sounded incredulous.

'It is. You can probably remember the name Billy Vanton,

removed from his mother's room in the maternity unit while she was haemorrhaging in the toilet? They had CCTV of the woman who took him making her escape with the baby, but nothing ever came of it.'

'Was it one of your cases, Tessa?' Beth asked, clearly intrigued by the strange turn of events.

'No, it was a South Yorkshire case, but we were sent all the details because we have adjoining county borders. I remembered it, but I wasn't involved in it. There were no clues, nobody ever came forward to say there was a baby crying where there shouldn't be one, nothing like that. It eventually went onto a back burner, but it's right at the front now.'

Beth looked troubled. 'I know I'm wrong, but I can't help feeling sorry for the poor woman, but also for the mum who had her baby stolen. What a mess. Tess, will you let me know when DNA is confirmed?'

'I will. It'll be later today, and if it is found to be little Billy, he'll be returned to his true parents immediately.'

31

As promised, Eileen rang Tessa as soon as she had the DNA result. It was Billy Vanton, and she expected to be accompanying someone from Children's Services in a couple of hours, as they returned Billy to his true parents.

'I didn't drop off to sleep too easily last night, wondering what today was going to bring. Have you interviewed Caroline Coates yet?' Tessa said.

'I've had her brought up to the interview room. She's no idea she won't be going home, but for her own safety we have to keep her. Finding little Billy is going to be big news, and all sorts of weirdos will be gunning for her. I spoke to John a few minutes ago, and I've advised him to move out for a short time, until everything quietens down. Unfortunately he has the issue of where his home is, his work is alongside it. He's going to speak to his employees this afternoon, tell them exactly what's happening, and I suspect they're going to be working from their homes on a temporary basis until the furore fades away.'

'I'll give John a ring. Thank you for letting me know, Eileen, it's appreciated.'

.   .   .

John Coates walked aimlessly around his home, steering clear of the nursery. It would be impossible to give up this house, they had loved it so much, and yet he felt it may come to that now.

He walked into the bedroom he had shared with Caroline for so long, and began to pack a small suitcase. For a couple of nights he would move into a hotel, then make decisions after that. He felt lost.

He reached the bottom of the stairs, left the suitcase by the front door and walked along the corridor leading to Code Blue.

Everyone stood as he entered the room. 'Are you okay?' was Flora's first question.

'I'm good,' was his short reply, and he walked to the front of the room where he faced everybody. Shelley slipped into the room from the reception area, and moved to sit on Ivan's chair.

'I don't know how much Flora has told y–'

'Nothing,' Flora interrupted him. 'You asked me to say nothing.'

'Then thank you. And thank you to all of you for carrying on with your work when it's been obvious I'm having issues. I have to reassure all five of you that nothing that has happened will in any way impinge on your jobs. However, we may have to make arrangements for you to work from home for a short while, so take home whatever you need to carry on working, and I'll make sure wages reflect the added inconvenience. I'm going away for a few days, but Dom will know where I am. If there are any major blips, get in touch with him, and he'll be able to pass things on.'

'I don't understand,' Brad Wells said. 'Are you closing this place?'

'Just until some adverse publicity dies down. I think the media will soon get bored, and we'll be able to come back to work, but they'll make your lives a living hell if you continue to come here. The problem is it's too close to where I live, and there are some things I have to tell you concerning... well, me, I suppose.'

There was silence in the room.

'Caroline was arrested yesterday, and it seems pretty conclusive that the charge will be kidnap. Fifteen months ago she stole a child, and yesterday it accidentally came to light. Casey was adopted, or so I was led to believe, but that turned out not to be the case. It also turned out that Casey wasn't a girl. He was really a little boy called Billy Vanton.'

There was a gasp from Kathy Easton. 'Kelly Vanton's newborn?'

He nodded. 'In retrospect, I believe I was stupid, putting my business first, but Caro took great delight in dealing with everything to do with Casey, and I hold up my hands and confess to never having changed a nappy in the fifteen months we were her parents. Which is why Flora came through to help me out yesterday. That put into action a chain of events, and I can't begin to imagine what's going on in Caroline's mind. She was taken to West Bar purely to give a statement, as she actually spoke to Ivan the Friday before he died on the Sunday. They wanted the conversation detailing, I believe. So that's where we are. The media will descend on us, and I don't want any of you feeling intimidated by it. I shall be in a hotel for a couple of days, but I promise I will be in touch. I need you all to go home now, because when this breaks it will be instant harassment, I can promise you that.' He stood and moved towards his own office. 'Dom, can I see you before you go home? Thank you, everybody, I'm so sorry for what's happening.'

Dom followed him, and closed the door. 'You okay?'

John shook his head. 'Far from it. I don't know when I'll be able to see her again, I've lost the little girl that I loved – life's pretty shit at the moment.'

'We've all got your back, you know. Nobody will talk, and

even Flora absolutely told us nothing. She said you'd had bad news.'

'Bloody Ivan. I feel as if he's the start of all this. Why would they want a statement from Caro? She hardly knew him, other than to say good morning.'

Dom frowned. 'He was grinning when he came back from taking that letter through to her. I can't remember exactly what he said, but it was something along the lines of rattling her cage, Miss High and Mighty in the big house. I was a bit short with him, to be honest, and I said you mean your employer's wife? He didn't say anything more, simply went back to his desk.'

'Have you told DI Haughton?'

'I told her he went through to deliver the letter, but nothing else. We are all a bit shocked by them finding his body, and I honestly never thought about it. It's only because you've been telling us about Caroline that I've remembered him being a bit of a smart arse.'

'Thanks, Dom. I'll pass it on, so expect a phone call at the very least. Now, I'm going to hide away for a couple of days, so I'll probably head to a Premier Inn, as the press will expect me to go to a five-star, but I'll let you know as soon as I've checked in. You're more than capable of sorting everybody out, but ring if you need me. If I find I'm getting phone calls from the press, I'll nip out and get another phone, and let you have the new number. I won't let this destroy the business as well as me.'

Dom turned to leave the room, but John spoke again. 'Did you get on okay with him? Ivan?'

Still with his back to John, Dom shrugged. 'I did, until he told me I was your second choice for supervisor.'

'Finally,' Caroline said, as Eileen and Aalia entered the interview room.

Eileen said nothing to her until she had confirmed who was present.

'Look,' Caroline said, 'can we get on with this statement or whatever you want from me, please? It's ridiculous that you kept me overnight. You know I have a baby at home who will be fretting without me.'

'The baby is fine. Your husband coped very well, he's quite proud of the fact that he can now change nappies.'

There was silence in the room, and Caroline leaned back, her face gargoyle-like in its stoniness.

Eileen opened her file, and stared at the woman across from her. 'Can you talk us through the adoption process when you received Casey?'

'Of course. We were promised a little girl, but she wasn't due to be born until the end of November, so John, my husband, took himself off on a tour of the States, promising to be back by the twentieth of November, ready for the birth. The baby came early, so I had to collect her on my own. John couldn't get back any earlier, he was booked in for all sorts of conventions, so he didn't get to meet Casey until around the twentieth.'

'So this isn't you?' Eileen showed Caroline a picture of the woman who had abducted Billy Vanton.

'No, it fucking isn't.' She tugged at her long hair. 'Mine's blonde.'

'Not when it's tucked inside a wig. Then it can be any colour. One thing I'm sure of, if that wig is still in existence and it's in your house, my team will find it.'

'You're searching my house?'

'We are.'

'You're searching my house because I haven't given a written statement about some yobbo my husband employs?'

'Oh no.' Eileen smiled. 'I doubt you'll be giving that statement, in fact I could release you now on that matter, you have a much more serious problem, believe me. I only brought you in to take your statement because you were starting to get antsy with me, and nobody does that, not in a murder case. But then we were called back to your house on this small matter.'

She took the DNA report out of her folder and pushed it across the table. 'This is a DNA report on a swab we took from the child who was resident in your house at the time, the child you called Casey. We had an expedited test done, and it appears that your child can't possibly belong to anybody else genetically, other than Mitchell and Kelly Vanton. And they certainly didn't put their first child, their one-day-old baby boy, up for adoption by you or anybody else. Do you have anything to say, Mrs Coates?'

'I need my solicitor.'

Thomas Overend, the Coates' solicitor who had taken care of them after the assault on Caroline, arrived within the hour, and he requested a period in which to speak to his client.

Eileen glanced at her watch. 'I'd like to resume questioning Mrs Coates at half past two.'

'Of course. I'm sure we can straighten all of this out.'

'I wouldn't count on it, Mr Overend, I really wouldn't count on it. I'll leave you to talk to her, but dig deeply. It seems she is hell bent on denying everything, but in front of a jury that simply won't work.'

'DI Haughton, aren't we getting a little in front of ourselves?'

'No we're not, remind me to introduce you to Mitch and Kelly Vanton sometime soon. Now when they get in front of that jury...'

.   .   .

By three thirteen precisely it was over. Caroline had been charged, Thomas was closeted in the cell with her, and Eileen was making arrangements for her to be brought before the magistrates court the following afternoon.

Eileen and Aalia walked to the car, still discussing the outcome. 'Overend knew she'd done it,' Eileen said, 'knew she stood no chance of walking away from this.'

'I was most shocked when she said she had chosen that particular baby because the nurses must have been stupid. She said if it had had on a blue woolly hat and not a white woolly hat, she would have known it was a boy, and if the nurse had spelt Billy properly and not the girls way of Billie, she wouldn't have taken it. She would have looked for a pink hat!' Aalia pushed her hands through her hair, almost a gesture of desperation. 'I can't wait to give this baby back to its proper mummy, and let's hope he doesn't remember anything of this crazy one.'

32

Eileen and Aalia walked towards the car they had been told would be parked around the corner from the Vanton home, and they were met by the same two ladies from Children's Services. Billy was lifted out of his car seat, and the small entourage walked around to Billy's new home.

Kelly was sitting in the window, waiting, head moving as if searching for a slow-moving vehicle that could possibly be looking for her address. Eileen saw her jump up, and seconds later Kelly threw the door open.

Eileen stepped between Kelly and her son, in the arms of one of the other ladies, and whispered, 'Slow down. He doesn't know who you are.'

Kelly lifted her head to Mitch, and he gave a gentle smile and a nod. 'I warned you, Kel. Let him get used to us.'

They all trooped through the front door, and Mitch and Kelly sat side by side on the sofa.

'Billy,' the taller of the two women said, 'this is your new mummy.'

'Peppa?' Billy queried.

'No, sweetheart, she's not called Peppa. She's called Mummy. Can you say that?'

'Peppa,' he repeated.

Kelly laughed. 'My God, he's gorgeous. And he can call me what the hell he likes, for him I'll answer to anything.'

'However,' Mitch said, 'despite my wife's words, I do not wish to be known as Daddy Pig.'

Mitch and Kelly had tears running down their faces, both oblivious to the floodgates having been opened. Kelly held out her arms, and Billy stared at her for a moment. 'Can I see Peppa?' she asked.

The little boy stared at the pink pig, thought about it for a minute, then walked over to his mother. 'Peppa,' he said once more and handed it to her.

Eileen rang Tessa later and gave her the blow-by-blow account of her very full day at work.

'You mean she chose him thinking he was a girl? That must have been a hell of a shock when she got him home.'

'But she blamed it on the nurses. They should have put him a blue hat on, not a white one, and then she would have known. And she said the nurse must have been really thick because she spelt his name on his crib the girls way, B I L L I E. She said if it had been spelt properly, as B I L L Y, she would have known. I think she wanted an apology for the failings of the NHS. You know, Tess, I felt sorry for her at the start, but not anymore. She's a proper nasty cow. And I still haven't got her statement from her about why she rang Ivan Newburg that Sunday morning. Not sure I can be arsed now, I only took her in 'cos she was pissing me off. She'll be shipped out tomorrow, pending Crown Court and her sentencing.'

'Does John know?'

'He does. Might call round to see him tomorrow. He's at the Premier Inn in the centre of Sheffield for tonight, so I'll ring him early tomorrow morning. I've asked him to keep me informed of his whereabouts while he's having to stay away from his home. I've got a forensics team in there today doing a search. I'm hoping they come across a short dark-haired wig, but I'm not holding my breath. She's pretty smart, she'll have got rid of that straight away.'

Eileen's last act of the day was to check in with John Coates. He answered at the first peal of his ringtone.

'DI Haughton?'

'Hi, John. I thought I should fill you in on developments, although no doubt you've heard from Thomas Overend by now.'

'I have. He says Caro is in front of the magistrates tomorrow afternoon and will be remanded into custody pending the case going to Crown Court for sentencing. What the fuck is happening to my life? And in all of this, how is little Billy?'

'Billy is back with the Vantons. He'll take a few days to settle, and Children's Services are keeping an initial watch on the situation, but he'll be fine. Children of that age have short memories and are very resilient, so while you'll never forget him, he'll definitely forget his start in life.'

'My mind won't stop. I'm in this hotel room, the TV is on and I've no idea what programme it is. I've spoken to my parents, but I can't really remember what I've said. They live in Spain, and both of them said they'll come over, but I hope I've talked them out of it.'

'And your wife's parents?'

'Both dead. We have very little family.'

'And the people who work for you at Code Blue. Have you warned them not to speak to the media?'

'I have. They're all currently working from home for a week or two – that's one of the advantages of being a technology business. I had a brief word with them, told them what had happened, and then put Dom Acton in overall charge as I'm not sure my mind's in any sort of position to make decisions. I'll be judging day by day whether it's safe to go back into work or not.'

'I'll keep in touch. I'll possibly have to talk to them as well, because despite everything that's happened in the last day or so, I still have a murder to solve.'

'Oh, thanks for reminding me. When I spoke to Dom earlier, he said something about when Ivan took the wrongly delivered letter through to Caroline. I have to stress that Caroline didn't mention anything, but when Ivan got back through from the house to his desk, he said something along the lines of he'd rattled Caroline's cage, and called her Miss High and Mighty in the big house. I have no idea what he said to her to rattle her, and she'd probably forgotten it by the time I arrived home on the Monday morning. Dom was more upset at the nasty way he referred to Caroline, called him out on it, he said.'

'Acton said nothing else with reference to it?'

'No, only about himself. It seems he was a bit aggrieved that he was second choice for office supervisor. I got the impression Ivan had rubbed it in a bit. Until yesterday I had no idea Dom felt like that, or that it had even been discussed. It's not that sort of environment where we chat to each other, it's a quiet space because concentration is key.'

Eileen gave a brief laugh, while scribbling down everything John was telling her. 'Tell me about it. If someone talks to me while I'm sending a text, there's more than half a chance it won't be sent. Thank you for these snippets, John, and take care. Will you be at court for Caroline tomorrow?'

'I will. And thank you, DI Haughton. You've been very kind, despite the awful circumstances.'

. . .

Eileen stared at the notes she had made. Caroline had been adamant that there had been no conversation of any interest between her and Ivan, that he had simply delivered the letter and gone back down the corridor to his own office space. So what had been said? What had she hidden?

Could he have suspected something about Casey? Could Caroline have taken advantage of her husband having set off for London and been changing the baby in the kitchen?

Would he, as a young man, have realised it was a little boy, given that she could have quickly covered his penis with a nappy? Eileen felt in her heart it was nothing to do with the baby. So what was it to do with?

What did this unlikely pair speak of that day, that had led to Ivan mentioning it in such a derogatory way when he returned to his desk?

She didn't know, but she'd damn well be in work early the next day and find out. She stared at her notes, particularly the one that she had circled. Dom Acton was pissed off that he wasn't first choice for supervisor, that had been Ivan Newburg who had turned it down.

How many times can you be reminded of that before you turn on somebody with a syringe full of heroin in your hand?

Tessa couldn't sleep. Caroline hadn't only been a victim of a cruel and unnecessary attack, she had been a friend. Tessa had seen her in court before, but that was to give evidence, not as a criminal.

She had been there for them both when Caroline was finally discharged from hospital, had been there when the pain was too intense to bear and standard painkillers didn't touch it, had watched as John got her stronger medication to help her, turning a blind eye to where he might have got it from, and then helping as she needed to be weaned off it. It had been a good day when Caroline finally admitted she was off drugs, and starting to re-build her fractured life. And they had initiated talk of adoption.

Tessa sighed. How can one life go from perfect to devastation in such a short time? And with no hint that it was coming. She could cry for John, and knew she would keep in touch with him. He would wait for Caro, that Tessa didn't doubt, but he would have to get through the intervening years when she would be locked away. And would he ever be able to trust her with anything when she was released?

Tessa picked up her phone as it pealed out. 'Hi, Luke. You can't sleep either?'

'No. I don't usually let cases get to me, I've learnt how to switch off, but this one isn't like that. How can I feel sorry for someone who's done what she's done? Tell me, Tess, because I sure as hell don't know how to handle this one.'

'I can't tell you because I don't know. I think it's hit us particularly hard because this wasn't what we were investigating. This aspect of our work has come to light and been solved in just over a day, and it's floored us. Have you spoken to Maria about it?'

'I have. Now she can't sleep either.'

'I can tell you it won't be a good day tomorrow, because if the neighbours of the Vantons haven't phoned the newspapers, the court reporters will see the lists first thing tomorrow morning and they'll be camped outside Code Blue by ten.'

'See, you're not making me feel any better, Tessa. I like John. Bit ambivalent about Caroline, but I think that's because she never said much. But John I liked, and he's going to have to carry the burden of this while keeping a business going and hanging on to employees who might decide it's not worth the hassle.'

'He'll cope. He coped with something far worse than this when he found Caro almost dead on that patio, and their babies dead. He handled that, he was there for her every step of the way, and to enable that to continue he sold his business. Massive changes in his life, so I don't doubt he'll cope this time. Now have some Horlicks and go to sleep. We don't know what we've to face yet tomorrow. Love to Maria.'

Eileen also had to make use of her phone. She sent a message to Thomas Overend.

Interviewing Coates on a different matter tomorrow at 9am.

She smiled as she imagined his reaction to the nine o'clock start, and switched her phone to silent. She could do without a late-night conversation with the solicitor, who would no doubt want her to start later. It wasn't going to happen – if there were to be extra charges, she wanted them done with as soon as possible.

33

Wednesday morning brought with it torrential rain. By the time Eileen reached her office she was dripping rainwater from her chin and nose, and struggling to get out of her coat.

Aalia had already arrived and had a coffee waiting for her boss. She handed her a towel. 'You'll need this.'

'Thanks, Aalia. Sorry to bring you in early, but I want to interview Caroline Coates before she disappears off to court, and depending how that interview goes, I may want to bring Dominic Acton in.'

'You notified her solicitor?'

Eileen laughed. 'At around eleven last night. I didn't get a response, so let's hope he gets up early. I'm starting at nine, no matter what. If he's not there, he'll have to catch up later.'

Overend was there, but not in a good mood. 'I don't appreciate you summoning me at eleven at night, DI Haughton.'

'Merely advance notification, not a summons,' she said, 'and it would have been no good notifying you at eight this morning, would it?'

He glared at her and walked to the coffee machine.

'It's in connection with a murder,' she called after him, and he stopped, his back to her.

Slowly he turned round. 'A murder? She stole a baby, she didn't kill it.'

'Our original investigation was for the murder of a young man called Ivan Newburg. Caroline Coates is the wife of Ivan Newburg's employer, but until last night wasn't suspected of any involvement in his death. However, as you know with murder cases, information keeps coming in from different angles, and the dead Ivan Newburg has provided something that may nicely draw Caroline into it. I suggest you leave that coffee machine alone, and go and speak to your client now, because in,' she glanced at her watch, 'fourteen minutes I'll be in that interview room.'

Just because he could, Overend turned back to the machine, selected a coffee, then carried it with him to the interview room.

Caroline looked wan. Lack of sleep had given her dark circles under her eyes, and her long blonde hair had seen only the briefest of connections with a hairbrush. She was slumped in her chair, and only her eyes moved when the door opened to admit Eileen and Aalia.

Aalia recorded the names of the people present, and still Caroline didn't react.

'My client categorically denies any involvement in the death of anyone.' Overend spoke before anyone else could, and Eileen smiled at him.

'Thank you, Mr Overend, I am grateful for your

contribution. Caroline, at any point in your life have you ever taken non-prescription drugs?'

For the first time there was movement from Caroline. She sat up, and looked at her solicitor. 'No comment.'

'Has your husband ever procured drugs for you to help with the pain after the attack and subsequent operations?'

'No comment.'

'Caroline, I am asking for a reason. Any admission of drug-taking will not produce charges against you. I'll ask you again, did you take non-prescription drugs to help with your pain?'

Caroline dipped her head almost in acknowledgement. 'Yes, for a short period.'

'Thank you. You came off them as the pain lessened?'

She nodded.

'For the tape, Coates is nodding,' Aalia said.

'Who did you buy them from?'

'No comment.'

'Did your husband get them for you?'

She thought for a moment. 'Initially, but then he stopped.'

'He thought you no longer needed them?'

'That's right.'

'But by this time you were hooked?'

Again she nodded.

'For the tape, Coates is nodding.'

'Caroline,' Eileen continued, 'where did you get them from once your husband stopped his supply?'

'No comment.'

'Would that be Jimmy B?'

There was silence in the room. Overend looked at Caroline and tapped her arm.

'It would.' Her response was muffled, her mouth hidden by her hand.

'For the tape, Coates said it would.'

'Is Jimmy B Jimmy Brownlow?'

'No comment.'

'For once I don't need a comment,' Eileen said with a smile. 'His name and his phone number, which is the same one against Jimmy B in your phone, are well known to us. When did you last buy drugs from Jimmy B? Before you answer, please remember that even though you may have deleted all phone calls to and from that number, O2 will have a full record of all calls made from your mobile. That list will be with us by the end of today.'

A tear trickled from Caroline's eye. 'No comment.'

'I don't need a comment.' Eileen turned over the page in her folder. 'Okay, on to the next point, which we have discussed before.'

Caroline pulled herself upright, as if preparing to do battle. 'If we've discussed it, why do we have to discuss it again?'

'New information has come to light. Simple as that.'

Overend shuffled uncomfortably.

'Caroline, on the Friday afternoon, seventh of February, your husband left to go to London for the weekend. Is that correct?'

'It is.'

'And shortly after he left a mail delivery was made, but one of the letters addressed to you was delivered to the company address of Code Blue.'

'Yes.'

'Ivan Newburg brought it through. Is that correct?'

'It is.'

'You had a conversation in which he said something that upset you?'

'No.'

'No conversation, or no upset?'

'No to both.'

'My information leads me to believe that Newburg told someone else that he had rattled your cage. He then went on to insult you by calling you Miss High and Mighty in the big house. Now, it's not the high and mighty stuff that bothers me, that's just the way he saw you, but the rattling of your cage is cause for concern. What did he say to you?'

'Nothing.' She cradled her arms against her chest. 'Leave me alone. Aren't you destroying my life enough?'

'Caroline, nobody here has destroyed your life. You did that when you walked into that maternity unit. I am now concerned with the death of a twenty-seven-year-old man that I believe you had a part in. What did he say to you when he brought that letter through to your home, to your kitchen. Did he see something he shouldn't have seen with regard to Billy? Did he make a personal comment – he obviously didn't like you? What did he say, Caroline?'

She began to sob and Overend held up his hand. 'Time out, DI Haughton. You can see my client is distressed. Can we please have a cup of tea for her?'

Eileen and Aalia stood, and Eileen gathered up her file. 'Ten minutes and I'll be back. I want answers about that conversation, Caroline.'

'What next?' Aalia asked as she sipped at her can of Coke. 'You have any thoughts on what he could have said to her?'

'None whatsoever. But it was something to do with going to her in the kitchen.'

'I saw her flinch when you mentioned it. But a kitchen's a kitchen. Heart of the home and all that. What spooked her by him going in it?'

I don't know. I keep going round and round that he could have seen something in the kitchen that he shouldn't have seen. Is she back on drugs? I don't honestly think she is, we would have had withdrawal signs by now.'

She took out her phone, and rang Tessa. 'As my Coates expert, is there something about the kitchen in the Coates house that could have affected Ivan Newburg in some way?'

'Let me think.' There was silence, and then a small sigh of satisfaction. 'Given that we now know who Ivan Newburg was, yes there is.'

Aalia re-logged them in, and Caroline shuffled in her chair.

'Okay, Caroline, back to the conversation that went on, probably a very short one, with Ivan Newburg before he headed back to his desk.'

'Please don't upset my client any more, DI Haughton. She's already said there wasn't a conversation of any length. Can we get by this issue, please. Time is passing, and I do have to prepare her for her court appearance.'

'Oh I'm sure we won't be much longer, Mr Overend. In fact, your client can expedite matters considerably if she'll tell us what was said in that kitchen.'

'I said nothing,' Caroline muttered, and Aalia asked her to repeat the comment for the tape. She did so without lifting her head.

'Let's retrace what happened. Ivan collected the mail, saw one was for you and went down the corridor that links the two buildings to deliver it to you. The corridor door leads off the hall?'

She nodded, and once again Aalia had to relay the nod to the tape.

'The kitchen door is at the end of the hall. Would it have been open?'

'Yes. I was doing something in there.'

'What?'

'Making some lunch for Casey. She had woken up.'

'And where was Billy?' Eileen deliberately gave the baby his proper name.

'In the high chair.'

'What happened next?'

'He threw the letter onto the kitchen table and I said thank you.'

'Then what?'

'He went back down the corridor.'

'So at what point was there some cage-rattling?'

'I don't know what you mean.'

'He told Dominic Acton he had rattled your cage, which as you know means he caused you some upset. This isn't going to go away, Caroline. I will find out what he said to you, I'm not known for giving up. Tears won't work this time, we're here in this room until you tell me.'

'That's enough, DI Haughton.' Overend frowned at her over the top of his glasses.

'It's nowhere near enough, Mr Overend. May I remind you this is a murder enquiry, and I believe your client, and her tears, are withholding information that I need.' Eileen slammed her hand down on the desk. 'Caroline Coates, what did Ivan Newburg say to you in your kitchen that told you exactly who he was?'

Caroline emitted a scream so loud that Overend moved his chair away from her. She burst into a torrent of tears.

'He said the kitchen was a nice replacement for the old one. He only saw the old one when he came to buy our car. I knew straight away who he was.'

'So she got the heroin from Jimmy B?' Tessa asked. 'Thought he would have been dead by now.'

'Unfortunately not,' was Eileen's dry response. 'She invented the beeping security box to get Ivan to call round, and she was ready for him with the syringe. She got him in the jugular as you know, and he never stood a chance. She waited till she'd put Billy to bed for the night with an extra dose of Calpol to make sure he didn't wake, then drove Newburg's body to Ecclesall Woods. She had a lot of luck on her side because she wasn't spotted at any point, and of course it was a clean kill. We've brought her car in now to do a full forensic on it, and there'll be something to place Newburg in it. You might want to contact John, he's falling apart as you can imagine. We've charged her, and it looks like it will be another guilty plea.'

'Well, thanks for letting me know, I guessed as soon as we realised the kitchen connection.'

'Oh and one little extra thing, Billy Vanton slept through the night, and is an absolute angel according to his mother.'

'Brilliant. She going to give you daily reports?'

'Probably, she's so grateful for us getting him back to her. She's already said she's never letting him out of her sight again.'

'So happy for them. And maybe I'll sleep through the night now. There wasn't much sleep last night, the intricacies of this case saw to that. I'll pass everything on to Luke, he was with me every step of the way in this one, and I don't think he slept much last night either.'

'Bye, Tess.'

'Bye, Eileen.'

Oliver felt so much better with his cone removed. He quite liked the new Dreamies that had appeared as extra special treats for him as well, but he wasn't too keen on everybody being a bit lackadaisical around him now they thought he was better. Even Luke had pushed him off his knee to go and stare out of the window. Everybody seemed put out by something, so he might just have to have a nap under Luke's desk until they all got over whatever was bothering them.

Luke stared out of his window, deep in thought. The events of the past couple of weeks seemed to be playing on continuous re-run through his mind, with the obvious conclusion that if they hadn't taken the case, Ivan Newburg would still be alive. Had their investigation and questioning of John's employees prompted Ivan to get just that little bit too cocky with Caroline, twisting the knife in her and knowing she was more than a trifle unbalanced?

Luke had finally spoken his thoughts as he and Maria had lain in bed the previous night. She had been unable to sleep because he was unable to sleep and so they had talked. He blessed her for her logic and common sense when she pointed out everything had started because two babies had died, not because he and Tessa had turned up at Code Blue and asked some questions.

They had fallen asleep in the early hours of the morning, holding each other, and he had felt 'thank goodness it was Monday and a new week'. She had gone into Connection first, checked out Oliver's wound was good, and removed his cone, before running across the road to check out her own new week.

Luke knew he would be glad when Tessa arrived, to see if it was affecting her in the same way, or if he was simply being oversensitive.

Tessa popped her head around Luke's door. He was standing by the window, holding his coffee, staring into space.

'Morning, partner. Any more of that coffee, or shall I make my own?'

He turned and she could see he was troubled. His smile was almost non-existent.

'I'll get you one,' he said.

'Thank you. I have news.' She moved to sit at his desk and waited until he handed her a cup. 'I had a phone call on the way into work.'

'Good Lord, other people get up at ungodly hours as well, do they?'

'They do if they're called Eileen Haughton, it seems. Anyway, her forensics team have been working on Caroline's car. They found a tiny amount of blood and one strand of hair which have proved to belong to Ivan Newburg, but, glory be, they have found a short dark wig stuffed in the back of the glovebox.'

'So they've got proof of everything...'

'They have. But it seems she's pleading guilty anyway. That's not going to shorten her sentence, pre-meditated murder is pre-meditated murder, not accidental. Did you like her?' The question was abrupt.

He sipped at his drink before answering. 'I did. All our subsequent findings have shocked me. And what John will do now, I can't imagine. She and Casey were his life.'

'Well, one thing he isn't doing is going to his mum and dad in Spain, they've closed everything down because of this coronavirus. I had a chat with John last night, and he's going to stay with a friend for a few weeks, but he said he'll keep in touch.'

'Good. So now what? Have you looked at your diary yet for this week?'

'Nope. Not given it a thought. Have you?'

'Not yet. My head will be ready for that at about ten, and it's only nine.'

'Good lad. Freshen up our coffees while I go and get us some croissants, and see if your mum's got any gossip for me.'

Fred was chatting to Naomi as Tessa entered the Co-op. When he heard of their plans for a second breakfast, he paid for the croissants and headed back over the road with Tessa.

'Go gentle on Luke,' she warned him. 'He's not taking it too well, the situation at Code Blue. I think he's shocked at the double whammy of Caroline being a kidnapper and a killer.'

'Must admit, it wasn't even my case but it's shocked me. It's all over the front pages.'

'You got anything on this morning?'

'Only a quick trip out to Bradwell to see Ken Freeman. I'm taking him our final bill and report.'

'Do me a favour and take Luke with you, unless he's got

something in his diary. He needs his mind switching to a different tack, and your giant will probably be a refreshing change for him.'

Fred laughed. 'He'll learn a whole new language and get his tongue burnt on Ken's Yorkshire tea. I'll be happy to take him, he'll enjoy Ken's company as much as I do.'

And Monday swung into action. It was a quiet day, and Luke spent the entire journey back from Bradwell to Eyam saying 'Ey up'; his intention was to impress Maria with his knowledge of the Yorkshire language.

Beth picked up on the general mood of the place, and made it her job to cheer everybody up, but by the time the clock reached four, she sent everybody home. Several new jobs had come in during the day, and she knew by Tuesday morning the general lassitude would have dissipated as they became embroiled in the new cases. She would soon have her merry band back to their cheerful normal selves.

She locked the Connection shutters and was inside Little Mouse Cottage before five. Joel arrived a few minutes after her and they were discussing what to do for food when there was a knock at the door.

Joel went to answer it, and Beth heard a mumbled conversation, then Joel called her name.

Alistair was standing away from the door, halfway down the path.

Joel pulled her close to him. 'It's Alistair,' he said quietly.

'Hi, Alistair. Where's Nan? Come in.'

Alistair shook his head. 'I can't come any closer.'

Beth started to shake. 'Alistair, where's my nan?'

'I'm sorry...' Alistair's head dropped and he fished in his pocket for a handkerchief. He held it against his eyes. 'We lost her in the early hours of this morning. I couldn't tell you over the phone...'

Joel held tightly to Beth. 'Nan's died? But she was fine last week!'

Alistair hadn't moved. 'She caught coronavirus. She was fighting it, but then suddenly she couldn't breathe. She was taken to hospital, and I was allowed to be with her at the end.' He staggered backwards as he spoke and Joel tried to balance Beth against the door frame to go to him, but Alistair held up a hand. 'Don't come near me, either of you. I've been in contact. I have to go now to protect you and to start making arrangements for Doris to come home to Bradwell.' He turned and stumbled down the path. 'I'll ring you tomorrow, Beth. I loved her so much, my Doris. I can't think at the moment...'

They watched speechless as he climbed into the car, and drove away.

Beth felt her legs begin to go and Joel helped her inside. He sat her on the sofa and within seconds had produced a glass holding brandy. 'Drink this,' he said. Don't think, just get this inside you and then we can talk.'

She stared at him. 'We feel immune to it, don't we, because we're British and stuff like this doesn't happen to us. What the hell is it, Joel, what the hell is this virus that it can take a strong woman like my nan? Tell me it isn't true, Joel. Tell me my nan hasn't left me.'

THE END

ACKNOWLEDGMENTS

My thanks as always go to the team at Bloodhound Books, who continue to publish my novels – this one is number nineteen. When I receive my first paperback of each one, the thrill is still just as great as it was when I first saw book number one, *Beautiful*. Thank you, team Bloodhound!

I also have thanks to go to Cheryl Dodd, Amanda Gilchrist and Caroline Coates for lending me their names! Thank you, ladies. I hope I did you proud.

Special thanks go to my beta-reading team of Tina Jackson, Marnie Harrison, Alyson Read, Sarah Hodgson and Denise Cutler – your thoughts, suggestions and approvals give me the strength to carry on writing. I am equally grateful for my forty-strong ARC team, who read the book before publication day and are ready with reviews on the day. An amazing group of people, believe me.

And where would this book be without its editor? Morgen Bailey, you are a star. You sort out my POV mishaps, my overuse of certain words, and generally turn a hit-and-miss manuscript into something I can be proud of. Thank you.

Thanks as always goes to my family, who support me with all of my writing, especially Dave who is my sounding board for plot issues. He really struggles with having a wife who sees murder in everything...

And my final round of thanks goes to my fans, the readers who buy my book because it says Anita Waller on the front, and don't bother to read the blurb because they know they will enjoy it. That gives me such a good feeling, and I hope this one captured you in the usual way.

Anita Waller
Sheffield, July 2021

A NOTE FROM THE PUBLISHER

Thank you for reading this book. If you enjoyed it please do consider leaving a review on Amazon to help others find it too.

We hate typos. All of our books have been rigorously edited and proofread, but sometimes mistakes do slip through. If you have spotted a typo, please do let us know and we can get it amended within hours.

info@bloodhoundbooks.com